TYLER WHITESIDES
JANITORS

TYLER WHITESIDES

JANITORS

CURSE OF THE BROOMSTAFF

ILLUSTRATED BY
BRANDON DORMAN

SHADOW
MOUNTAIN

Visit us at ShadowMountain.com

First printing in hardbound 2013
First printing in paperbound 2014

Library of Congress Cataloging-in-Publication Data
Whitesides, Tyler, author.
  Curse of the broomstaff / Tyler Whitesides.
     pages cm. — (Janitors ; book 3)
  Summary: Spencer, Daisy, and their little team of rebels must find the source of all magical Glop and destroy it before it destroys the world as they know it.
  ISBN 978-1-60907-605-4 (hardbound : alk. paper)
  ISBN 978-1-60907-874-4 (paperbound)
  [1. Friendship—Fiction. 2. Schools—Fiction. 3. School custodians—Fiction. 4. Magic—Fiction.] I. Title. II. Series: Whitesides, Tyler. Janitors ; bk. 3.
  PZ7.W58793Cu 2013
  [Fic]—dc23   2013019598

Printed in the United States of America
R. R. Donnelley, Harrisonburg, VA

10   9   8   7   6   5   4   3   2   1

For anyone who has ever felt
down in the dumps.

And for Mom and Dad,
who always made me feel the opposite.

CONTENTS

CONTENTS

Contents

CHAPTER I

"THE CLEAN WAY."

Mrs. Natcher's chalk squeaked against the board, and Spencer shuddered at the sound. The teacher stepped away from the chalkboard so the students could see what she'd drawn. It was another story problem. And this time there was a pie chart to go with it.

Why did Mrs. Natcher have to ruin pie by turning it into a math problem?

Spencer sighed and picked up his pencil. He finished the problem quickly and still had time to double-check his work.

Class was different without Dez. Spencer found that it was much easier to finish his assignments without the bully's grubby hands poking him. Dez's absence, under any other conditions, would have been a great relief. But Spencer was troubled.

Three months had passed without any word from Dez. Under Slick's persuasion, the bully had stayed at New Forest Academy. But Slick was long gone, eaten by his own overgrown Grime. So what was keeping Dez from coming home? Had the bully given in to the BEM? Was he truly one of them now?

Glancing around the classroom, Spencer saw that he was practically the first student finished with the pie chart problem. Daisy sat a few desks away, her nose an inch off the math notebook as she scribbled out numbers.

Spencer sighed as he thought through the rest of his day. It was Max's fourth birthday. Spencer's mom would be busy planning a party for his little brother. They'd have cake. But Max would probably slobber when he blew out the candles, getting his germs all over, so Spencer probably wouldn't eat any.

Life had actually become quite boring lately. If it weren't for his bronze visions, Spencer would feel completely left out of what the Rebel Underground was doing. Ever since Walter had escaped through the woods around New Forest Academy, Spencer liked to check on the old warlock. Just to make sure everything was all right.

Spencer's hand drifted to his left pocket. He knew he shouldn't do it. Not during class. But a quick checkup wouldn't take long. Spencer could be back before Mrs. Natcher sliced the pie chart.

Spencer plunged his hand into his pocket, his fingers slowly lowering to the object concealed there. It was an old high school swimming medal that his sister had bought at a yard sale. It wasn't gold or silver. It was third place—bronze.

Spencer's hand closed around the cold medallion. He tried to keep a casual gaze forward, but almost immediately, Mrs. Natcher and the chalkboard were blurred away in a blizzard of white. It spread, consuming his entire vision, until it fell away, point by blinding point.

He stood in a parking lot only fifty-two miles west of Welcher Elementary. Spencer tried to remain calm. His power was still new and, in many ways, uncontrollable. Even though he'd been able to increase the length of his warlock visions, Spencer still didn't know who he would be spying on at any given time. He had hoped for a glimpse of Walter, but the man in the parking lot was too broad and tall.

Spencer knew at once who it was.

The man was Mr. Clean, the president of the BEM and the most mysterious of the three warlocks. The name was clearly an alias, which prevented Walter from discovering his true identity or anything about Mr. Clean's past.

Spencer had seen through Mr. Clean's eyes a number of times. The warlock was usually at his BEM office in Washington, DC, causing everyone nearby to cower in fear. But not this time. What was Mr. Clean doing in Idaho, standing in the parking lot of a prison?

The sun was brilliant, sparkling on the mounds of snow at the edge of the parking lot. The warlock looked down, his breath billowing in the frosty February morning. He was wearing a long white lab coat, but as his gloved hand moved the lapel aside, Spencer saw that something was attached to his belt.

It was a large black battery pack with a dial in the center. Plugged into one end was a thick orange extension cord. Mr. Clean's eyes followed the trailing cord, and as he looked over his shoulder, Spencer gasped.

Not three feet behind the warlock crouched a gigantic Filth. The rodent's face was downturned, its hideous buck-teeth jutting crookedly from a slobbering mouth. It was purring softly, a deep-throated, phlegmy sound that caused the deadly sharp quills on its back to rise and fall.

The other end of the cord was nestled into the monster's dingy fur, plugging into the gray flesh near the spine. The Filth's eyes were half closed and the beast pulsated lazily as energy flowed through the extension cord and into the creature's body.

The warlock did not seem the least bit terrified that an overgrown Toxite was breathing down his neck in the open parking lot. In fact, the broad man reached out a gloved hand and stroked the creature's muzzle.

Then, with a blur of movement, the man leapt into the air, his white lab coat swinging wide. To Spencer's surprise, the warlock landed atop the huge Filth, straddling it like a warhorse. The Filth made no reaction, completely contented, apparently due to the energy coming through the cord.

The warlock adjusted his weight, and Spencer noticed that there was a floor mat draped across the Filth's back like some kind of primitive saddle. The man's hand dropped to the battery pack at his waist. As soon as he twisted the dial, the Filth roared to life.

The huge creature leapt forward, bounding across the parking lot with a snarl. When it reached the doors of the prison, the Toxite lowered its broad head. Spencer flinched at the sound as both doors were ripped open, the Toxite and rider tumbling into the reception area. The Filth stomped its clawed feet, shaking broken glass from its fur as the alarm blared.

There was a uniformed woman behind the reception desk. She sprang from her seat, fumbling to draw her gun. The warlock and his beast paused in the center of the room, reveling in the chaos they had just created.

In seconds, the reception area was swarming with armed guards. But Spencer couldn't understand what was happening. The guards raced past the warlock, inspecting the walls and shattered doors. Of course they wouldn't be able to see the huge Toxite, but had Mr. Clean somehow made himself invisible as well?

"Was it a bomb?" asked the uniformed woman.

The warlock drew a deep breath. "No," Mr. Clean said aloud. Every guard turned, pistols aimed randomly across the room. "It was a phantom."

Then, with terrifying speed, both gloved hands plunged into his lab coat. Two plastic spray bottles flashed from concealment. He took aim and pulled the triggers.

It was over in a moment. A drip of green solution glistened on the nozzle of each spray bottle, and an emerald mist hung in the room. The guards collapsed into a heap on the hard floor, their guns slipping from limp hands.

Spencer felt a stab of fear pass through him. He was aware of himself, sitting stock straight in his school desk, hand gripping the bronze medallion so tightly that the edge dug into his palm. He wanted to let go, to end the vision on his terms. But the fallen security guards, the green spray, the warlock atop that fearsome creature . . .

Mr. Clean twisted his head from side to side in satisfaction, his neck popping from the motion. The reception area was littered with bodies—all of them trained security guards, but none of them a match for the warlock in the white coat.

The big man touched the dial on his belt, and the Filth moved away from the wreckage. They walked down the hallway, the warlock holding his spray bottles like dual pistols in his gloved hands.

In a moment, Mr. Clean had found the cell he was looking for. He twisted the dial and dismounted the giant Filth in the middle of the hall, keeping the extension cord stretched between them. Peering through the bars, Spencer saw the limited contents of the cell. Curled upon the bed was a figure in an orange jumpsuit.

"Knock, knock," the warlock whispered through the bars.

The startled prisoner leapt from the bed, tripped in surprise, and came to rest on her knees not three feet away. Her thin face upturned, she stared through the bars.

It was Leslie Sharmelle!

Spencer's breath caught when he recognized her. *Leslie Sharmelle!* She was a BEM worker who had substituted for Mrs. Natcher at the beginning of the year. Leslie was the one who had teamed up with Garth Hadley to get Spencer involved with the BEM. She had survived the Vortex, but the classroom had collapsed on her. Walter had framed her for the accident, and once she was released from the hospital she had gone to jail.

Now she knelt before the mysterious warlock. And with fear and respect in her eyes, she muttered his name.

"Mr. Clean."

"Aren't you going to invite me in?"

Leslie swallowed hard. "You . . . you have the key?"

"Why would I need a key," Mr. Clean asked, "when I have this?"

His fingers turned the dial on the battery pack, and the Filth bellowed. Leslie jumped away from the bars, but it was too late. The creature had already caught sight of her.

Mr. Clean stepped aside as the Filth sprang at the cell bars. Its jaws snapped through the metal. Clawed toes scraped, bending and twisting the bars aside. In less than a heartbeat, the Filth was inside the cell.

In panicked shock, Leslie collapsed against the back wall, shielding her face as fragments of metal fell around her. Her hands reached out and she screamed as the slavering jowls of the beast opened to destroy her.

But the Filth did not bite. It bowed its head in relaxation as a surge of electricity flowed down the Glopified extension cord. Mr. Clean stepped through the twisted bars and approached the cowering woman.

"I see you've met the Bureau's newest weapon," the warlock said, one hand scratching the creature behind the ears. "An Extension Filth."

Leslie did not move from her place against the wall, the Filth's face inches from hers. Mr. Clean reached out for her. Leslie put her thin hand into his, carefully sliding away from the huge Filth as he hoisted her up.

The warlock drew a strip of gray cloth from his white lab coat. "Do you know what this is?" he asked. "It is the cuff of a shirtsleeve, ripped from the arm of a very elusive man." He held up the scrap. "But I'm about to make sure that he never escapes again."

Mr. Clean paused. For a moment, Spencer was afraid that the man had somehow detected his spying eyes. Then the warlock continued, his voice metered and steady. "You're going to bring me Alan Zumbro—dead or alive."

Spencer almost lost contact, his hand slipping on the bronze medal in his pocket. He forced himself to linger in the vision a moment longer, to face Mr. Clean's terrible pronouncement.

Leslie wrinkled her forehead. "I thought Alan was—"

"The Rebels rescued him," the warlock cut her off. "But he doesn't have the package. He's out there now, looking for it."

"Where?" Leslie asked.

Mr. Clean approached the Extension Filth. He adjusted the dial on the battery pack just enough to cause the creature's head to perk up. Then he lowered the scrap of cloth to the beast's nose.

The Toxite inhaled sharply, its slit nostrils opening wide to take in the scent. Then the warlock dropped his hand lower. The Filth's coarse tongue emerged and the razor teeth snapped together, Mr. Clean barely pulling away his hand in time. The creature chewed noisily on the scrap of cloth and then swallowed.

"All is ready now," said the warlock. "The Extension Filth has been baited."

"So your beast will lead me to Alan?"

Mr. Clean laughed. "It's not *my* beast." He unclipped the belt and battery pack. "It's *yours*." He held the items out. "On its own, an Extension Toxite is reckless. Plug it in, wear the battery pack, and you have the power to control it. Saddle up, Leslie. Become a Plugger."

With shaking hands, Leslie Sharmelle accepted the pack. She turned to the huge Filth, and Spencer could see her reluctance to climb onto its back.

"I have a gang of Pluggers waiting to meet you at the edge of town," Mr. Clean said. "They will teach you to control your beast and prepare you for the manhunt."

The big warlock stepped away, passing through the wrecked bars. "I'm trusting you to prove yourself," he said. "To do better than your previous assignment." Mr. Clean turned away from the cell. "If you fail me again, Leslie, there will be no forgiveness. I'll have no choice but to deal with you . . . the *Clean* way."

CHAPTER 2

"THAT'S JAYWALKING!"

Spencer's head slammed against his desk. His hand slipped from his pocket, releasing his clutch on the bronze medallion. He snapped his head back, gasping for air as he sat bolt upright in his desk.

"Spencer Zumbro!" Mrs. Natcher's voice cut through the stillness of the math-enveloped classroom. "It seems you would like to share your answer with the class."

Answer? What answer? Mr. Clean had just broken into prison and put a death sentence on Alan Zumbro! How could Spencer possibly think about math?

"Uh . . ." Spencer glanced down at his notebook, but he couldn't focus on the page. He had to get home and call his dad immediately. He had to warn Alan that a giant Filth was out to hunt him!

"My socks are warm and fuzzy," Spencer said. His face

flushed with embarrassment, his eyes darting over to Daisy's desk. But his classmate was somehow the only person in the room who still appeared to be working on the math problem.

"Excuse me?" Mrs. Natcher's gray eyebrows rose, further wrinkling her forehead and pushing back her impossibly tight hairline.

"My socks are warm and fuzzy!" Spencer said it loud and clear this time, wondering why Daisy hadn't come up with a less conspicuous code phrase.

They had decided that they needed something to shout out in case of an emergency Toxite infestation. Spencer had suggested several phrases that might not seem out of place in a classroom: "I'm downright confused," or, "I don't understand this concept." But Daisy was too afraid that she'd forget. Or worse, that she'd use the phrase in a nonemergency situation. So Daisy insisted on the Gates family emergency code phrase.

"Your socks are warm and fuzzy?" Mrs. Natcher said.

Daisy sprang into action, slamming her math notebook closed and jumping to her feet. Mrs. Natcher spun to face Daisy, giving Spencer a moment to gather some Glopified supplies from his desk: a Ziploc bag of vacuum dust, a latex glove, and a chalkboard eraser. He most likely wouldn't return to the classroom today, and he didn't want Mrs. Natcher to find anything if she went snooping.

"I've got to go," Daisy said.

"You need a note for an early checkout," answered Mrs. Natcher.

Daisy shook her head. "To the bathroom!" she whispered.

"Take the hall pass," came the usual answer. Without delay, Daisy crossed the room, grabbed the doll pass, Baybee, and ducked out the door.

Okay, that was *not* the plan. When the code phrase was spoken, Spencer and Daisy were supposed to help each other leave the classroom. They had rehearsed a number of scenarios that would do the trick. Now Daisy had skipped out the easy way, leaving Spencer to fend for himself. And Baybee, the only real ticket out of the classroom, was gone too.

Mrs. Natcher swept down the aisle between desks, a piece of chalk still gripped between her fingers. Spencer sat stunned, partly from Daisy's retreat, and partly from Mrs. Natcher's advance. He didn't even realize that he was clutching his Glopified chalkboard eraser until the teacher pointed it out.

"So that's what happened to my missing eraser!" She reached for the object, but Spencer pulled away.

"What? No," he said. "This one's mine." He couldn't let Mrs. Natcher get her hands on a Glopified weapon. "I brought it from home!"

"Don't be ridiculous." Mrs. Natcher turned up her nose at him. She held out her hand, palm as flat and stiff as a ruler. She wasn't going to wrestle him for it. "Mine, Spencer."

What could he do? Gently, like he was placing the winning block in a game of Jenga, Spencer laid the Glopified eraser on the teacher's outstretched hand. She closed her fingers around it and returned to the front of the room.

Even on the best of days, Mrs. Natcher wasn't the most delicate flower. When upset, Spencer knew she was especially heavy-handed at erasing the chalkboard. All she'd have to do was erase her pie chart, and the whole classroom would fill with paralyzing white dust! Unless he could somehow contain the explosion . . .

"The correct answer is: 23 more apples than bananas," Mrs. Natcher said. Without even asking who got it right, the teacher swiveled on her hard heel and slammed the eraser against the chalkboard.

As soon as the Glopified weapon made contact, Mrs. Natcher disappeared in a puff of white chalk dust. It swirled up her arm, overtaking her face and gray hair bun faster than anyone could react.

Anyone except Spencer, of course. He had been expecting the worst from the moment he handed over the eraser. As the teacher coughed from within the quickly expanding cloud, Spencer sprinted toward the front of the room, weaving between desks.

The classroom was a mix of emotions now. The students began talking all at once, some conversations laced with subdued chuckles. Chalkboard erasers were known to puff if not properly cleaned. And so far, the Glopified cloud hadn't spread enough to look too unnatural.

Having previously been a victim of chalk dust, Spencer wisely held his breath. He dove into the puff of whiteness at the front of the room, finding Mrs. Natcher's arm and ripping the eraser out of her grasp. The weapon fell to the floor, and Spencer pounced on it . . . with his lunch box.

He slammed the metal box closed, wondering what was happening to his sandwich and pudding pack as the eraser continued to detonate inside. The cloud in the classroom was already thinning, Mrs. Natcher leaning against the board. The dust on her face and hands made her look somewhat like a zombie, all pale and creepy.

Spencer staggered to his feet, gripping his lunch box in both hands. The thing was shaking as pressure built to a dangerous level. He skirted around the edge of the classroom until he reached the window. Ripping aside the thick paisley curtains, he pulled open the glass, pushed out the screen, and threw his lunch box as far as he possibly could.

Spencer yanked the curtains closed, not even waiting to see if the lunch box exploded. His classmates were crowding around Mrs. Natcher as she coughed and wheezed. They had no idea that Spencer had just saved them from temporary paralysis. And Spencer had a feeling that *thank you* would not be among the words he'd hear from Mrs. Natcher if he waited for her to make a full recovery.

Spencer quietly backed across the classroom and pushed open the door. He slipped into the hallway just as Daisy rounded the corner. They stopped, face-to-face—one with a baby-doll hall pass, the other with chalky white hands.

Finally, Spencer shrugged. "What happened to our escape plan?"

"Sorry," Daisy shrugged back. "It was an emergency." She hefted Baybee as proof.

"I know it was an emergency," Spencer said. "That's why I said *my socks are warm and fuzzy!*"

Daisy's eyes widened. "You mean . . . there really is an emergency? I just had to go to the bathroom."

Spencer rolled his eyes. "Come on!" He set off down the hallway, hoping Daisy would follow before Mrs. Natcher came looking. "We've got to call my dad!"

"From the front office?"

"No," Spencer said. "It's got to be more private. Maybe your dad can give us a ride to my house."

"But," Daisy stammered, "you heard Mrs. Natcher. We can't check out early without a note!"

Spencer stopped to face her. She hadn't seen Mr. Clean ride into that prison on a giant Extension Filth. Daisy didn't understand the danger. "It's a matter of life and death," he said. "If you want to go back to class, then do it now and pretend like you never saw me out here!"

"But I did see you," Daisy said. "So let's go."

As soon as they burst through the school's front door, Spencer and Daisy felt the sting of winter on their skin. There hadn't been time to grab coats—especially for Daisy, who had thought she was just going to the bathroom.

It was a deceptively bright day, with plenty of sunshine but no warmth from it. Spencer and Daisy ran across the parking lot, trying not to slip on patches of ice. Just outside Mrs. Natcher's classroom was a cloud of white dust from the chalk eraser explosion. So his lunch box *had* blown up after all. Good thing he wasn't hungry.

Spencer jumped off the sidewalk, his shoes breaking through the crunchy upper layer of snow. "This way!"

"That's jaywalking!" Daisy said. "There's no crosswalk there!"

Spencer paused in the road. "We're running away from school and you're worried about crosswalks?"

A silver Cadillac suddenly turned the corner, emerging from behind a snow-covered pine tree. Spencer spun around, making eye contact with the driver as the car slipped toward him on the icy road.

It was Principal Poach. And he had a mouthful of French fries.

The principal screamed, spraying fries onto the windshield. Spencer dove aside, landing safely in the crusty snowbank as the principal jerked on the wheel. The Cadillac crossed the road, skipped up the curb, and smashed into a streetlight.

Daisy was at Spencer's side in a minute, Baybee tucked under her arm. "I'm fine," Spencer said, rising to his feet. "That was Poach. We've got to check on him!"

The hood of the Cadillac was folded around the streetlight. Peering through the driver's window, the kids saw a streak of red oozing from the corner of Principal Poach's mustache. His eyes were closed.

"He's bleeding!" Daisy said. She thrust Baybee into Spencer's hand and jerked open the car door.

But Spencer shook his head, pointing to the McDonald's bag on the seat and the spewed French fries on the dashboard. "It's ketchup."

The word *ketchup* seemed to bring Principal Poach around. His little tongue reached out, lapping at the red sauce in his mustache. He muttered something under his breath. Spencer thought it was *cheeseburger*. Then, suddenly, Principal Poach was completely revived and alert.

"Twenty-four years I have driven this road to Welcher Elementary and I have never—*never*—seen such behavior!" The principal struggled to climb from the crashed car, his weight wedging him behind the steering wheel. He threw his bulk forward once, twice. Third time was the charm, and Poach rolled out onto the snowbank.

"Should have known it would be you." The principal looked at Spencer as he rose, panting, to his feet. "Should have known you'd be standing in the middle of the road with your baby doll, trying to make me crash."

"It's not *my* doll," Spencer said. "It's Mrs. Natcher's."

The principal's face, already a reddish hue from anger and exertion, turned a shade of purple as he pointed a hot-dog-shaped finger directly at Spencer. "Stealing Mrs. Natcher's things, eh? Theft of school property!"

"We didn't steal it," Spencer said, holding out the doll. "It's the hall pass."

"Hahaha!" Principal Poach laughed. The creaking sounds of his wrecked car were working him into unhealthy hysteria. "Hall passes are for hallways, not for roads!"

"Sorry," Daisy said. "We got lost."

The big man rested a pudgy hand on the crumpled hood of his once-shiny vehicle. "It was new, you know." He nodded, jowls quavering. "New car. Christmas gift from the missus." A tear slipped down his ample cheek. "Now how am I supposed to explain the ketchup stain on the front seat?"

Spencer started backing away. He'd heard about people going into shock after a car crash. But this didn't look like shock. Principal Poach was going crazy!

"Suspended!" Poach shouted. "Both of you are suspended for the rest of the month!"

"Wait a minute," Spencer said. "What? You can't suspend us like this!" Getting suspended was for kids like Dez, not hardworking students like Spencer and Daisy!

"Suspended!" He shooed them away, clearly wanting some time alone to grieve over his smashed Cadillac. Spencer tugged at Daisy's arm and the two of them began a hesitant retreat.

"And when you come back . . ." Poach shouted. "No—*if* you come back . . . you better bring that stolen doll pass!"

CHAPTER 3

"YOU WOULDN'T GET IT."

By the time they reached the Gates home, Spencer had explained everything to Daisy. She might have been terrified by Mr. Clean's visit to Leslie Sharmelle; she should have been upset by Leslie's pending escape and the death sentence on Alan Zumbro. But Daisy Gates was hung up on one little detail.

"We just got suspended!" she said again, walking up her driveway.

"Don't think of it like that," Spencer said. He paused at the edge of the sidewalk, eyeing the big black dog chained to the front porch. "Maybe Principal Poach didn't mean it . . ."

A head poked out of the garage beside the house. It was prematurely bald, with a ring of hair around the side that managed to hold its color. Daisy froze, making eye contact with her dad.

"Early release today?" Mr. Gates asked, strolling down the driveway. He had a greasy tool in one hand and a denim coat flung over his smudged coveralls.

"Bad news, Pops," Daisy said. "We just got suspended!"

Mr. Gates stopped, his eyebrows meeting in confusion. "Suspended?" He whistled through his teeth. "That sounds horrid, Daisy. What happened?

Daisy took a deep breath. "We ran away from school and then Principal Poach crashed into a pole because Spencer was jaywalking."

Spencer rolled his eyes. Daisy didn't know how to sugarcoat the story. She was giving her dad the hard facts, and Spencer braced himself for the reaction.

"How long are you out for?" Mr. Gates asked.

"Rest of the month," answered Daisy.

Mr. Gates nodded solemnly. "At least it's February," he said. "Shortest month of the year." He absently wiped a bit of grease from the wrench in his hand. "Was it worth it? Leaving school. Did you have a good reason?"

Daisy pointed back to where Spencer stood at the edge of the sidewalk. "Spencer's worried about his dad . . ."

"He's out of town . . . again." Spencer said the last word with a trace of bitterness. "I'm worried about the weather. Got to check on him."

Mr. Gates turned to his daughter. "Your mother's gonna turn the color of beet juice when she finds out you got suspended." Daisy hung her head, and Mr. Gates glanced

nervously toward the house. "I don't like beet juice." He dug
in his pocket until he found a little ring of keys. "Quick!" he
whispered. "To the truck!"

Spencer and Daisy clambered after him, ascending the
red Ford pickup parked against the curb. Daisy claimed the
hump as Spencer shook the snow off his feet and hoisted
himself into the huge passenger seat. The cushion was worn
thin, and a few springs rose uncomfortably against his backside, but Spencer didn't complain.

The ignition cranked a few times before Mr. Gates managed to get the truck bouncing down the frosty road toward
Spencer's Hillside Estates neighborhood. The heater was on
full blast, but the air hadn't warmed yet.

"Why don't you two stick together this afternoon?"
Mr. Gates said. "Hide out at the Zumbros' for a while." He
tapped Daisy's knee with a greasy finger. "Mom's all worked
up about that storytime presentation she's supposed to give
at the library tonight. It would be best for everyone if she
doesn't find out you were suspended." He rubbed a hand
along the steering wheel. "At least till tomorrow."

Daisy shivered without her coat, clutching Baybee close.
"Thanks, Dad. For not being too mad," she said. "We left for
a reason. Spencer's really worried about his dad."

Mr. Gates nodded. "Can't say I blame him." He whistled
through his teeth again. "Poor kid."

Spencer sighed, letting his head rest against the window. Daisy and her dad had an obnoxious way of talking as
if they were alone, regardless of who else was listening. It

was most awkward in moments like these, when the subject of the conversation was sitting only inches away.

"You gotta help him through it, Daisy," said Mr. Gates. "I mean, his dad came back almost three months ago, but I still haven't seen them down at the baseball diamond together."

Daisy pointed out at the crusted snowbanks whipping past the window. "Maybe 'cause it's winter."

"Baseball was a metaphor," Mr. Gates said. "I've just noticed that his dad hasn't been around much since he came back."

"He's a really busy guy," Spencer finally cut in. He didn't want to know where the conversation was headed. He didn't want to compare Mr. Gates's involvement in Daisy's life to his own father's absence. Alan Zumbro was alive. Spencer was supposed to be happy.

"My dad's doing something important," Spencer said. "And he's in danger. That's why we had to leave school." He stared out the window, his breath fogging the glass. "You wouldn't get it."

Mr. Gates turned up the steep road toward the lavish mansions of Hillside Estates. "I might not get it," said Mr. Gates. "But the two of you better have this sorted out before you go back to school next month."

Daisy nodded. "That gives us . . ." she counted on her fingers, "ten days to find the package?"

Spencer tried to nudge her inconspicuously but only managed to elbow Baybee in the head. Why did Daisy have to mention the package in front of Mr. Gates? It was that mysterious parcel that kept Alan away, kept him searching across the country. Kept him from being a real dad.

Mr. Gates leaned forward, squinting out the windshield. "You guys get a new automobile?" he asked, a half-grin spreading across his face.

Spencer peered ahead to see a large blue garbage truck idling on the street in front of Aunt Avril's house, exhaust pipe chugging diesel pollutants into the cold midmorning air.

The huge vehicle was completely blocking the Zumbro driveway, so Mr. Gates did a quick U-turn in the street to drop off the kids. They jumped out, Daisy nearly slipping on a patch of ice in the road. Mr. Gates waved a greasy hand, and his pickup rolled out of sight.

"Ooh, good timing." Daisy turned her attention to the big blue garbage truck. "I always like to watch it dump the stuff."

Spencer stepped toward the front of the garbage truck. Straining against the glint on the glass, he saw that the cab was empty. "That's weird."

"Not too weird," Daisy said. "In my neighborhood it happens every Monday morning and I stand out on the front porch and watch. I'm usually not fast enough to see the part where the big metal claw grabs the trash can, but I get to see it all come tumbling out. And sometimes, if I look really close, I can even catch a glimpse of something that I threw away just a day or two before."

"There's no driver." Spencer pointed to the empty cab. "And garbage pickup isn't till tomorrow." He looked around the truck to the front of Aunt Avril's house. There was no movement in the windows, and the Zumbro SUV wasn't parked in the driveway. That meant no one was home but the idling garbage truck.

"So what's this guy doing here?" Daisy asked.

There was a crash, a bang, and the sound of shattered glass, momentarily rising above the monotonous purr of the garbage truck's diesel engine. Spencer and Daisy dropped to their knees at the edge of the driveway, taking shelter behind an icy bank of dirty snow that had been pushed up by the plows.

"What was that?" Daisy whispered. "That crash! It was like someone breaking into the side of your house!"

Spencer dug in his pocket for the vac dust and Glopified latex glove. "I'm going to check it out," he said. "You be my backup. Do you have any supplies?"

Daisy hoisted the hall pass. "Just Baybee," she whispered. That would have to be good enough. Besides, Daisy had once used Baybee as a club against Dez. The doll could be quite deadly.

Pinching out a strong dose of vacuum dust, Spencer sprinted across his driveway. He paused momentarily at the corner of the house, just long enough to take two steadying breaths. Then he leapt around the frozen downspout and came face-to-face with a pile of garbage.

CHAPTER 4

"I'M THE FIRST ONE HERE, THEN?"

In truth, there were many piles of garbage littering the snow beside Aunt Avril's house. They were heaped in tidy mounds, like a dozen multicolored molehills.

The big waste bins that were normally tucked against the side of the fence had been tipped over, their lids askew. A week's worth of Zumbro trash and recycling had been recklessly dumped.

At first, Spencer thought it was an animal. Raccoons, skunks . . . any number of critters could have ventured into Hillside Estates and torn into the garbage. But that didn't explain the sorted piles. Spencer didn't know of a single creature that would ransack a recycle bin and then separate the plastics from the newspapers. . . .

Spencer saw a blur of movement as something rounded the corner from the back of the house. He leapt forward,

25

hurling his vac dust in a widespread Palm Blast. The Glopified dust struck dead-on, sending the approaching figure toppling into the overturned garbage can. The lid flopped shut and the black can quivered, pivoting in the snow and grating against the side of the house.

Daisy appeared at Spencer's side, Baybee raised aggressively in her hand. "Are you all right?" she asked Spencer as the vac dust subsided.

"Fine, actually!" shouted a response from the depths of the black trash can. "I'm . . . I'm fine!" The lid of the garbage can snapped back as someone kicked from within.

Spencer readied a second blast of vacuum dust, but the stranger who emerged from the trash can looked so peculiar that any sense of threat was momentarily forgotten.

He was a short man, Spencer could tell once he managed to get on his feet. His striped overalls were tucked into tall yellow rubber boots that squeaked underfoot as he righted himself in the snow.

The man tugged at his unbuttoned coat—a tan tweed jacket with patches sewn onto the elbows. It looked nice, like something a businessman might wear to a meeting. But the man's long necktie, made entirely of duct tape, didn't seem to match.

To round off the whole attire, the stranger was wearing a leather aviator cap, like an air force pilot from World War II. The brown cap was worn and weathered, the straps flapping against the man's cheeks and the buckle jingling beneath his chin.

The man straightened his cap, twitched his pencil-thin

mustache from side to side, and took a step toward Spencer and Daisy.

"I'm the first one here, then?" His voice had an unusual accent, but Spencer couldn't place it. New York, maybe?

"Who are you?" Spencer asked, his fingers tightening on the vacuum dust.

"Who am *I*?" He looked around, his face long with mock astonishment that no one had recognized him. "The name is Bernard Weizmann. *Dr*. Bernard Weizmann."

"Dr. Bernard Weizmann?" Daisy whispered.

"You know him?" Spencer glanced at his shivering classmate.

Daisy shook her head. "Never heard of him. But he sounds like a wise man."

The man chuckled, smoothed his duct-tape tie, and took a bow. "Call me Bern, Bernie, Bernard. Whichever you prefer."

"What are you doing at my house?" Spencer said.

"Ahh!" Bernard gave an overexaggerated wink. "But this isn't your house, is it? The Zumbro family appears to be renting here—more likely tending, free of charge. No doubt a generous offer from Uncle Wyatt and Aunt Avril."

Spencer swallowed a lump in his throat. He wasn't cold, despite the frigid air. "Who sent you?" Was this common information among the BEM? "How do you know all this?"

"I just read the piles, kid." Bernard pointed to the multicolored mounds of trash and recycling in the snow.

"Wow!" Daisy said. "You're like some kind of garbage-reading fortune-teller?"

Bernard shook his head, aviator straps flapping. "Garbologist," he said. "I'm a garbologist."

"Wait," Spencer said. "Garbologist? Like someone who studies . . . *garbage?*"

Bernard held up a hand. "Don't act so disgusted. The garbage is my friend."

"What does it tell you?" Daisy asked.

A smile flashed across Bernard's face. "Anything I want to know." He took a knee in the snow, surrounded on all sides by organized piles of Zumbro trash. His eyes, stark blue in the bright reflection from the snow, danced from mound to mound.

"Your mum'll be back in a flash," Bernard said, glancing briefly at Spencer. "Not yet noon and she's had quite a hectic day. Preparing a birthday party for a younger sibling."

Bernard's hand darted out, scattering one of the piles. He lifted a shred of orange gift wrap and let it flutter back to the snow. "Max, I assume. Judging by the gift receipts, I'd say he's turning four, maybe five."

Bernard picked up an empty sugar box. "Max won't settle for a party without cake." Bernard's tongue came out, carefully licking a dark smudge on the side of the box. "Chocolate cake. Your mother hoped to have enough sugar for the recipe." He tossed the box. "And indeed she did. But it was the eggs . . ."

Bernard lifted an egg carton from the trash and opened it to reveal jagged shells still glistening from a fresh crack. "She needed three eggs. And she only had two." The garbologist shrugged. "So she ran to Food Mart. Be back in a flash, though."

A sudden, prolonged honking rang out from the street. Spencer swiveled to see the Zumbro SUV trying to pull into the blocked driveway.

"That was amazing!" Daisy said. "Is it really Max's birthday?" Spencer could only nod. "How'd you do that?"

Bernard Weizmann stretched his hands over the trash and grinned. "It's all here. You just gotta know what you're looking for."

The SUV finally parked against the roadside. Spencer saw Alice and Max climb out. His mom had a Food Mart bag in one hand, the clear outline of a rectangular egg carton hanging gently in the bottom.

"So what if you guessed it right," Spencer said. "That doesn't explain what you're doing here, sorting through my family's trash!"

Bernard clucked his tongue defensively. "I wasn't sure if this was the right place. I can't go ringing doorbells without doing a bit of research on the family." He stood up, dusting the snow off his striped overalls. "Turns out that it is the right place, though. So we can go inside now, if you please."

"No, I don't please," Spencer said. "Not until you clean up this mess!"

"This is not a mess!" Bernard shouted back. "This is scientific research!" The garbologist took a deep breath. "Look, Spencer. Your dad handpicked me to be on this team. The pieces are moving. So we can stand out here and bicker like schoolgirls." He turned to Daisy. "No offense." Then back at Spencer. "Or, we can get inside and figure out who called the team."

"What team?" Daisy said. "I thought Alan didn't play baseball."

"It's not about baseball," Bernard said. "It's about saving the world."

"I thought we were trying to save education," Daisy said.

"Destroying education is only the BEM's first step toward world domination. If education fails, the rest of the nation will follow too easily," Bernard continued. "But we have a chance to stop them this very day!" The garbologist turned his blue eyes on Spencer. "Didn't you hear? Someone found the package."

CHAPTER 5

"YOU ARE A STRANGER."

Spencer and Daisy led Bernard Weizmann through the back door of the house. They entered directly into the kitchen, taking Alice Zumbro by such surprise that her fingers slipped on the eggbeaters, spraying chocolate cake batter everywhere.

"Spencer!" Her eyes went to the clock on the wall. "What are you . . . ?" Then she saw Bernard, standing in the doorway with his dripping yellow boots. "Who is . . . ?"

"Dad's in trouble," Spencer said. "The BEM's going for him. They have a group of . . ." He stopped, not knowing how to describe what he'd seen at Leslie Sharmelle's prison cell. "It's bad, Mom. I've got to warn him!"

Spencer crossed to the table, grabbed the phone, and began dialing.

"No way he'll answer," said Bernard, clomping to the center of the kitchen in his shiny boots.

"Excuse me?" Alice said. "Who are you?"

He smoothed his tie and took a bow. "The name's Dr. Bernard Weizmann."

Daisy stepped forward. "He's a garbologist."

"A gar-whoola-what?" Alice said.

"Come on!" Spencer started dialing again. "Pick up the phone, Dad! He's not answering."

"Of course not," Bernard said. "The whole team's been off the grid for almost twelve hours already." He glanced at the clock on the wall. "Since midnight last night."

"Off the grid?" Daisy said. "What's that supposed to mean?"

Bernard crossed the room, and Spencer let him take the phone. He'd dialed the number three times, but Alan's phone was definitely turned off.

Bernard seated himself at the head of the kitchen table. Wordlessly, the others filed around him. The garbologist cleared his throat, as though he were some college professor about to begin a sophisticated lecture.

"Since Alan's return last November, the Rebels have been pouring everything into his mission. Top priority is to find that package. Problem is, nobody knows what's in it. Last thing Alan remembers was mailing it to you," Bernard pointed at Spencer. "But that was more than two years ago, and you clearly never got it."

Spencer nodded in agreement. That misunderstanding

had led him to New Forest Academy and a series of dangerous events.

"A few months ago, Alan assembled a small Rebel team—specialists devoted full-time to searching for the package," Bernard continued. "But we knew that the BEM would have eyes and ears on us at all times. So if one of us actually did find the package, how could we gather the team without bringing half the BEM on top of us?"

Bernard reached inside his tan tweed jacket and unclipped something. It was a two-way radio. Spencer had seen them at school. The front office used similar walkie-talkies to contact the custodians about messes or other problems.

"Walter Jamison set up a communication grid of Glopified walkie-talkies. They operate on a modulating frequency over any distance. That makes it hard for the BEM to listen in, but easy for us to communicate with each other. Everybody on the team has a walkie-talkie. They've got everlasting battery power and unlimited range, so the radios stay on at all times. But here's the catch. If one person switches off his walkie-talkie, the whole grid comes down. All the walkie-talkies shut off."

"Why?" Spencer said. "That doesn't make sense."

"Of course it does!" Bernard picked up the walkie-talkie. "It makes scads of sense! If one of us finds the package, we don't go blabbing it over the radio for any BEM spy to hear. We quietly switch off the walkie-talkie and head to the nearest predetermined rendezvous point." Bernard reached inside his jacket and clipped the radio back in place.

"Who found the package, then?" Daisy asked.

Bernard shrugged. "Won't find out till we get the whole team together."

"Here?" It was the first thing Alice had said since sitting down. "The team's coming here?"

"There are three rendezvous locations," Bernard said. "Zumbro household on Hillside Estates is number one. We have twelve hours to get here, hoping that everybody shows. If not, we move quickly and quietly to the second rendezvous, and so on to the third. Once everybody makes it, we open the package and do whatever it takes to complete the mission."

"Who else is coming?" Spencer asked. "Who's on the team?"

"Alan Zumbro, mission leader and Toxite scientist." Bernard said it like he was reading a roster. "Walter Jamison, Rebel warlock. Penny Jamison, Glopified weapons specialist." He paused for effect. "And of course, the one and only . . . Dr. Bernard Weizmann, garbologist."

"Four of you?" Alice said.

"Four? No, no," Bernard said. "Six." He pointed across the table at Spencer and Daisy. "You two have been part of the team since Alan handpicked it in November."

"Hold on a minute," Alice cut in. "My husband picked a couple of twelve-year-olds to be part of a top-secret mission?"

Bernard made a nonconfrontational expression. "They saved his life, you know. The man has serious trust issues. He's just surrounding himself with people he can depend on." Bernard shrugged. "Besides, we'll need Spencer for his . . . *visions.*"

"Absolutely not," Alice said. She muttered Alan's name

under her breath. "This is unbelievable." Alice leaned forward, and Spencer could see a monologue brewing at her lips. Dr. Bernard Weizmann was about to see his mother's fury.

"I try very hard," Alice began, "not to judge people. I like to consider myself fairly tolerant." She took a deep breath. "Then you show up. A *garbologist*. You walk in here with your yellow boots and duct-tape tie and expect me to turn these kids over to you?" She pinched her lips together. "Oh, no, sir! First it was Garth Hadley. Then it was Slick at New Forest Academy. Now it's you. You are a stranger. And you are a *strange* stranger!" She slammed her hand against the table for emphasis.

Bernard remained surprisingly calm in the face of mother Zumbro. "I assure you, my allegiance is with the Rebel Underground," he said. "And you can verify that with anyone you trust."

Alice smirked. "Conveniently for you, everyone I trust is now off the grid."

Spencer and Daisy watched the debate unfold. Alice was a thorough interrogator, but Bernard's composure and self-confidence did not betray him. But even though Spencer's first impression of Bernard was that he was genuine, the BEM was ever sly and manipulative.

"What about the visions?" Bernard pointed at Spencer. "I've heard the kid can see the warlocks. Is it true?"

Spencer shifted under the sudden change in conversation. The debate had fallen out of his mom's hands and into his own. He stammered, unsure now if he should trust Bernard with any information about his special Auran powers.

"Do your thing," Bernard said. "Check on Walter. If I'm telling the truth, then he'll be making his way to one of the rendezvous points to meet with the team."

Spencer looked at Daisy, then at his mom. He felt the weight of the bronze medallion in his left pocket. He'd tried to see Walter earlier, but that vision had led to something really frightening and upsetting. Spencer didn't want to risk seeing Mr. Clean again. But Bernard had a point. The only way to verify his allegiance would be to check on Walter.

"Okay," Spencer said. He reached into his pocket, digging until he came to the hard, cold medallion. His fingertips brushed the metal, and the kitchen instantly went white.

Spencer braced himself for the worst and was pleasantly relieved to find himself in the driver's seat of a familiar janitorial van. Walter's old hands turned the wheel, guiding the big vehicle around a corner.

He glanced at his watch and muttered something. "This is a message for Spencer. I'm repeating it every three minutes, in case you're watching me. I'm too late to reach the first rendezvous point in Welcher. Hopefully Alan, Penny, or Bernard will make it. Go with them. I'll meet you at the third site."

Spencer didn't need anything more. He released the bronze medal in his pocket, instantly reviving to the Zumbro kitchen table. With everyone watching him, Spencer realized that he was about to resolve everything by stating Bernard's loyalties.

He looked at his mom. "Bernard's with us," he said. "Walter said we should go with him."

Alice gave a defeated moan while Bernard let out a victorious chuckle. "That's some talent you got, kid." He grinned at Spencer. "I see why Alan wants you on the team."

"Look," Alice said, "it doesn't really matter what Alan wants. The mother in me isn't going to let you take these kids."

"Too late," Bernard said. "The kids are already here. Already off the grid."

"To be honest," Daisy said, "I never really felt like I was *on* the grid."

"Yeah," said Spencer. "If we've always been part of the team, then how come nobody told us about the walkie-talkies?"

Alice pushed away from the table, her face flushed. She stalked out of the kitchen. Bernard watched until she was out of earshot. "Pass me the beaters," he said.

Spencer glanced at the eggbeaters propped against the mixing bowl, still sticky with chocolate cake batter. "You're not licking the beaters," Spencer said. He shivered at the thought of Bernard contaminating the whole cake with his spit.

Bernard held up a finger. "Just one?"

Alice appeared around the corner and Bernard dropped his plea. Her jaw was tight as she reseated herself beside Bernard. Alice leaned forward and set something on the table in front of Spencer.

It was another walkie-talkie. Just like Bernard's.

"I was supposed to give it to you," Alice said. Her voice was tight, her eyes watery. "Your dad said that if you found the package you should turn off the radio and stay home."

Spencer felt a shock of betrayal. "Why didn't you tell me?"

"It's been three months since you brought him back, Spence," Alice whispered. "Since then, I have seen my husband twice. *Twice!*" She took a gasping breath to steady herself. "He has no right to involve you like this! If Alan thinks he can just stand on the sidelines and call for help whenever he needs it—"

"With all due respect, Mrs. Z," Bernard cut in, "Alan is out there doing everything in his power to save education and stop the fall of this great country."

"Well, maybe he should worry more about saving his family," Alice said. The room drooped in awkward silence. Alice lowered her face into her hands. She held her breath for a long moment.

Spencer felt a wash of similar emotions. What had been the point of rescuing his dad if they never got to see him anyway? It was jealous thinking, and it made Spencer angry. Angry at Alan for loving his secret work more than his family. Angry at Alice for not trusting her husband more.

Alice let out a long and deliberate sigh. Her hands slipped from her now-red eyes. She looked at Spencer, Daisy, and Dr. Bernard Weizmann. Then she whispered, "The package is downstairs."

"THAT'S IRONY."

It took a moment for Alice's words to ring around the kitchen table. Bernard stood up slowly. "Wait a minute," he said. "You're talking about *the* package?"

Alice nodded, her expression blank.

"How long has it been here?" Spencer had to ask the question. Had his mom been hoarding this information for all these months?

"I don't know," Alice said. "I just found it last night."

"It's been in the mail for over two years?" Daisy exhaled. "Slow delivery."

"It was delivered to our old house," Alice said, "years ago. It's addressed to Spencer, from Alan. And the postage date is a match. It must have gotten lost in the clutter of the old house. Somebody packed it when we moved and it's been sitting in a box downstairs for who knows how long. I was just looking for birthday candles."

A deep shred of anxiety entered Spencer's heart. A question came to his mind that he and Alan had both been interrogated for. "Did you open the package, Mom?" Spencer asked.

She turned to her son, managing to shake her head. "Your father said not to."

Spencer felt a rush of relief, dispelling his unease from the moment before. If Alice hadn't looked inside the package, then she posed no threat to the BEM. Now Spencer could leave safely, knowing that the Bureau wouldn't come after the rest of his family on Hillside Estates.

"Then it was you who took the radios off the grid?" Bernard asked, glancing at the walkie-talkie on the table in front of Spencer.

Alice nodded. "I thought he would come," she said.

"Oh, he's coming, all right." Bernard looked at the clock. "But not here. First rendezvous time expires in half an hour. We've got to take the package and move on to the next site."

"Happy birthday to me!" shouted a little voice from the entryway. The birthday boy stood with a mischievous glint in his eye, brown hair shaggy and unkempt. Max was pulling something wrapped in a bedsheet over one shoulder like a big makeshift sack. He'd dragged the load up the stairs when he saw the visitors at the table.

"Presents!" Max shouted, throwing back the sheet to expose his loot. The four-year-old had gathered anything that looked like it might be a birthday gift and piled it into his sack.

"Remember, Max," Alice said, "we're not opening presents till the party tonight."

Max threw his head back and growled. Then he dove into his pile of gifts and grabbed the biggest box in bright *happy birthday* wrapping. He shook the present with all his strength, listening to the way the box's contents clanked around.

"Presto Racing Police Edition Remote Control Car!" Max shouted at the top of his lungs. He did a little happy dance, kicking and scattering presents from his pile. Max's foot caught on something. He tripped, sending a parcel skidding across the hardwood floor to rest at Spencer's feet.

It was a white mailing tube, about a foot long, with plastic caps over both ends. There was a set of postage stamps at one end, slightly bent and crinkled from neglect.

Spencer reached down. His chair shifted, and the mailing tube rolled another half-turn, exposing a smudged address label in Alan Zumbro's distinctive handwriting.

To: Spencer Zumbro
477 Winowah Way
Spokane, WA 99223

From: Dad

Spencer's hand closed over the mailing tube, his heart hammering as he realized the significance.

"Mine!" Max threw himself at Spencer, gripping the

package with both hands. Spencer jerked back, feeling the mysterious contents of the mailing tube slide from one end to the other. The brother tug-of-war lasted only a moment.

Alice descended upon Max, prying him away from the important package, trying to explain that it wasn't another birthday gift. The conflict ended poorly, with Max abandoning his entire pile of presents and running, sobbing, to his bedroom.

"Poor little guy," Daisy said. She turned a disapproving stare at Spencer. "Why would you steal his presents?"

Spencer set the postal tube on the table, checking that the end caps were still secure. "Because it wasn't for him." Spencer pointed to the address label. "This is it."

Alice nodded in agreement, a trace of embarrassment on her face for having already lost track of the package's whereabouts.

Bernard put a hand to his forehead, as if the strain of the situation were too much to handle. It was clear how easily things could go missing in the Zumbro house. Only twelve hours after the vital package had been discovered, Max had almost thieved it for a birthday gift.

"Hmm," Daisy said. "I didn't think the package would look like that."

"What did you think?" Spencer said.

Daisy shrugged. "I thought it'd be a little black box covered in stickers that say *top secret*."

"Something you should know about top-secret packages," Bernard said. "They never say *top secret*." He leaned forward and picked up the mailing tube. He examined the postage stamps and the address label.

"Oh, the irony," Bernard muttered. "After all his time out searching, Alan could have found what he was looking for right here at home." Bernard shook his head. "That's irony."

Bernard sighed and tucked the package into the front of his striped overalls. Standing, he glanced at the clock once more. "Time's up," he said. "Best be getting on the road." He turned to Spencer and Daisy. "You two got any luggage?"

"They're not going with you," Alice said.

"Whoa, lady!" Bernard held out his hands. "You can't go making statements like that. These kids are part of the team. They're off the grid now, so regardless of what happens, they're going into hiding until the mission is over."

"What about school?" Alice said.

"About school . . ." Spencer muttered.

"We're good!" Daisy said. "We just got suspended. Can't go back till March."

Alice shook her head, as if she couldn't allow the idea of suspension to enter her brain right now. "What about your parents?" she said to Daisy. "You can't go off the grid with your parents!"

Daisy scratched her forehead. "Actually, I think they'd be okay with it."

"Are you kidding?" Spencer said. "Your parents are, like . . . *super* protective!"

Alice threw her hands in the air. "What does that make me?"

Daisy turned to Spencer, her eyes full of sincerity. "I think it's time to tell my parents."

"Tell them what?"

"The truth," Daisy said. "About everything."

"We've been over this, Daisy," said Alice. "Telling your parents would put them onto the BEM's radar. It would make your whole family a target. I promised Walter that I wouldn't—"

"But they'll believe me!" Daisy said. "They'll believe anything I say!" Again it was quiet around the kitchen table.

"Problem is," said Bernard, "you can't say anything. I'm no parent, but I don't imagine your folks will let you ride out of town in a stranger's garbage truck. We'll have to slip out quietly without confronting your parents."

"That's not my way," Daisy said. "I tell them everything!" She looked from face to face, but no one would hold eye contact. "At least a note!"

Bernard nodded. "Keep it vague. We can't have anyone finding out where we're going or how long we'll be there."

"Disneyland," Daisy said. "We're going to Disneyland."

Spencer fished a paper and pen from a drawer and passed them to Daisy. She stooped low over the page, her tongue sneaking out in concentration. When she began to write, Spencer, Alice, and Bernard couldn't help but watch every unconvincing word unfold.

Dear Mom and Dad,

Spencer needs some help. He's going to Disneyland with his dad and I have to go along. Luckily, we've been suspended from school, so we won't miss anything important. Be back soon!

Love, Daisy

She dotted the *i* in her name and sat back.

"Lovely note," Bernard muttered.

Alice sighed. "That's it?" she said. "Your folks are going to buy that?" She shook her head. "Of course, *I* have to be the bad guy again. *I* have to deliver the note and answer phone call after phone call from your parents."

Daisy tapped her chin with the pen. "One more thing!" She bent over and scratched out a final sentence at the bottom of the page:

P.S. My socks are warm and fuzzy!

Then she folded the note and slid it across the table to Alice. Daisy set down the pen. No one said anything about her quick postscript. It was gibberish to Alice and Bernard. But Spencer's mouth had fallen slightly open, and he studied Daisy with a curious expression.

Daisy finally looked over at him, a pleased smile across her face. "Well," she said, "I'm ready when you are. I've always wanted to go to Disneyland!"

CHAPTER 7

"TREASURE!"

A light snowfall flittered in the headlights of Bernard's garbage truck. The flurries had come and gone since dinner—never enough to whiten the road, but keeping the windshield wet so that Bernard had to use the wipers.

Bernard's garbage truck smelled weird. Spencer hadn't expected a nice scent, but the sight of so many car fresheners had momentarily lifted his hopes. Bernard had at least a few dozen pine-tree-shaped fresheners dangling from the truck's rearview mirror.

There was a myriad of scents: cinnamon, coconut, vanilla, sprucewood, lavender, and even bacon. The hodgepodge of fragrances, combined with the truck's preexisting odor of garbage, had been terrible at first. But after so many hours in the truck, Spencer had grown accustomed to the smell.

Spencer yawned. They were somewhere in eastern Wyoming. The Mickey Mouse clock on the dashboard said it was just after ten o'clock. They'd been driving steadily since noon, stopping only to refuel the garbage truck. Even lunch and dinner were eaten on the go. Alice had packed a cooler with enough food for the three of them.

Once she had finally agreed to let Spencer and Daisy go, Alice had gone above and beyond to prepare them for the journey. In addition to the meals, Alice had packed a gigantic duffel bag with blankets, sleeping bags, and clothes. Spencer's sister had a few clothes that would fit Daisy, as well as a coat, gloves, and hat. Thanks to Alice Zumbro, they were prepared.

"Ahh, goodie," Bernard said, cranking the big garbage truck around a corner. "Here we are at last."

Through the headlights and falling snow, Spencer saw a parking lot. Along both sides were rows of yellow school buses. There must have been more than fifty, all lined up and carefully parked. The windows were dark, and a bit of snow had started to gather on the roofs of the vehicles.

"It's like a bus cemetery," Daisy whispered as they pulled into the lot.

"Actually," Bernard said, "it's a district bus depot. This is where all the buses park overnight."

"Where are all the bus drivers?" Daisy asked.

"Probably at home sleeping," answered Bernard.

"But how'd they get home if all the buses are here? Ooh, maybe there's a special bus that all the bus drivers ride." She scratched her head. "But who would drive it?"

"Is this the second rendezvous point?" Spencer asked, distracting Daisy from her chain of useless questions.

"That's right," said Bernard. "We've got about two hours here." He parked the garbage truck in the center of the lot, with rows of quiet school buses on either side. "See if anybody from the team shows."

In Spencer's vision of Walter, the warlock had mentioned that he wouldn't meet them until the third rendezvous point. But that still left Penny and Alan unaccounted for. Either one could show up here.

Bernard's blue eyes scanned the area, pausing on a distant dumpster. "I'm going to check out the trash," he said. Reaching over, he opened the glove compartment and fished out a headlamp. Bernard strapped the light over his aviator cap, clicked on the bulb, and turned to the kids. "You two stay here." Then he lowered himself from the truck and took off at a jog toward the dumpster.

"Guy's crazy," Spencer said. "We've been with him for ten hours and don't know a thing about him."

"We know he likes garbage," Daisy said. She pulled a battered CD case from a pocket on the passenger door. "And he listens to *They Might Be Giants*."

"So he likes weird music and digs through people's trash." Spencer shrugged. "He's crazy."

"We know he's a good guy," Daisy said.

Spencer sighed. At least they had that assurance, directly from Walter's mouth. There was no questioning the garbologist's loyalty. Bernard was weird, but he was also a faithful Rebel.

"I mean, it's a good thing Bernard came to get us," Daisy said. "Without him, we wouldn't have even known we were on the team. I'd be back at home, listening to my mom's library presentation." Daisy glanced at the clock. "Actually, that's probably over by now."

Thoughts of home and Daisy's parents brought something back to Spencer's mind. It was something that he hadn't dared mention with Bernard in the truck. But now that he and Daisy were alone . . .

"My socks are warm and fuzzy," Spencer said.

Daisy instinctively flinched and ducked low in her seat. But Spencer shook his head. "I saw you write that at the bottom of your note."

Daisy relaxed a bit, seeing that there was no real danger. "It's a family phrase," she said.

"But it means something," said Spencer. "Something about danger."

Daisy shook her head. "Not danger. It means something Toxite-related is going on."

"But that doesn't make sense. Why would your parents use that phrase? They don't even know—"

"I need to tell you something," Daisy cut him off. "But you have to promise not to tell the others. Not your mom, not Walter, not anybody. Promise?" She stuck out her pinkie.

Spencer hadn't pinkie-promised in years. He'd grown out of it, realizing that a pinkie couldn't magically make someone keep a promise. But the look in Daisy's eye and the sincerity in her voice caused Spencer to offer up his pinkie without question.

Daisy linked her little finger around his. The cab of the garbage truck was already chilling off, and Spencer could see her breath against the passenger window.

"My parents know, Spencer."

Spencer should have seen it coming. The family phrase, Mr. Gates's unquestioning trust in his daughter . . . all the evidence led to this conclusion. But how could Daisy have kept this from Spencer?

"They've known from the very beginning," she continued. "When you left the soap at my house, I told my dad about it. I was scared to try, so he said he'd use the soap with me."

Spencer's pinkie slipped from their grasp. Part of him was impressed at Daisy's faithfulness in keeping it secret for so long. But another part of him felt utterly betrayed.

"That's how I knew your mom would believe us if we told the truth," Daisy said. "'Cause my parents already had. I've told them all about the BEM's plan to ruin education and take over the world. That's why they let me go to New Forest Academy. And that's why they're going to be okay with me going on this mission."

"You've got to tell Walter!" Spencer said. "Your parents could be in danger!"

"No!" Daisy held up her pinkie to reaffirm their promise. "The only reason they're safe is because no one knows that they know. It's our family strategy. We're the Gullible Gates family."

There, in the dim cab of Bernard Weizmann's garbage truck, Spencer sensed a depth to Daisy Gates. Her face half illuminated by a snowy streetlamp, Spencer saw a complexity and wisdom that he'd never noticed before.

"Promise?" Daisy said.

He nodded, taking her outstretched pinkie once again. "I promise."

The driver's door jerked open, and a little flurry of snow whipped into the truck. Bernard scampered up the steps, clutching something small in his hand. He was shivering, but there was a smile on his face.

"What did you find?" Spencer asked.

Bernard's headlamp shone on his hand. "Treasure!" His fingers uncurled to reveal the item he'd brought from the dumpster.

"A retainer!" Daisy said. Sure enough, Bernard was holding a dental retainer. The kind people wore to keep their teeth straight after braces.

"Not just any retainer," Bernard said. "Rainbow colored!" He held it outstretched, shining his light through it. "Red, orange, yellow, green, blue, indigo, *and* violet." He grinned, and Spencer thought he looked nuttier than ever. "Never found one like this before!"

"Uhh . . ." Spencer fidgeted in his seat. As far as he was concerned, retainers were one of the favorite hangouts for germs. What was Bernard doing, waving it around like he'd found treasure?

Bernard reached behind his seat and withdrew a battered steel briefcase. He flipped the clasps and folded back the lid. As his headlamp illuminated the contents, Spencer almost gagged.

The entire briefcase was full of used retainers! There must have been at least thirty, all different shapes and colors. The briefcase was lined with foam, and Bernard had pinned the retainers in place like specimens in a bug collection!

"Time out," Spencer said. "Why do you have a briefcase full of retainers?"

Bernard took an extra pin and carefully hooked the rainbow retainer next to the others. "You have any idea how many kids lose their retainers?" Bernard asked. "Leave them on the bus, throw them out with lunch . . ."

"That happened to me last year," Daisy said. "I've been retainerless ever since."

Bernard turned the briefcase toward her. "Any of these look like yours?"

Daisy squinted across the cab. "Yeah," she said. "Maybe that pink one . . ."

Bernard pulled out the pins and lifted the pink retainer from his briefcase. "This one's from Minnesota." He handed the object to Daisy. "See if it fits."

"No!" Spencer shouted, but Daisy was already tucking the retainer into her pocket for safekeeping. Spencer leaned over and shut Bernard's briefcase. "That's disgusting. We're putting the retainers away now."

Bernard shrugged and clasped the briefcase. "You should see my other collections." He turned around to reach behind the seat again.

Spencer stared out the windshield, bracing himself for whatever Bernard might have in store. In the frosty glow of the streetlamp, he noticed something. One of the school buses was gone.

Spencer leaned forward. His view through the windshield was blurred by slushy snow, but there was no mistaking it. In the solid row of school buses, one had suddenly vanished.

Then he saw a figure sprinting directly toward the garbage truck. Her distinct athletic movement identified her immediately.

"Penny," whispered Spencer.

"Nah," Bernard said. "I don't collect coins. But you'd be surprised at how many pennies end up in the trash. . . ."

"Penny!" Spencer shouted. But before Bernard could turn around, a yellow school bus came hurtling through the snowy night and slammed into the side of the garbage truck.

CHAPTER 8

"A JOYSTICK!"

There was a deafening crunch, followed by a moment of sheer disorientation. The school bus glanced off the garbage truck in a shower of glass. Bernard's sturdy truck teetered for a split second as half the wheels came off the pavement. Spencer and Bernard slid sideways across the seat. Daisy, who hadn't unbuckled her seat belt, whiplashed against the strap. Then the garbage truck tipped upright once more, rocking violently against the vehicle's shocks.

Bernard twisted the truck keys, muttering under his breath. The big engine cranked and the headlights flared up. It seemed as though the snow had suddenly increased. Visibility was obscured in a blanket of white.

Spencer squinted forward as the engine finally came to life. Penny was nowhere to be seen. Instead, the truck's headlights glinted against the reflective eyes of a giant creature.

It raced toward them through the snowy night, every stride revealing a new detail. It was an overgrown Filth, just like the kind Slick had been growing with Glopified extension cords at New Forest Academy. Just like the kind Mr. Clean had ridden into the prison to rescue Leslie Sharmelle.

The Filth was massive. Foamy white saliva streamed from its jowls. Sharp teeth gnashed with an insatiable hunger. The creature's deadly long quills were lying back, sleek and aerodynamic for speed.

There was something else that Spencer noticed as the Filth drew nearer. The sight of it confirmed his fears and caused his hands to shake.

This was more than just an angry relocated Toxite. There was a rider on the Filth's back! There was no doubt about it now. The Pluggers were here.

Bernard fumbled with the gears, finally sliding the truck into drive. He stepped on the gas, building momentum as he drove directly toward the charging Filth.

"What are you doing?" Spencer shouted. Hitting the huge Toxite could devastate the garbage truck, ruining their only chance of escape.

"You never played chicken?" Bernard said, closing the distance to impact.

"That's not a chicken!" screamed Daisy.

Spencer scrambled for his seat belt and braced himself against the dashboard. They were close enough to see the Filth rider. It was not Leslie Sharmelle, but a man wearing a winter face mask and heavy coat. His gloved hands clung to the mangy brown fur at the base of the Filth's neck. Spencer couldn't see the battery pack on his belt, but a thick exten-sion cord trailed out from under the man's coat.

"Yaahh!" Bernard shouted, frantically spinning the wheel. The garbage truck veered hard to the right, missing the Filth by mere inches. There was a harsh grating sound as the Filth flared its quills, raking the sharp points against the side of the truck.

Bernard spun the truck around, narrowly missing the row of school buses. Through the flurry of snow, they could see the parking lot exit. If they drove fast enough, they might be able to escape before the Filth caught up.

"Wait," Spencer said. "Penny was out there!"

Bernard scanned the bus depot. "Are you sure you saw—" He was cut off as the truck shuddered under a loud thump. Spencer looked out Daisy's window, glimpsing the truck's side mirror.

A huge Grime had latched onto the side of the vehicle. Its slimy body inched forward silently, venom oozing from its bulbous fingertips. Again there was a rider, masked and hooded. He clung to the Grime's back, seated on a floor mat draped across the creature's middle like a saddle.

The Grime advanced, its black tongue flicking out to taste the cab of the garbage truck. Its face was dangerously close to Daisy's window, and its potent distractor breath seeped through the glass.

Daisy giggled.

"Drive!" Spencer shouted. But Bernard was also watch-ing the Grime through the side mirror. He held up a finger for patience as he put the truck into park.

"You know," said Daisy, "I never really noticed how many cool buttons and switches there are in this truck."

There was no need for the side mirror now. The Grime's massive head was in view through the window. Spencer could see pale sacks on the creature's throat, pulsing with an eerie green light. In moments, the Grime's mouth would fill with deadly venom and the creature would sear its way into the truck.

"I love switches!" Daisy said. She flicked a black switch on the control panel. A bright light turned on at the back of the truck. "Ooh! A joystick!"

The Grime's sticky hand flashed into sight. It clamped onto Daisy's window and instantly shattered the glass into tiny fragments.

Spencer lunged sideways, jerking Daisy away from the control panel and pinning her down against the seat. The Grime's gigantic face pressed through the broken window just as Bernard grabbed the joystick.

The garbologist pulled the joystick back, and the truck's mechanical trash-collecting arm sprang into action. The claw closed around the Grime's middle. Bernard tugged the joystick to the right. The mechanical arm extended, stripping the Grime away from the garbage truck with a squelch. Bernard pushed the joystick in a new direction and the arm came down, pinning the creature to the pavement.

Spencer peered out the shattered window, the cold air forcing him to squint. The Grime wriggled free in a heartbeat, easily compressing its slimy body to escape the mechanical claw. But the fallen rider was trapped under the crushing arm of the garbage truck. The Grime crouched patiently nearby, like it was waiting for the human to break free.

Spencer could clearly see the battery pack around the man's waist. Extending from one end of the black box was a thick extension cord, frighteningly similar to Slick's old cord. The line extended from the man's belt, stretched tightly across the pavement, and plugged into the waiting Grime.

Spencer unbuckled his seat belt and leaned farther out the window. He needed to get a better view, to find out how the extension cord was controlling these massive Toxites.

There was a bloodcurdling screech from above. Spencer looked skyward, but before he could withdraw his head, a giant Rubbish was upon him. Its rough talons snatched the neck of his coat and yanked him through the open window.

Daisy screamed and grabbed his legs. For one hopeful moment, she held tight to Spencer's foot. Then his shoe came off, and he was soaring upward into the snowy night.

CHAPTER 9

"WHO'S NEXT?"

Spencer wasn't twenty feet up when he saw a blur of action on an aerial intercept course. It was Penny, a flying broom tucked tightly under one arm as she strained upward. Her second hand swung into action, a familiar short-handled mop flicking out. The white strings lassoed tightly around the huge Rubbish, trapping one wing against its hairy body and causing the creature to hiss in pain.

Then began the sick-stomach plunge toward the ground. The Rubbish spun earthward, completely out of control. The mop flew from Penny's grasp, but the Rubbish refused to release Spencer. Up became down. Spencer glimpsed a human rider clinging to the Rubbish's neck while the extension cord that joined them tangled around his chest.

From the tool belt at her waist, Penny drew another mop, casting the strings downward toward the falling monster. The mop wrapped tightly around Spencer's leg. The collar of his coat finally ripped, and the Rubbish's talons came free. The creature and its rider struck the ground in a painful heap. But Spencer dangled upside down from the mop, only a foot above the pavement.

The strings retracted as Penny touched down. Spencer staggered to his feet. With only one shoe on, his left toes were numb in his wet sock. Penny put a reassuring hand on his shoulder.

Only three months had passed since New Forest Academy, but Penny looked worn and weathered. Her gymnastics letter jacket was tattered and filthy, her red hair unkempt. Her slim figure was draped in Glopified janitorial weapons, and her eyes had a deadly edge.

The crashed Rubbish hopped upright, clacking its massive beak. The extension cord trailed back to the prone rider, but the Rubbish stood defensively over the human, its leathery wings stretching for intimidation.

"Here," Penny said, reaching into her janitorial belt. She handed Spencer a retractable razorblade. He'd used one of them before, months ago, when Marv had made him scrape old gum off desks at Welcher Elementary. Now he held it in his hand, wondering what such a tiny tool could do against a fearsome overgrown Toxite.

"I'll distract it," Penny said. "When the cord goes tight, cut it!"

Spencer looked hopelessly at the little blade. "With this?" But Penny was already moving off, a pushbroom in her hands.

Spencer put his thumb on the little button and pushed the blade up out of the handle. The sound of ringing metal caused him to jump back as a full, two-edged sword rose from the razorblade handle.

"Whoa!" He held the sword before him, amazed at how lightweight and agile it felt. "Definitely Glopified!"

The Rubbish croaked like a raven and hopped toward Penny. The rider moaned and pushed himself onto hands and knees. Penny went into a deep lunge, thrusting the pushbroom under the Rubbish's beak. The action sent the creature skyward, pulling tight the extension cord between man and Rubbish.

"Now!" Penny screamed.

Spencer leapt forward. His razorblade sword flashed through the falling snow and sliced the extension cord. There was a zap of electricity and a shower of sparks as Spencer rolled away.

The Rubbish twitched midair. Its mighty wings flapped and its head cocked, like an animal suddenly realizing its freedom. The rider groaned, trying to strip off the severed battery pack.

With a cry, the Rubbish went into a tight dive. Its sharp talons ripped into the man, jerking him from the ground and tossing him over the row of buses like a rag doll.

"Over here!" It was Daisy's voice, but Spencer couldn't find her. He looked back to the garbage truck. The huge Grime had climbed through the broken window, filling the entire cab. Only its yellow tail protruded from the window, flicking back and forth. The human rider stood by the cab, still attached to the creature by the extension cord trailing through the window.

"Spencer!" Daisy shouted again. Then Spencer saw the flicker of Bernard's headlamp coming from the back of the garbage truck, safely hidden from the rampaging Grime and its terrible breath. The hatchlike tailgate had lifted partway, and Daisy and Bernard were hunkered in the dark opening.

Penny must have seen them too. She grabbed Spencer's arm and took off for the garbage truck at a sprint. Spencer's soggy sock flapped against the pavement. His numb foot skimmed along painfully as Penny pulled him forward.

Out of the snowy darkness, a Filth snarled. The rider urged it forward, letting the beast fall into a charge.

"Close the razorblade!" Penny shouted. Spencer could barely comprehend. His heart was hammering, his head spinning with snowfall. His thumb slid onto the button and he clicked it back. Instantly, the sword blade collapsed into the handle. Spencer shoved it into his pocket just as they reached the garbage truck.

Penny flung Spencer through the opening and leapt up into the back of the truck. Her feet had barely cleared when the charging Filth smashed into the vehicle. Its ugly face pressed up through the opening, tongue lapping.

"Shut the hatch!" Penny yelled. But Spencer didn't see the wisdom in that plan. If the tailgate closed, they would be enclosed—*trapped*—in a place meant only for trash.

"No can do, kid!" Bernard shouted back. "Controls are in the cab!"

The Filth had a paw up now, its forked toe claws

scratching against the metal floor of the truck. It strained its neck, bristling a few quills.

Penny grunted in frustration as she unstrapped a large weapon from her back. Bernard's headlamp shone on the small handheld motor as Penny pulled the ripcord.

It was a leaf blower. Spencer felt a shiver pass through him. A few months ago, he'd seen Walter's early sketches to Glopify a leaf blower. It was part of Operation Vortex: a strategy to rescue Marv from his imprisonment in the overcharged Vortex vacuum bag. If Walter had completed work on the leaf blower, then maybe it was time! Maybe Marv was coming back!

But there was no time to ask Penny questions. The little motor roared to life, reverberating loudly in the empty metal garbage truck. Penny swung the long nozzle around, setting it inches from the slavering Filth. Narrowing her eyes, she pulled the trigger and sent a 200-mile-an-hour blast of Glopified wind into the creature's face.

The Filth's jaw instantly disintegrated into a puff of dust. The huge Toxite went skittering backward, rolling over its human rider and sliding out of sight.

"Who's next?" Penny shouted, revving the motor on her deadly leaf blower.

Spencer stood petrified in the center of the garbage truck, trying not to gag from the stench. At least the cab had air fresheners. Back here, it was the smell of pure trash. Even though the truck was empty, Spencer could feel a slick sludge on the floor, squishing against his sock. He kept his arms tucked close, as if worried that the grubby walls might reach out for him.

The back of the truck fell silent. Bernard stood next to Penny, guarding the only way in. But there was no movement at the tailgate, only an odiferous breeze that caused the snowflakes to swirl at the opening.

"I got your shoe," Daisy whispered. Spencer jumped to find her standing so close, holding out his shoe. The laces were still tied from when he'd slipped out in the cab.

Stripping away his wet and filthy sock, Spencer took the shoe from Daisy and slipped his bare foot inside. He hated the feeling of shoes without socks, but the alternative was worse.

"Thanks," Spencer said. He had to grin. Through all the danger, Daisy had managed to hold on to Spencer's shoe. Something so small suddenly meant a lot, when they were standing in an inch of garbage sludge.

"I think they're gone," whispered Bernard, backing away from the tailgate.

"Who were they?" Daisy asked.

"BEM workers," answered the garbologist. "I bet my life on it." He shook his head, leather aviator straps flapping. "I've never seen anything like it. They were—"

With a deafening clang, the roof of the garbage truck was stripped back like aluminum foil. Spencer pulled Daisy against the wall as an overgrown Grime head appeared at the opening above. Its long black tongue shot out with lightning speed. It wrapped around Bernard's arm and jerked him out the top of the truck like a puppet on a string.

CHAPTER 10

"PLUGGERS."

Daisy screamed. Penny whirled around, aiming her leaf blower upward. But Bernard was gone.

With Daisy and Penny looking skyward, Spencer was the only one who saw a masked face appear in the open tailgate. It was a human rider, dismounted from his giant Toxite so he could fit through the narrow opening. His gloved hands came up, flicking a Glopified mop.

The strings tangled both of Penny's legs. She pitched forward, dropping her leaf blower and trying to grasp anything. She shouted as the strings retracted, dragging her through the sludge toward the enemy.

Daisy lunged, grabbing Penny's hands, but she just slid uselessly across the truck floor. Spencer dug the small razor-blade from his pocket and pushed the button. The blade rang out and he dove forward, slicing through the Glopified mop strings.

Daisy and Penny tumbled across the truck. Spencer rocked back on his knees, the razorblade tight in his grasp. With his attack thwarted, the BEM worker ducked out of sight.

"They took Bernard," Daisy said, staring up at the tear in the truck's roof.

Then, as if in answer to her statement, the garbologist came hurtling through the snowy opening and landed with a clang not three feet from Spencer.

Bernard was limp and motionless. His body steamed, covered in glowing green slime. Penny scrambled forward, pulling off his headlamp and turning the light on Bernard. Daisy stared in shock, but Spencer had to look away.

"Is he . . ." Daisy swallowed. "You know, D-E-A-D?"

"He's going to be in a minute," Penny said. Her hands were passing over Bernard, carefully stripping back his dissolving clothing and checking his pulse. Oozing burns covered his shoulders and neck.

"What did they do to him?" Daisy asked.

"Grime slime," answered Spencer. He recognized the glowing gunk from the parking garage below New Forest Academy. The enlarged Grimes had the capability of filling their throats with poisonous slime. "It spat on him."

Daisy gulped. "I don't think his arm is supposed to bend that way." Spencer made the mistake of looking. It was like Bernard had two elbows in one arm.

"Yeah," Penny said. "His arm's busted. I think he's got a concussion, too."

Penny's hand went to her waist. Spencer hadn't noticed before, but there was a set of spray bottles dangling from her janitor belt. Seeing them reminded him of the terrifying vision of Mr. Clean, unstoppable with such weapons.

Penny unclipped one of the bottles and flashed her headlamp across it. A bright orange liquid sloshed about halfway up the bottle. Penny adjusted the spray nozzle and pointed it at Bernard's neck. Giving a few sprays, she misted the entire wounded area. Immediately, it began to foam and bubble, filling the garbage truck with the clean scent of citrus.

"My dad says we're not supposed to spray people with cleaning liquids," Daisy said. "My cousins did it one time and they got nasty rashes."

Ignoring Daisy's warning, Penny carefully removed Bernard's aviator cap. There was a deep gash in his scalp, streaking his short dark hair with red. Penny squirted the cut from one end to the other until the entire gash had foamed over.

"What is that stuff?" Spencer asked.

But Penny was too focused on first aid to talk. She moved on to Bernard's broken arm. Spencer couldn't watch as she tugged away the sleeve. He heard the distinct spray of the bottle, and then Penny sighed.

"It's an all-purpose cleaning solution," Penny said, "with peroxide." She turned the headlamp back to Bernard's neck.

The foamy cleaner was receding from his shoulder, leaving the skin pink and fresh, as if it had never been burned.

"And it's a healing spray," Penny said. She clipped the bottle back onto her belt. "It's a race now."

"Relay race, or normal race?" Daisy asked. "Or three-legged race? I'm good at those."

"A life-and-death race," Penny said. "If his wounds kill him before the cleaning solution takes effect, then there's nothing we can do. Twenty . . . thirty minutes, and we'll know."

Penny rose to her feet. "You two stay with him. If he wakes up, try to get him talking." She headed for the open tailgate.

"Where are you going?" Spencer asked. "They might still be out there!"

"That's what I intend to find out." Penny dropped through the opening and out of sight.

Spencer and Daisy turned back to Bernard. They didn't dare say anything, as if speaking of death might bring it closer. They simply watched the garbologist, prone on the floor of his garbage truck, covered in foamy, citrus-smelling, all-purpose cleaning solution. His chest rose and fell with labored breaths, and the rhythm of it seemed to put the two kids into a worried reverie.

They had no idea how much time had passed before Penny returned. The agile young woman boosted herself into the back of the truck, something dangling from her hand.

"They're gone," Penny said. "But I found this." She held

out the object, illuminating it with her headlamp. Spencer recognized it immediately as the extension cord he had severed with the razorblade. It was still attached to the battery pack the rider had strapped around his waist.

"Is that what they use to ride the Toxites?" Daisy asked.

"Looks like it." Penny crouched next to the kids to inspect the battery pack. There was a dial in the center with a little blinking yellow light. When Penny turned the dial left, the exposed end of the extension cord sparked and the blinking light turned green. Penny twisted the dial the other direction. The electricity decreased and the light turned from yellow to amber to red.

"The dial regulates the flow of Glopified electricity," Penny said.

"That's how they control them," Spencer said. "Remember the cords at New Forest Academy? When the Toxites were plugged in, they were calm. They like the electricity because it makes them grow."

"So," Penny said, turning the dial back to green and increasing the electricity, "the Toxite won't go anywhere if it's on green. Like parking your car."

"But if you turn it to yellow, the Toxite starts getting angry. It realizes that it's relocated and wants to attack."

"I don't even want to imagine what happens if you turn it to red," Daisy said.

"Closer to red means less electricity," Penny summed up. "Less electricity means angrier Toxites." Penny blew a strand of red hair from her face. "This is bad. The BEM has a huge advantage with these . . . these Toxite-riders."

"Pluggers," Spencer said. That was what Mr. Clean had called them when he rescued Leslie from prison. "The BEM calls the overgrown monsters Extension Toxites. The riders are called Pluggers. "

"You've seen them before?" Penny asked.

Spencer nodded. "In a vision. Mr. Clean used an Extension Filth to rescue Leslie Sharmelle from prison. She's a Plugger now."

Penny pointed outside. "That was your old substitute teacher out there?"

Spencer shook his head. "I didn't see Leslie tonight. But there's a whole gang of Pluggers under her command," he said. "Mr. Clean sent them on a manhunt to find my dad."

"Maybe that's why they left," Daisy said. "They realized that Alan wasn't with us."

"But why were they here in the first place?" Penny said. "They followed me into the bus depot."

Bernard suddenly sat bolt upright, causing everyone else to jump back in surprise. "Which way did they go!" he shouted. "Where are they?"

"Relax." Penny put a hand on his knee. "It's all right, it's just us. They're long gone by now."

Bernard closed his eyes in misery, and for a moment Spencer thought he might see the grown man cry. "They took the package!"

CHAPTER 11

"IT'S A PATTERN."

Spencer awoke as the garbage truck's engine roared to life. He blinked against the sunlight coming through the windshield. The Mickey Mouse clock on the dashboard said it was eight o'clock in the morning.

Spencer hadn't even realized that they'd stopped for gas until Penny restarted the truck and pulled away from the pump. Daisy was trying to wake up in the passenger seat next to him. Penny had duct taped a piece of tarp over the broken window. As the garbage truck pulled onto the highway and gathered speed, the tarp began to flap noisily.

The package was gone. As horrible as it was, there was nothing to be done. The Pluggers were too far away by the time Bernard awakened. And with only one more rendezvous point, the most important thing was to get the team assembled. Alan would know what to do.

Bernard snored softly in the space behind the seats. The garbage truck had an extended cab, but that didn't mean there was room to get comfy.

The garbologist had made a rapid recovery from his injuries. Penny's Glopified all-purpose healing spray was truly magical. By the time the foamy orange cleaner had dried, Bernard was back to full health. The cut on his scalp had vanished as he dusted the dried foam from his hair. And his broken arm was functioning without so much as a bruise.

Despite Bernard's miraculous recovery, Penny had insisted that she drive through the night, giving him a chance to rest up.

"Where are we?" Spencer asked. His voice was raspy from sleep. Penny handed him a plastic sack from the gas station. Chocolate milk, a granola bar, and some muffins.

"Breakfast," Penny said. "We're in Kansas."

Either the mention of breakfast or the thought of Kansas seemed to bring Daisy fully awake. "Better watch out for tornados," she said, grabbing a chocolate milk from the sack. "That's what got Dorothy, you know."

Penny grinned. "Looks like a clear day to me."

"Where's the third rendezvous point?" Spencer opened his granola bar, careful to touch only the wrapper since he hadn't washed his hands.

"Triton Charter School," Penny said. "Couple hours ahead. North of Wichita."

"Triton," Spencer said under his breath. "Why does that name sound so familiar?"

"Maybe 'cause it's Ariel's dad," said Daisy.

Then it came to him. Spencer snapped his fingers. "Aaron!"

"No, it's *Ariel*," Daisy said.

Spencer rolled his eyes. "I'm not talking about *The Little Mermaid*, Daisy." He turned to Penny. "Triton Charter is one of our schools."

"Of course it is," said Penny. "We've got a good Rebel working there. We wouldn't set up a rendezvous point at a BEM school."

"No, I mean one of *our* schools." He pointed at himself and Daisy. "We've got a Monitor at Triton Charter. His name is Aaron."

"Nice memory," Daisy said. "I can't remember where anybody is."

"I only remember because there was a special report from Triton just last week. Aaron sent me an email."

"Slow it down," Bernard said, suddenly sitting up in the backseat. "What's a Monitor?" Daisy passed him the breakfast sack while Spencer explained.

"Last November, we escaped from New Forest Academy with about thirty other students," Spencer said. "The bus driver, Meredith List . . ."

"She's actually our lunch lady," Daisy interjected.

"Meredith got everybody home," Spencer continued. "But the students were pretty shaken up. They knew something magical had happened. They wanted to talk about it, so I gave them a way to get some answers. I told everybody to go back to their schools and get detention with the janitors."

"Good advice," Penny muttered sarcastically.

"It was the only way to find out if the janitors are Rebels or BEM. We watch the janitors, and my Monitors send reports about suspicious activity."

"Do you get a lot of reports?" Bernard asked.

Spencer nodded. "Everybody writes in from time to time."

"Well, not everybody," Daisy cut in. "We're still waiting to hear from Jenna."

"Who's Jenna?" asked Bernard.

Spencer could feel his face going red. Jenna was a girl he'd spent a lot of time with at New Forest Academy. It was fairly common knowledge that she liked Spencer. He was secretly surprised that she'd never written to him, despite her promise to do so.

Spencer didn't want to answer Bernard's question. He wasn't there to talk about Jenna—not when there were much more important things happening at Triton Charter School.

"Anyway," Spencer said, abruptly changing the subject, "the reason I remember hearing about Triton Charter School is because Aaron reported an incident last Monday."

"What kind of incident?" Penny asked.

"The Rebel janitor at Triton slipped on the stairs and broke his leg," Spencer said. "So they've hired a temporary. Aaron thinks the new lady is just a custodian. Thinks she doesn't know anything about magic or Toxites. We told him to be extra careful and keep a close eye on the new worker. I haven't heard from him since. But it's been a couple of days since I've checked my email."

"Hmm . . ." Bernard said. "This is going to complicate our rendezvous."

"Just because they hired a temporary custodian doesn't mean she's part of the BEM," Penny said. "We'll be extra careful and we'll be fine."

"I wish there were a way to warn Walter and Alan," Daisy said.

"What about your visions, kid?" Bernard asked.

"It doesn't work like that," answered Spencer. "The warlocks never know I'm watching."

"At least you could check on old Walter," Bernard suggested. "See what he's up to."

It was a good idea, even though Spencer wasn't keen on it. He reached into his pocket for the bronze medallion. "Be right back," he said, wrapping his fingers around the medal.

The cab of the garbage truck disintegrated, his head reeled in the whiteness, and then he was brushing his teeth. With a mirror directly in front of him, there was no mistaking the warlock.

It was Director Carlos Garcia.

His dark hair was combed and gelled, the collar of his white shirt pressed. Spencer got an immediate location on him. The director was northwest of Denver, nestled into the mountains at New Forest Academy. The location didn't surprise Spencer since he knew that Garcia lived in a house on campus. Spencer choked back his anger over Director

Garcia. Not only was he a corrupt warlock, but he was the creator and principal of the elite Academy.

Spencer had learned that the BEM had established New Forest Academy to be a safe haven for education. The Academy would be kept Toxite-free while all other schools in America were left unattended and infested. In this way, the BEM could handpick the future leaders of the country while everyone else got dumber from Toxite breath.

There was a knock at the door. Garcia bent over and spat into the sink. He wiped his mouth on a soft towel and threw it over his shoulder as he pulled open the door. Spencer recognized the man in the doorway as one of the Academy teachers.

"Sorry to bother you, sir," the man said. "But you have a visitor."

"A visitor?" Director Garcia repeated.

The messenger swallowed nervously. "It's . . . it's Mr. Clean, sir."

Garcia took a cautious step back. "Where is he? What's he doing here?" There was definitely terror in the director's voice.

"He's waiting for you in the underground parking garage. First level."

"What does he want?" Garcia asked.

"He said we should expect more company within the hour." The man paused. "Pluggers."

"Pluggers? Here?" That obviously angered Director Garcia. "I've had enough of those overgrown beasts. Why is he bringing them here?"

"The Academy was the only secure location along the Pluggers' route. Mr. Clean said the Extension Toxites needed improvements," the messenger answered. "I believe his exact words were, 'I'm going to turn those hunting beasts into war machines.'"

Garcia responded, but the vision was already blanching, Spencer's concern over the conversation pushed him away. What was Mr. Clean planning to do to Leslie's Extension Toxites? Spencer couldn't think about it now. A new vision was taking shape, whiteness fading into black.

Spencer waited patiently, but nothing came into view. He almost panicked, wondering if his Auran ability had suddenly ended. Then he realized that, despite the blackness, he could still hear, and he had a specific location.

What he heard was the distinctive sound of a school bell ringing to announce the beginning of a new day. And the location was just where he suspected.

Spencer pulled his hand away from the bronze medallion, and the cab of the truck shimmered back into view.

"Walter's already at Triton Charter School, and I think he's in trouble," Spencer blurted.

"What did you see?" Penny asked.

Spencer decided not to mention Garcia's vision yet. Walter was in danger, and they needed to focus on him. "Nothing. I couldn't see anything, which means that Walter's eyes were closed—or covered."

"Maybe he's sleeping," Daisy suggested.

"Definitely not sleeping," said Spencer. "He's at Triton

Charter School. I heard the first bell ring. Walter's been captured! And my dad might be with him."

"You don't know that." Penny was trying to keep him calm.

"It's a pattern," Spencer said. "Every time the BEM knows we're coming, they replace our Rebel with a bad guy. They do it so fast there's never enough time to change plans. That's how Slick got us at New Forest Academy. And that's what is happening at Triton."

"Kid's got a point," Bernard said. "And if the BEM knows where we're headed, then those nasty Pluggers might be waiting for us."

Spencer knew the Extension Toxites weren't at the school. But again, he decided not to mention them. He didn't want to give anyone a false sense of security. Just because the Pluggers had made a pit stop at New Forest Academy didn't mean they were giving up the manhunt. In fact, from what Spencer gathered from his vision, Mr. Clean was giving them some kind of upgrade, making the Extension Toxites even more deadly.

Penny let go of the wheel just long enough to throw her hands up. "So, what are we supposed to do?"

"I've got an idea," Spencer said. "But I'm going to need to make a phone call."

"We're supposed to be off the grid," Penny said. "No communication with anyone outside the team."

"One call. It'll be fast." Spencer put his hands together in pleading. "I've got to talk to the president of the Monitors."

"I thought you were in charge," Bernard said.

Spencer shook his head. "I'm just the one with the answers. The real brain behind the Monitors is another kid. His name is Min Lee. And he's a genius."

CHAPTER 12

"IT DOESN'T REALLY WORK LIKE THAT."

Triton Charter School was just ahead, the playground covered in a skiff of trampled snow. This was definitely the right location from Spencer's vision. Walter was somewhere in the building, his eyes still closed.

The garbage truck idled at the corner of the block, its passengers keeping a close eye on the school as they waited for the phone to ring.

Penny drummed her fingers on the steering wheel, her green eyes never straying far from the clock on the dashboard. "It's time to think of a backup plan," Penny said. "In case your little friend doesn't call back."

"He'll call," Daisy said. "Min's the best."

Penny sighed. "It's been almost two hours. I say we give it another thirty minutes. At eleven thirty, we go in, mops blazing."

Spencer looked at the cell phone in his hands. He hadn't let go of it since Penny had handed it to him for the first call. She didn't believe in Min because she'd never seen him in action. The Asian boy could rewire a computer in his sleep. Getting a message to Aaron at school would be child's play. But Spencer did wonder what was taking so long.

The phone vibrated in his hand, the screen lighting up to show an unknown caller.

"Hello?" Spencer said.

"Greetings." It was Min, his voice as steady and businesslike as ever.

"Did you get a message through?"

"All is in order. Aaron stands ready to assist you."

Spencer smiled. "Great! What's the plan?"

"Walter is most likely being detained in the janitor's closet," Min said. "In order to rescue him, we'll need to lure the temporary janitor out, giving you time and safe passage to find him."

"Are you thinking what I'm thinking?" Spencer said.

"It has already been arranged," said Min. "At precisely eleven thirty, Aaron's class will go to lunch. Once in the cafeteria, he has agreed to create a janitorial diversion, by any means necessary."

"Is that your way of saying that Aaron's going to start a food fight?"

"Regardless of the mess that Aaron makes, you must be otherwise engaged. Do not go near the cafeteria. Find the janitor's closet, rescue Walter, and get out."

"Easier said than done, Min."

"To facilitate your entrance, I have some simple directions," said Min. "Enter the school through the front doors.
Take your first left. Follow the hallway until you pass the
bathrooms, then take a right. The janitorial closet is at the
corner."

"Wow." Spencer was amazed at Min's detailed instructions. "How'd you figure that out?"

"I found a satellite image of the school and determined
the year it was built. Then I overlaid a series of standard
school blueprints from that era until I found a match."

"Min Lee, you are a genius!" Spencer said.

"Did you ever think I wasn't?" Through Min's tone on
the phone, Spencer could imagine his face, mouth tilted in
an arrogant smirk. "One last thing. If you are approached
by Triton Charter School staff, you and Daisy are in Ms.
Bellingham's class, room 17."

"Got it," Spencer said, glancing at the clock. "It's almost time."

"On behalf of the Organization of Janitor Monitors, I
wish you luck."

"And I say thanks," said Spencer. "On behalf of education's future."

"Until next time," Min said. Without waiting for a response, he hung up the phone. Spencer grinned.

"What did he say?" Penny asked, taking her cell phone
from Spencer and tucking it away.

"In ten minutes, me and Daisy are going through the
front doors," Spencer explained.

"Okay." Penny nodded. "Bernard and I will come in through the back, meet you in the hallway."

"No." Spencer shook his head. "You two have to wait in the truck and watch out for the Pluggers." The giant Extension Toxites were probably still behind. But Spencer didn't know how long it would take the Pluggers to travel from New Forest Academy, and he didn't want to be taken by surprise again.

"I'm not sending you in there alone!" Penny clearly didn't want to miss out on the action.

"We belong in there!" Spencer said. "We're kids. It's the middle of the school day. If you and Bernard go in armed, the office staff will be all over you." Spencer took a deep breath. "We're going to do this the old-fashioned way. Just me and Daisy, some latex gloves, and a food fight."

"Where are we going to get the food?" Daisy asked.

"That's Aaron's job. He'll be in the cafeteria." Spencer clapped his hands. "We're losing time. Let's go."

In a moment everyone was standing on the sidewalk next to the garbage truck. Bernard didn't have much to say about the plan, but Penny was spewing precautions and safety tips.

Even though Spencer wanted to go unarmed, Penny filled their pockets with vacuum dust. She produced two latex gloves from a pouch on her Glopified janitorial belt. Spencer and Daisy felt significantly safer as they pulled them on. As long as they each wore a glove, no one would be able to catch them.

"Give me your coats," Bernard said. When the kids

hesitated, Bernard explained, "You don't want to look like you just blew in from Kansas."

"But we *are* in Kansas," Daisy said.

Bernard beckoned for the coats again, and Spencer and Daisy handed them over.

"Wait!" Daisy suddenly seemed to remember something important. She clambered into the garbage truck, and Spencer saw her reaching behind the seat for a moment. When she emerged from the cab, an old familiar friend dangled in Daisy's grasp.

It was Mrs. Natcher's hall pass, Baybee.

"You brought Baybee?" Spencer raised an eyebrow.

"I put her in the duffel bag," Daisy said. "I couldn't leave her behind! What if something happened to her?" Daisy tucked Baybee under one arm. "Besides, if we're going to go wandering through the halls of Triton Charter School, then we'd better have a hall pass."

Spencer rolled his eyes. "It doesn't really work like that. Baybee isn't exactly a universal hall pass. Outside of Welcher Elementary, she's just a doll."

Daisy's forehead wrinkled as she contemplated this. But it was Penny who cut in.

"Actually, I think it's a good idea." Penny reached into her belt. "It's one more way to sneak in some weaponry." She snatched Baybee and turned the plastic doll upside down. With a swift jerk, Penny pulled down the diaper. Spencer looked away, embarrassed. Daisy gasped.

A razorblade sword extended from Penny's other hand.

Before anyone could stop her, she spun the blade around and sliced a gash in the doll's bottom.

"Penny!" Daisy was distraught. "That's toy torture!"

Penny closed the razorblade and dropped it back into her belt. At the same time, she withdrew a chalkboard eraser. Lining it up, Penny gave a push, sliding the dangerous eraser through Baybee's bum and out of sight. Then she pulled the diaper over the cut and handed the doll back to Daisy.

"If things go wrong in there, just pull out the eraser and detonate it," Penny said.

"I'm not pulling anything out of Baybee's diaper!" Spencer made a disgusted face.

Daisy held the doll protectively, as though Penny might grab Baybee and start slicing again. Bernard pulled a pocket watch from his charred overalls.

"Lunchtime," the garbologist said. "Better get going. And may the Force be with you."

"Force?" Daisy said. "What force?"

"Haven't you seen *Star Wars?*" asked Bernard.

Daisy shook her head. "Too scary for me. I don't like outer space."

"For someone who doesn't like outer space," Bernard said, "you sure seem to spend a lot of time there."

"Come on!" Spencer said, pulling Daisy away before she had a chance to figure out what Bernard meant. The kids jogged to the front of the school while Bernard and Penny climbed back in the garbage truck.

"Stay close," Spencer said as he pulled open the school

doors. They slipped inside, grateful for the warmth on their bare arms. Luckily, the secretary was distracted, and they sneaked past the front office with no trouble. Spencer turned left and headed down a long hallway.

The resonant rowdiness of the cafeteria was behind them. Spencer hoped that Aaron already had a mess going so the janitor would be gone by the time he and Daisy reached the maintenance closet.

"And where are you two headed?"

Spencer froze, Daisy bumping into him as a teacher's voice sounded behind them. He turned to face the speaker as she strode toward them. She was a sharply dressed black lady, about his mom's age.

"Think you can ditch out on lunch duty?" the woman said.

"It's okay," Spencer said, trying to keep composed. "We're in Ms. Bellingham's class."

"And we have a hall pass!" Daisy held out Baybee by one arm.

The lady put her hands on her hips. "Looks like we got a couple of smart alecks."

"No, really," Spencer said. "You can ask Ms. Bellingham."

The woman's face tightened. "I *am* Ms. Bellingham."

A lump formed in Spencer's throat as his eyes strayed to the name tag on a lanyard around her neck.

Ms. Julia Bellingham.

"Oops," Daisy said.

"The way I see it, you have two options," Ms. Bellingham

said. "We can either take a trip to the principal's office, or you can go back to lunch duty."

Spencer could think of a third option—to run. But that would most likely lead to a chase, and then they would never have time to rescue Walter.

"But we're not on lunch duty!" Daisy said.

"Then how do you explain this?" Ms. Bellingham reached out and grabbed Spencer's arm. She held up his hand, sweaty under the Glopified latex glove. Spencer could have easily slid through her grasp, but he didn't want to raise suspicion.

"Everyone takes a turn on lunch duty," the teacher said. "So let's head on back to the kitchen and do your part."

Min's only advice had been to stay away from the cafeteria. But as Ms. Bellingham pulled the two kids down the hallway, Spencer realized that the plan was about to change.

CHAPTER 13

"WE WON'T FORGET THIS."

The lunch lady was a man. He was burly and greasy, with gray chest hair sprouting out the top of his shirt. He acknowledged Spencer and Daisy with a wave of his rolling pin as Ms. Bellingham motioned them into the kitchen.

"What do you think we have to do?" Daisy whispered as the kitchen door closed behind them. "We don't have lunch duty at Welcher Elementary."

"We're supposed to help serve lunch," Spencer said. "I had to do this at my old school." There were four other kids in the kitchen. They stood at the serving counter, handing food under the plastic sneeze guard to their classmates.

"HAIRNETS!" the lunch man yelled. Daisy jumped as he slammed his rolling pin onto the countertop. In three steps the big man was looming over them with a hairnet and apron in each hand.

Daisy had some trouble trapping her thick braid under the hairnet, but in a moment, she and Spencer were ready for lunch duty.

The lunch man pointed one hairy finger at Spencer and shouted, "SPAGHETTI!" Then he turned to Daisy. "MEATBALLS!" Then he lumbered back to the rolling pin, as if his one-word instructions were sufficient.

Daisy had threaded her apron strings under Baybee's arms so the doll dangled at her waist. "Come on, spaghetti man." She strode past Spencer and approached a steaming vat of meatballs at the counter. Spencer was at her side, and before they knew it, they were serving spaghetti and meatballs to the students of Triton Charter School.

Between each serving, Spencer stole a glance into the cafeteria. The students were pretty rowdy, but food wasn't flying yet. The rambunctious behavior made sense as Spencer caught sight of six or seven little Toxites skittering around the cafeteria. The presence of the creatures was more evidence that the temporary janitor at Triton Charter was working for the BEM. A Rebel school would have had those Toxites under control.

In a way, the creatures would be helpful today. The Toxites in the cafeteria would make the students far more likely to join in the food fight.

But Spencer grimaced. Why hadn't the fight started yet? For a moment, Spencer wondered if Aaron had chickened out. If he didn't make a mess soon, the BEM janitor would never leave the maintenance closet. Spencer mindlessly served spaghetti as he scanned the tables for his Monitor friend.

"No way!" said one of the students as a few noodles slipped off the side of his tray. Spencer's attention turned back to his serving. Standing on the other side of the plastic sneeze guard was Aaron.

"There you are!" Spencer said.

"I got held up in class," Aaron said. "Had to finish a writing assignment."

"Make sure to get extra sauce and meatballs," Spencer said, ladling a second serving of noodles onto his tray.

"But I really wanted pizza today," Aaron said, glancing down the line to the students serving pepperoni pizza. He shook his head. "I don't know if I can do this, Spencer."

"Of course you can," Spencer urged. "All you have to do is get somebody to throw back at you. In a couple of minutes the place will be a mess and no one will remember who started it."

"What if nobody throws back? What if I'm the only one?" He was shaking. "I'll get suspended! Banned from the cafeteria!"

"They'll throw," Spencer promised. "Everyone's looking for an excuse to start a food fight." Spencer leaned forward. "You know how important this is, Aaron! Remember New Forest Academy? Remember what they did to us there?"

Aaron nodded. Wordlessly he slid his tray along, accepting extra sauce and meatballs from Daisy. Spencer watched him stop at the salad bar, heaping lettuce and tomatoes onto the corner of his tray. Aaron glanced toward the kitchen one last time. Spencer caught his eye and gave a silent nod of encouragement.

Aaron suddenly whirled around, lifting the tray above his head and flinging his lunch into the air. It was an excellent spread, showering more than half of the tables with red sauce, meatballs, and spaghetti noodles.

The cafeteria fell silent. Students turned in their seats, expressions of shock and disbelief on their faces. Aaron lowered his tray and backed up to the salad bar.

"Come on, throw something back," Spencer muttered under his breath. "Somebody throw something . . ."

There was a war cry at Spencer's side. He turned to see Daisy leap across the kitchen counter, duck under the sneeze guard, and hurl a handful of meatballs at the back of Aaron's head. Her aim was mostly off, sending three of the meatballs splattering onto the table by the salad bar.

Then, with the rowdiness of school lunch and a haze of Toxite breath in the cafeteria, a full-scale food fight broke loose.

A flying fruit cup hit Daisy in the shoulder, flinging pineapple chunks into her ear. A piece of pizza struck Aaron in the chest, and he went down under the salad bar. Somebody's steamed broccoli hit the ceiling, while the corner table was caught in an onslaught of stringy spaghetti.

"CAFETERIA!" the burly lunch man roared. He raced from the back of the kitchen, brandishing his rolling pin. Spencer couldn't let the lunch man break up the food fight. Not when it had just started getting good!

Spencer grabbed the huge pot of red sauce. Heaving it off the serving counter, he knocked it to the kitchen floor, covering the tiles in Ragu. The lunch man slipped in the sauce and went down, rolling pin flying out of his hand. His momentum carried him across the kitchen and smashed him into the serving counter. The force of impact tipped the pot of noodles.

"SPAGHETTI!" yelled the lunch man as fifteen pounds of wet noodles landed on his head. Instantly, two of the lunch duty students latched on to Spencer. They grabbed his arms, trying to pull him down. But Spencer's latex glove was not a normal lunch duty glove. He slipped out of their grasp like Jell-O.

The kitchen was no longer safe. And even though the cafeteria was a virtual war zone, Spencer decided to take his chances out there. He dove across the serving counter, grabbing the vat of meatballs as he slid under the sneeze guard.

Spencer had thrown at least a dozen meatballs when a piece of pizza slapped him in the face. Before he could recover, the vat was swiped away by another student, forcing Spencer to retreat.

He slid through fruit juice and ducked under the salad bar. Daisy was hunkered low, a couple of olives in each hand. Her head was covered in Ragu. Reddish noodles wrapped around her neck like an edible scarf.

Aaron was next to her, one eye squinted shut, Thousand Island dressing oozing down his face. He had half a banana in one hand and some steamed broccoli in the other.

"I'm really starting to wonder if this was a bad idea,"

Aaron said to Spencer as a lunch tray clattered to the floor next to him.

"Take it up with the president of the Monitors," Spencer said, dodging a cucumber slice. "This was Min's planning."

"I don't know how much longer we can hold out!" Aaron hurled his broccoli like green grenades. "You guys should get out of here while you still can!"

"Not until that janitor shows up!" said Spencer.

"Is that her?" Daisy pointed across the chaos of the cafeteria. A lean woman in blue coveralls was rolling a cleaning machine into the lunchroom.

"That's her!" Aaron shouted. "Now go! I'll cover you!"

"Thanks, man," Spencer said. "We won't forget this." Spencer slid out from under the salad bar just in time to see a big pair of sneakers tromping forward.

"SALAD BAR!" roared the lunch man.

"Not you again!" Spencer reached into the salad bar and grabbed a bottle of dressing. Squeezing with all his might, he sent a stream of white shooting from the bottle and into the lunch man's face.

"DRESSING!" He blundered, trying to wipe his eyes. At the same time, Aaron pitched his half banana under the big guy's foot. The lunch man toppled with a grunt.

"Is he okay?" Daisy asked, scooting out from under the salad bar.

"I bleu-cheesed him!" Spencer said, throwing down the empty bottle of salad dressing.

Spencer and Daisy sprinted across the filthy cafeteria. Teachers and staff were everywhere, getting caught in the crossfire as they tried to break up the massive food fight. Twice, teachers reached out for Spencer and Daisy, but the Glopified latex gloves made them uncatchable.

Spencer took a chocolate pudding to the back of the head. Daisy slipped on some mandarin oranges. They each caught a splatter of Ragu to the face before they burst through the door and into the quiet hallway.

Spencer got his bearings and raced back the way they'd come. With all eyes on the cafeteria, the way to the janitorial closet was wide open. The cafeteria was a mess, but Aaron was a hero.

They passed the bathrooms, took a right, and came to a halt in front of the maintenance closet. A pineapple chunk fell from Spencer's chest and splatted on the floor. Daisy absently tucked a strand of spaghetti behind her ear.

Spencer reached into his pocket for a bit of vacuum dust as Daisy untied Baybee from her apron strings. Then Spencer threw open the closet door and they raced inside.

"SHAKE YOUR LEG!"

By this point, Spencer had visited enough janitorial closets to know the similarities. They were always highly stocked and fairly cluttered, with a bit of grit built up in the corners. Lighting was usually poor, and they often smelled of cleaning chemicals.

The closet at Triton Charter School was no different. The room was long and narrow, and Spencer and Daisy had it searched in less than a minute.

"He's not here," Daisy said, keeping watch at the door.

"But this is the right location!" said Spencer. "I know I sensed him here." He began scanning the back wall for another common feature among janitorial closets. "There's got to be a secret passageway!"

Then he noticed a symbol on one of the bricks. It was small and carefully painted in gold. It was a ring, with dozens of keys splaying out like rays from the sun. Spencer had seen it before. The icon was painted on a secret door in the janitor's closet at Welcher Elementary. The keyring symbol was also embossed on the cover of *The Janitor Handbook*.

Without thinking, Spencer pressed on the painted brick. The sound of mechanical gears cranked as the brick depressed into the wall. Spencer jumped back, bumping into Daisy, who had come to see what he'd discovered. A portion of the wall swung upward to reveal a dim ramp angling down.

"Where does that go?" Daisy asked, gently rocking Baybee with one arm.

"Let's find out." Spencer went first, vacuum dust ready between his fingers. The ramp led down to another room stocked with janitorial supplies. Bare pipes networked the ceiling and a single bulb lit the area.

"I don't think he's down here, either," Daisy said.

"He's got to be. I sensed him!" Spencer closed his eyes, trying desperately to recall the vision. He knew he was within feet of the location he had sensed, so where was Walter? He crossed over to the ramp, a strange tingling in his fingertips as he drew even nearer.

Then he saw it: the sole of a shoe barely sticking out from under the ramp. It was almost lost in the shadows of the dim room, but Spencer recognized it immediately. He raced around, grabbed Walter's feet, and dragged him out from under the ramp.

"How'd you know he was under there?" Daisy asked.

Spencer didn't answer. He had just known Walter was here. His Auran sense was too keen and sharp to be wrong.

Spencer stared at Walter, who was wearing khaki cargo pants and a plaid shirt. The bald warlock was in a deep slumber, his chest gently rising and falling. Spencer tried to lift the man, but the effort was futile.

"Try to wake him up," Spencer said. He scanned the closet for a way to get Walter out. Crossing the cluttered room, he took one of the toilet plungers from a shelf.

Daisy gave Walter's arm a timid poke. When nothing happened, she poked harder. Then she grabbed the warlock by the shoulders and shook. Daisy hovered over him for a moment, waiting for some kind of reaction, but the man slept on. Finally, Daisy lowered her face to within an inch of Walter's and held very still.

"BOO!" Daisy shouted. Spencer looked over at her, putting a finger to his lips for silence.

"It's okay," said Daisy. "I don't think he's going to wake up. Heavy sleeper."

Spencer glanced back up the ramp. "We've got to get him out of here," he whispered. "Do you think you can plunge him?"

Glopified toilet plungers magically reduced the weight of whatever object they were clamped onto. At New Forest Academy, Daisy had easily carried Dez after plunging him on the stomach. Maybe they could do the same to Walter now.

Daisy nodded, taking the plunger from Spencer. "Help me roll him over."

Spencer tilted Walter onto his side while Daisy pulled up the back of his shirt. "Sorry if this is cold," Daisy said, clamping the toilet plunger to Walter's back. But when she lifted, nothing happened. Daisy tugged harder, and the plunger popped off.

"What happened?" Spencer asked.

"I don't think it's Glopified." Daisy held out the plunger for inspection. "I think it's used!"

Spencer shuddered and wiped his hand against his jeans. "We just stuck a used toilet plunger to Walter's back?"

They both glanced at the sleeping warlock. Daisy set the plunger in the corner of the room and went to get a second one from the shelf.

"What are you doing?" Spencer stepped out of her path.

"Maybe this one's Glopified," said Daisy.

"So you're just going to keep plunging till you find one that works?" Spencer was disgusted. "He's a person, not a toilet!"

Daisy shrugged. "We don't have to tell him." She stuck the new plunger onto Walter's back and lifted the warlock off the floor. "There we go. This one works like a charm!"

Daisy held Walter at an upward angle so his feet didn't drag. It looked like a painful position, bent over backward with his head flopped back.

Spencer grimaced, wondering what kind of stiff neck Walter would have upon waking. "I guess plungers weren't designed for comfort."

"Nope," Daisy said. "They were designed for toilet clogs."

Spencer tried not to think about it. Feeling sorry for Walter, he scanned the room for a more humane mode of transportation.

"Over here." Spencer found something tucked against the wall.

It was a janitorial cleaning cart, with four sturdy wheels and a yellow trash bag hanging off the front rack. He'd used a cart like this at New Forest Academy. If this one was Glopified, then Spencer knew just what to do.

He stepped onto the cart, leaning his weight forward. The cart sped ahead, turning as he leaned to the side. Spencer wheeled over to where Daisy stood with Walter propped on the plunger.

"Set him down on the rack," Spencer suggested.

Daisy swung the warlock around, accidentally bumping his head as she draped him across the front of the cart. Walter lay motionless, the plunger handle rising from his back like a mini flagpole.

"Is there another cart back there?" Daisy asked.

Spencer shook his head. "Just this one. You want it?"

"Nah," said Daisy. "I'm better on foot."

"Let's get out of here." Spencer leaned hard and drove up the ramp. Daisy jogged after him as they entered the hallway.

The fastest way out of Triton Charter School was through some double doors at the end of the hallway. The coast was clear, not a teacher in sight.

Spencer was almost there when he realized that Daisy

wasn't behind him. She was casually headed the wrong direction, Baybee tucked under her arm.

He wanted to shout for her, but that might bring teachers out of their classrooms. Right as Spencer made the decision to go back for Daisy, the BEM janitor rounded the corner. In a single bound she was onto the girl, grabbing Daisy by the shoulders.

"Let me go!" Daisy shouted. "I've got to check out that wall!" She twisted easily out of the janitor's grasp, latex glove working its magic.

As she turned, Spencer saw the reason for Daisy's odd behavior. A little Grime was clinging passively to the leg of her jeans. It was enjoying Daisy's brain waves while exhaling potent distraction.

The janitor, realizing that getting a hold on Daisy would be impossible without a glove of her own, raced toward the closet of supplies. Leaning into his cart, Spencer gathered speed. Once in range, he pinched out a Funnel Throw of vac dust and sent it hurling. It struck the janitor just as she reached the doorway.

Spencer was past her in a flash. Drawing alongside Daisy, he shifted his balance and spun the cart around, Walter's weight on the front nearly causing them to topple. Armed only with vac dust, Spencer didn't know how to knock out the Grime without taking Daisy down too. But if he didn't do something fast, the janitor would recover.

"Listen, Daisy," Spencer said. "I need you to shake your leg."

She was standing with her nose an inch from the wall,

staring intently at the blank space. "This would be a great spot to paint a picture of King Triton," she said. "Wonder why they haven't done that yet . . ."

"Shake your leg!" Spencer steered closer to her, but the Grime scurried around Daisy's thigh, like a squirrel on a tree trunk. "There's a Grime on you!" he tried, but Daisy was too distracted. Now she had an imaginary paintbrush in her hand, making invisible brushstrokes against the white wall.

Spencer leaned on his cart, brought it swinging around and crashed into Daisy from behind. She slammed against the wall, forcing the Grime to leap away to safety. The moment its slimy fingers touched the floor, Spencer hit it with a Palm Blast of vacuum dust. The Grime's breath caught in its throat, and Daisy instantly revived.

"Go!" Spencer shouted.

Daisy spun around once, getting her bearings. Then she sprinted down the hallway toward the double doors, the BEM janitor struggling to rise and stop her.

Spencer turned back to the little Grime on the floor. He had to finish it off, like a good Rebel janitor. Otherwise the creature would continue to distract the students of Triton Charter School.

Spencer lined up the wheels of his cleaning cart and leaned back sharply. He felt a thump as the Glopified wheels passed over the Toxite. As the cart rolled clear, there was nothing left but a splatter of pale slime on the hard floor.

When he looked up from the task, Spencer saw that Daisy was free. She must have pressed the wheelchair access button, opening the automatic doors to make a quick escape.

But between Spencer and his way out stood the BEM janitor. Reaching into a deep pocket on her coveralls, she withdrew a spray bottle. The liquid inside was green, just like the solution that Mr. Clean had used at the prison.

Spencer felt his knees weaken. The latex glove wouldn't protect him from the green spray. He needed to find another way out. But riding through the school with an unconscious Walter draped across his cart was not an option.

Stripping off his latex glove, Spencer reached for Walter's limp hand. He curled the warlock's fingers into a fist and stuffed on the glove. Spencer's sweat trickled out of the glove and ran down Walter's arm. It wasn't pretty, but it would do the trick.

Spencer leaned hard and fast. The cart raced forward, building speed and momentum as Spencer tried to line it up with the distant door. He held on till the last second, seeing the janitor raise her green spray bottle.

She pulled the trigger, sending a green mist at the cart. But Spencer was gone. He had bailed from the speeding cleaning cart, tumbling painfully to the hard floor and rolling twice before he managed to get back on his feet.

The janitor shouted in surprise. She threw down the bottle and lunged for Walter. Her hands gripped his ankles, but the latex glove pulled him free as he zoomed past.

Sprinting back toward the front office, Spencer looked over his shoulder only once to see Walter's cart speed through the open doors and into the midday air. Now it was up to Daisy to get Walter safely to the garbage truck.

The BEM janitor was coming after him. Spencer heard her footsteps but didn't dare look back. Without his latex glove, there would be no way to escape if she caught him.

Spencer was so worried about the pursuing janitor that he didn't even see Ms. Bellingham as he rounded the corner. He was almost to the front doors when her firm hand snatched him by the elbow.

"Going somewhere?" she asked.

Spencer didn't even attempt an escape as the BEM janitor caught up to him. At least for the moment, he was safer in Ms. Bellingham's grasp.

But the moment didn't last. The teacher pulled him down the hallway, escorting him once more to the cafeteria. Pushing open the lunchroom doors, Ms. Bellingham ushered Spencer in.

"MESS!" roared the ogrelike voice of the lunch man. With one hairy, tomato-sauced hand, he seized Spencer by the back of the neck and pressed him up against the wall.

"IT'S ALL IN THE SYSTEM."

As soon as the lunch man released his grip, Spencer realized that he was not alone. There were probably twenty or thirty students standing with their backs against the cafeteria wall. The kids were covered in food, some of their faces barely visible beneath a layer of Ragu. And as bad as the students looked, the lunchroom was worse.

Spaghetti dangled from the ceiling like limp stalactites. The floor was a swamp of red sauce and milk, with pieces of pepperoni pizza floating like lily pads. Fruits and vegetables were smeared on the walls, and steamed broccoli was smashed all over the tables. It was as if the food pyramid had exploded and left no survivors.

The lunch man looked like a human salad. His face was still dripping bleu cheese dressing, and a leaf of lettuce covered his head like a skullcap. None of this stopped him from producing a powerful scowl with enough intimidation to keep all the students quietly against the wall.

The cafeteria door opened once more, and a stern-looking woman entered.

"PRINCIPAL!" the lunch man announced.

The principal carefully maneuvered through the mess, careful not to put her pointy heel through a piece of pizza. At last she stopped, just a few feet in front of the dripping students. She gave a sharp clap of her hands, not unlike a gunshot from a firing squad, and everyone jumped.

"I will be contacting your parents," the principal began. "You'll have some explaining to do to them. And you have some explaining to do to me."

Under the intensity of her gaze, a meatball fell from one trembling student and landed with a splat.

"This cafeteria is your responsibility," said the principal. "Our substitute janitor has other things to do besides clean up your mess."

Spencer rolled his eyes. Little did the principal know that the substitute janitor's "other things" involved abducting the good guys.

"So *you* will clean it." She pointed down the line at every student. "And you will not leave the lunchroom until it is spick-and-span."

The students nodded in submission, bits of food flecking from their faces. "I expect more out of you," she said. "Now, would someone like to tell me how this started?"

A profound silence overtook the cafeteria. Even the lunch man seemed to hold his breath in anticipation. The students didn't dare look at each other, for fear of where the blame might land.

Spencer stole a quick glance down the line. Aaron was looking back at him. The Monitor had a pineapple chunk stuck to his nose and a mournful expression on his face.

Spencer thought back to his own mess at Welcher Elementary. Five months ago, he'd caused a disaster at the ice-cream social, hurling cans of root beer like grenades. After it was over, he'd felt horrible. He had disappointed his family and his school and wished there were some way to take it back.

"I started the food fight," Spencer said, stepping forward. "I got mad at Aaron and threw some spaghetti at him. He wouldn't fight back, so I threw some food at his friends."

The principal listened to his false confession with squinted eyes. When he was finished, she tilted her head. "What's your name?"

"Spencer Zumbro," he said. "I'm a new student. Like, really new."

"You clearly don't understand our expectations at Triton Charter School. Perhaps we should go to my office and discuss them."

Spencer nodded, wondering how all of this was about to play out. He followed the principal out of the cafeteria, glancing back at Aaron as he slipped through the door. The Monitor put his hands together and mouthed the words *thank you!*

A moment later, Spencer was seated in the principal's office. She drummed her fingers against the table, and

Spencer wondered if that was standard procedure for all principals.

"Whose class are you in, Spencer?" the principal finally asked.

Spencer shrugged. It looked insubordinate, but he didn't know how to answer.

The principal pursed her lips. "Okay, so you want to play the hard way." She grabbed the computer mouse, clicked twice, and typed his name into the system.

Spencer braced himself. He knew what would happen once she discovered that he wasn't actually a Triton student. The police would have to get involved. He'd be cited for trespassing and who knew what else.

"Hmm . . ." the principal squinted at the computer screen. "So you're in Ms. Bellingham's sixth-grade class. She'll be disappointed in you." The principal scrolled down. "But I'm afraid that Mr. Alan Zumbro will be even more upset. I'm afraid I have to call your father."

Spencer's eyes grew wider as she went on. "How do you know my dad's name . . . ?" He was so ripe with astonishment that he could barely get the question out.

"It's all in the system." The principal swiveled the computer screen so Spencer could see. How was it possible? There was a complete student profile for Spencer Zumbro!

"Min," Spencer mumbled. Somehow he had hacked Triton Charter School's system and written a false profile.

The principal dialed Alan's phone number and waited. "He's not answering."

Of course not. Alan was off the grid with the rest of

the team. And now Alan was the only team member unaccounted for. Spencer found a clock on the wall. It was 11:58. In two minutes the final rendezvous time would expire. Once Spencer got free of the principal's office, the team would have to move on without Alan.

The principal had just started to leave a message when the office door suddenly burst open. Spencer went rigid with astonishment.

"I hate to barge in like this, but I got a call from my son's teacher, saying he was involved in some kind of food fight?"

Alan Zumbro stood in the doorway.

CHAPTER 16

"SMELLED LIKE ORANGES."

Alan's short brown hair was nicely combed, and a trim beard outlined his face. He wore black slacks and a gray, button-down shirt under his coat. For a moment, Spencer remembered what his dad used to look like when he taught biology at the junior high. But at second glance, Spencer noticed a rip in his pants and a dark stain on his shirt.

"Is it true?" Alan asked, looking at Spencer for the first time in over a month. The principal set down the telephone as Spencer nodded wordlessly.

Alan looked away and ran a hand through his beard, as if trying to calm his temper. Then he turned back to his son. "Get up. We're going." His voice was cold and hard. "Get up before you disappoint me further."

Spencer felt a pang of hurt strike his heart. His dad was

acting, right? Did Alan have to say it with such conviction? Spencer rose onto numb feet.

"Mr. Zumbro," said the principal, "your son needs to return to the cafeteria and help his classmates with the cleanup."

"No," Alan said, "he needs to go home where I can teach him a lesson. Believe me, he's about to spend a lot of time with cleaning supplies." Alan took his son firmly by the elbow and nodded to the principal. "Good day."

He dragged Spencer out of the office, past the entryway, and through the school's front doors. As soon as Spencer felt the cold air on his face, Alan let go.

"Haha!" his dad laughed. "I think we sold it! Was I convincing enough?"

Spencer was speed-walking ahead, upset with himself for not feeling more joy at his dad's sudden arrival.

"Whoa, slow down!" Alan said. "We're free."

"Let's just get to Bernard's truck," said Spencer. "Before I disappoint you further."

"You know I didn't mean that stuff I said." Alan jogged a few steps to catch up. "I'm proud of the work you did in there. You single-handedly rescued Walter."

For some reason, Spencer didn't like the praise. "Daisy did most of it." They walked the rest of the way in silence. Alan didn't ask about the family, didn't ask about life. It made Spencer feel a kind of festering resentment that lasted until he saw Walter Jamison standing in front of the garbage truck. The old warlock smiled warmly, and Spencer ran to him.

111

"You all right?" Spencer said.

"Better now, thanks to you and the Organization of Janitor Monitors."

Penny and Daisy climbed down from the cab of the truck. "The orange healing spray woke him right up," Penny said. "We just finished unloading Uncle Walter's van into the garbage truck. We stay together from here on out."

"What about the bronze nail and hammer?" Spencer asked. Walter always carried the hammer, and the nail had previously been inside his van.

Walter held out his hand. The antique nail was safe in his palm. "Whoever captured me must not have recognized who I was. Ninfa never left my side."

He patted a cargo pocket on his pants where the bronze hammer was tucked away. It was the hammer and nail that gave Walter his warlock powers. Without them, there would be no way to Glopify new supplies.

"Who did capture you?" Daisy asked. "Was it that temporary janitor lady?"

"I'm sure it was," said Walter. "Though I don't remember."

"The janitor used green spray," Penny said, touching a stain on her uncle's shirt collar. "Green spray puts you to sleep and erases your recent memory of the person who sprayed you."

"How did they know you were coming?" Spencer asked.

"The BEM always has ears on me," said Walter. "Lately, they seem to be making a move on any school that I mention by name. It's likely that I accidentally let Triton

Charter slip, so they took out the Rebel Janitor and replaced him with that substitute BEM worker."

Bernard came around the side of the garbage truck. The garbologist stopped a foot away from Spencer and sniffed the air.

"I'm guessing spaghetti and meatballs in a heavy marinara sauce," Bernard said. He wiped a smudge off Spencer's forehead. "You sure stink, kid."

"That means a lot coming from the garbage man," Spencer said.

"Hey." Bernard held up his hands. "My nose doesn't lie."

Alan Zumbro stepped into the center of the group. "Well," he said, "we're all here. But we shouldn't stay much longer. That BEM janitor has probably already sent word. When last I checked, there were about a dozen Pluggers on my trail. We need to go somewhere safe before they find us again." He paused and looked at each face. "We need to get the package open."

Bernard coughed nervously. "About the package . . ."

"Who found it?" Walter cut in. "Which one of you?"

"Actually," Spencer said, "it was my mom. The package was at home all along." He looked directly at Alan. "Funny you didn't spend more time there, looking." His dad's eyes flicked away.

"About the package . . ." Bernard tried again.

"We should inspect it before opening," Alan said. "Somewhere quiet, with a lot of light."

"I lost the package!" Bernard finally shouted. "At the bus depot."

"It wasn't his fault," Penny vouched. "Couple of Pluggers attacked us. The Extension Grime nearly killed Bernard."

Daisy nodded. "His head was cracked open. I could almost see his brains! Smelled like oranges."

"That was the healing spray," Penny reminded.

"Argh!" Bernard grunted. "It was my responsibility and it got away from me!"

"By the time we realized it was missing," Penny said, "the Pluggers were long gone."

"They didn't make it far," Alan said. "I was also at the bus depot rendezvous point. The Pluggers had been following me for hours. I thought I'd lost them, but they found me again in Wyoming. When I realized how close they were, I decided not to lead them into the bus depot. Problem was, a few of them picked up Penny's trail and followed her in."

"So that's how they found us," Penny muttered.

"I hid out down the road and waited for them to leave the bus depot," Alan explained. "I spent a long time trapped in a dumpster, thinking about that package, remembering every detail of the way I mailed it. So you can imagine how I felt when I saw that one of the Pluggers had it. I just had to get it back."

Alan reached into his coat and withdrew the white mailing tube. "The package is safe," Alan said. "And I don't know about you guys, but I'm dying to find out what's inside."

CHAPTER 17

"POTATO, POTAHTO."

Spencer thought it was strange to watch the sun set through the windows of an elementary school. Stranger still to know that he would probably see it rise through the same window.

The team had made camp inside Woodbury Elementary School, about two hours south of Triton Charter. The janitor at Woodbury was a friend of Walter's and a highly trusted Rebel. He had let them into the school as soon as the students had gone home.

The Rebel team members had made themselves comfortable in the janitor's closet, while Spencer and Daisy were led to the gym so they could finally shower off the crusty spaghetti sauce.

The Woodbury janitor brought them dinner and gave

Walter instructions on how to lock the school. Then he departed, leaving the team alone as the sun set.

"How does it feel to have your dad back?" Daisy asked, coming alongside Spencer in the dim hallway.

He shrugged. "Not all that different from when he was gone."

"But he saved you from the principal's office," Daisy said. "That's got to feel good."

"He chewed me out." Spencer looked at his feet. "He didn't even say hello."

"He was just pretending." Daisy paused. "Right?"

Footsteps in the hallway caused them both to turn. It was Walter, both hands in his pockets. "We're ready to begin," Walter said. "Your dad has inspected the package for traps and safeguards. The time has come to open it."

Spencer and Daisy followed Walter into the janitor's closet. It was larger than usual, with a round table in the middle of the room. Bernard and Penny were already seated. Alan stood, the package resting in his hands. Spencer, Daisy, and Walter took the three remaining chairs.

A reverential hush settled over the janitor's closet. Alan looked briefly at each member of the team. It was as though he were making a last-minute decision whether to let them see the contents of the package. Then his eyes turned to the white mailing tube in his hands.

"Let me start at the beginning." Alan's tone was dark and somber. "Back when there were two of us." His brow wrinkled at a bitter memory. "Did any of you ever have the pleasure of meeting Rodney Grush?"

Alan looked around the table, but all heads were shaking no. Spencer had heard the name a hundred times. Rod Grush was his dad's science partner. For a long time, Alice had blamed Rod for Alan's sudden disappearance.

"Rod was my friend and colleague. We worked together at Winowah Junior High School in Washington. He taught chemistry and I taught biology. We were both heavily involved in the science division for the Bureau of Educational Maintenance."

"You worked for the BEM?" Daisy asked.

"Back when they were good," Alan answered. "About three years ago, the BEM approached us, asking Rod and me to head up a top secret mission. The warlocks had discovered a clue. Something that would lead us to the source of all Glop."

"What's so important about the source?" Penny asked.

"The source is where it all began." Alan's face flushed with the importance of what he was about to say. "Toxites are born from Glop."

There was a moment of thoughtful silence, and then Bernard raised his hand. "So you mean to tell me," he said, "that there's no such thing as mommy and daddy Toxites? The little creatures just pop out of the Glop on their own?"

"Exactly," Alan said.

"No parents?" Daisy said. "Sad for them."

Walter's face was more intent than Spencer had ever seen it. He obviously understood the magnitude of Alan's discovery. "This changes everything," the warlock said.

"Indeed it does," Alan said. "If Toxites are born in Glop, then we finally know how to get rid of them permanently."

"Find the source of Glop and destroy it," Walter finished.

It was quiet again, and then Spencer spoke up. "But if we destroy Glop, there wouldn't be any more magical supplies."

"We wouldn't need magical supplies," his dad said. "There would be no more Toxites to fight."

A life without Toxites. It was indeed a wild idea.

"But no one knows where Glop originated," Walter said. "How did you expect to find it?"

"We were looking for help from the only people who know how to find it." Alan turned to Spencer. "We were looking for the Aurans."

Spencer felt all eyes shift to him. He cowered in his seat, feeling his face turn hot from the unwanted attention. "I don't . . ." he said, head shaking. "I don't know how to find the source of Glop."

"The *other* Aurans," Alan clarified. "The original thirteen. They will tell us how to find the source."

"The Aurans don't speak to us," Walter said. "Few warlocks have ever even seen them. Most of the time the Glop is delivered during the night. I awake to find it at the foot of my bed."

"Sounds like they're in league with the tooth fairy," Daisy interjected.

Walter continued, ignoring the girl's comment. "We

don't even know how to find the Aurans, let alone get them to divulge the location of the source."

"Maybe we can use Spencer," Penny said. "If we could find a way to reveal that he's an Auran, maybe it would lure the original thirteen out to find him."

"No." Alan shook his head. "We must keep Spencer's status secret for as long as possible. That means we don't mention a word of it to anyone outside this room. Can we agree on that?" Alan looked around the room, accepting either a verbal "yes" or a head nod from everyone at the table.

The attention bothered Spencer. Why did his dad have to treat him like he was a dangerous secret? Spencer wondered if his dad would take such an interest in him if he weren't an Auran.

"There is a way," Alan continued. "A way to find the Aurans and gain their cooperation that doesn't involve putting Spencer at risk. That's the secret mission that Rod and I were supposed to accomplish. The BEM gave us a clue, the first in a sequence of thirteen. It took Rod and me the better part of a year to solve the first twelve clues." Alan paused, brushing his hand over his eyes. "We passed through our fair share of dangers and difficulties, and I learned to trust Rod Grush with my life. It was late August when we found the final, thirteenth clue. Dallas, Texas. At an intermediate school.

"Rod and I broke into the principal's office late one night. Following instructions from the previous clue, we began peeling back a strip of carpet in the corner. There was noise in the hallway, and before we knew it, we were under attack. We didn't know who it was, but they were armed with Glopified weapons and wore the seal of the BEM.

"We locked ourselves into the principal's office, but it was clear that the door wouldn't hold for long. I returned to the corner, frantically tearing up floorboards. But Rod . . ." Alan swallowed hard. "Rod went out to buy me time. His surprise attack was so sudden that he drove them down the hallway, giving me time to find *this* under the floorboards."

Alan tipped the mailing tube, and something slid out of the package. It was a shiny metal cylinder, about an inch wide and just under a foot long. There was a black cap at one end, held in place by a metal clasp. Alan held up the cylinder so the whole team could see the number 13 written in dripping red paint.

"The BEM workers were returning, and I had no time," said Alan. "It was a matter of minutes before they captured me. I couldn't let the cylinder fall into their hands. I couldn't let them steal what I'd worked for. I found the mailing tube and stamps in the principal's desk. I'd seen a secure mailbox just outside the office, so I made a run for it. The attackers didn't see me slip the package through the opening, but before I could get away, they were onto me."

He looked down for a moment, taking deep, steadying breaths. "They dragged me outside. Rod was on the steps of the school, tangled in mop strings. One of them tied my hands, and I heard him say, 'We'll leave this one alive for questioning.' That was when I knew that Rod Grush was already dead." Alan paused, giving his old friend a moment of respectful silence.

"I was sent to a BEM compound and questioned for a year and a half. Then, as if I wasn't miserable enough, they threw me into a dumpster for six months. I hadn't opened the cylinder, so I could tell them nothing. Only two words escaped my lips: *Spencer. Son.*" He looked at his boy. "I had mailed the package to Spencer, where it sat untouched for over two years. Now it is found. And we're here to open it." He held up the silver cylinder.

"What happens when we solve the last clue?" Daisy pointed to the cylinder in Alan's hand.

"This clue should direct us to a map. The map will lead us to a hidden landfill. That is where we'll meet the Aurans."

"The Aurans live at a landfill?" Spencer raised his eyebrows, not so sure if he wanted to be associated with kids who'd been living in a trash heap for a few hundred years.

"What makes you think the Aurans will cooperate once we find them?" Penny asked.

"They left the clues for someone to solve. I think the Aurans want to be found. Maybe this is their very purpose. Maybe the Founding Witches left them here so that whoever solved the clues could put an end to Glop and Toxites forever."

"If the Aurans are hundreds of years old," Penny said, "then how come that cylinder looks so new and shiny?"

"The Aurans periodically updated the thirteen clues, keeping with the times as technology advanced," Alan said. "I have learned never to underestimate the Aurans. They want to make it as difficult as humanly possible to find the map to their landfill. We have to earn the right to speak with them."

"Mmm, landfill . . ." Bernard said, a grin spreading across his face. "So there's gonna be garbage?"

"Lots of garbage," said Alan. "Which is why I put you on the team."

Bernard rubbed his hands together in pure joy. "I love a good dump."

"It's not a dump," Penny cut in. "It's a landfill."

"Dump, landfill. Potato, potahto." Bernard shrugged. "Same dif."

"No," Penny persisted. "A dump is *not* a landfill. I did a report on it in high school. There's a big difference."

"No difference," Bernard said stubbornly. "Place for garbage."

Penny leaned across the table. "Dumps aren't even legal anymore. Once upon a time, people heaped their hazardous waste into holes in the ground and called it good. Now we have landfills—well-engineered disposal sites for nonhazardous solids."

"Bern! Penny!" Walter finally cut in. "Can you have this discussion later?"

"Same thing." The garbologist sat back, smiling as he managed to sneak in the final word.

"Let's suppose we find the Aurans and they tell us the location of the Glop source," Walter mused. "How do you plan to destroy it?"

Alan had an answer ready. "The Aurans have been destroying Glop for centuries. They collect old maxed-out

Glopified supplies. Somehow they extract the Glop, deliver a small portion back to the warlocks, and destroy the rest."

Penny sat forward, a scheming look in her eye. "If we can find out what the Aurans use to destroy the Glop, then we might be able to use the same method to destroy the source."

"I think we're getting ahead of ourselves," Bernard said. "We've got to find the map to the dump first."

"Which is why we have this." Alan hefted the cylinder and took a deep breath. "Let's find out what's inside."

His thumb flipped the clasp, and the black lid sprang open.

"IT'S ALL RIGHT HERE."

Alan upturned the cylinder and dumped the contents onto the table. There was a quiet stupor as they all stared blankly at the item.

Finally, Bernard threw his hands in the air. "You gotta be kidding me!"

"That's a little disappointing." Penny raised an eyebrow.

"It's a . . ." Spencer stammered. "A . . ."

"It's a roll of paper towels!" Bernard shouted.

"But without the paper towels," added Daisy.

And that was exactly what it was: a brown cardboard tube, about eight inches long, slightly wrinkled at both ends.

"There's something inside it," Walter said, bending close to the table.

Alan picked it up and peered through it. Carefully, he

reached his fingers into the end of the roll and pinched out a scrap of old newspaper, stuffed tightly, as if to hold something in. Alan tossed the paper into the trash can and grabbed a second wrinkled scrap from the other end of the tube. This time, something fell from the cardboard roll and landed with a tinkle on the table.

It was a tiny silver key, maybe half the size of Spencer's thumb. He'd never seen one quite like it before. Alan dropped the scrap of paper and the cardboard tube in the trash and bent over to inspect the key.

"Why's it so . . . small?" Daisy asked.

"It's the economy," Bernard said. "Everyone's downsizing."

"It's small," Walter said, "because the lock is small." He reached across the table and picked up the key. "Anyone who's spent time as a janitor ought to know exactly what this key is for." He pinched it between his fingers for all to see.

The garbologist and the biology teacher shrugged. Spencer and Daisy had both spent time as janitors, but they didn't have keys to the school. It was Penny who finally answered: "It opens a paper-towel dispenser."

Walter nodded. "Every paper-towel dispenser has a tiny keyhole, usually on the side or the top. That's how the janitor opens the dispenser to put in a fresh roll of paper."

"Then the map to the Auran landfill must be hidden inside a dispenser somewhere!" Alan said.

"How many paper-towel dispensers do you think there

are in the United States?" Penny asked. "Millions? Billions?" She shook her head. "Where do we even start looking?"

"I just have to point this out," Daisy cut in, holding up a finger. "Has anyone else noticed that the word *dispenser* sounds a lot like, you know, *Spencer?*"

"What does that have to do with anything?" Spencer said.

Daisy shrugged. "Just an interesting coincidence."

"Did the twelfth clue give you any direction on where we could find this dispenser?" Walter asked.

"No, I don't think so." Alan rubbed a hand through his beard. "But that was more than two years ago. I could be wrong."

"We've got to find a way to narrow down the search," Penny said.

"I might start by searching Alsbury High School." Everyone turned to Bernard. The garbologist was rocked back on his chair, yellow boots resting on the edge of the table. He was holding a newspaper in front of his face, as though casually reading at the breakfast table.

"Would you get your nose out of the trash and start taking things more seriously?" Penny snapped at him.

Bernard lowered the wrinkled newspaper just enough to peer over the top. "One man's trash is another man's reading material. Very interesting report about the janitor at Alsbury High School. Looks like the article continues on page A3."

He dropped his boots to the floor and reached into the trash can for the second scrap of newspaper that Alan had plucked from the tube. Carefully, Bernard unfolded the page and smoothed it against the tabletop.

"Yup!" Bernard said. "Sure as shooting. It's page A3."

The whole team was staring at the garbologist, waiting for an explanation of what was written on the newspaper.

"It's all right here." Bernard hoisted the trash can onto the table. "You were all so worked up about the tiny key that you didn't think twice about throwing away the real clue."

He lifted the cardboard tube out of the trash and waved it around. "This tells you that the key belongs to a paper-towel dispenser." Bernard set down the tube and lifted the newspaper. "And this tells you that the paper-towel dispenser belongs to Alsbury High School. Are you following me?"

Walter sighed. "Just read the article, Bern."

"Ahem." Bernard cleared his throat and straightened his duct-tape tie. "Police are investigating the death of Alsbury High School's night janitor, Rico Chavez."

"Wait!" Walter held out his hand.

Bernard flinched. "I haven't even gotten to the tragic part yet."

"What's the date on the paper?" the warlock asked.

Bernard squinted at the corner of the page. "Let's see . . . Friday, January 13, 1993."

Daisy did some quick math on her fingers. "That newspaper's more than twenty years old!"

"It's a warning," Walter said. "I remember the Rico

Chavez incident in '93. The Bureau wasn't happy about it going public."

"What happened to Rico?" Spencer asked.

"It isn't pretty, kid," Bernard said. "Says here he was found—"

Walter held up his hand again, cutting off Bernard before he could share the gruesome details. "The press found Rico before the BEM could cover it up. The news reporters couldn't fathom what got him. There were even outrageous theories about wild animals in the school. But every janitor knew without a doubt. Rico Chavez was killed by Toxites."

"How could that be?" Penny asked. "Toxites don't live in high schools."

"Toxites feed on active brain waves," Walter said. "High school air is too rotten for them. They'd feel relocated and would do anything to escape."

"Okay," Alan said. "Let's suppose the Toxites were trapped in the high school, getting angry. Rico must have accidentally released them, and before he knew it, the creatures got him."

"Right," said Penny. "I'm still wondering how a swarm of angry Toxites ended up trapped in a high school."

"They must have been planted there," Alan said. "I bet the Aurans put them there to guard the final clue."

Walter picked up the small key. "If the paper-towel dispenser is at Alsbury High School, then Rico Chavez might have given his life to pave the way for us."

"Don't take anything for granted," Alan said. "Just

because Rico sprang the first trap doesn't mean there won't be others. I'm guessing we can still expect to run into danger."

"I don't think any of you know this," Bernard said, fishing around in the trash can again, "but my middle name is actually Danger."

"Dr. Bernard Danger Weizmann." Daisy said it softly to hear what it sounded like.

"It's got a nice ring to it!" Bernard found what he was digging for and produced a half-empty bottle of Dr. Pepper from the trash can. He unscrewed the lid and took a swig. The garbologist smacked his lips. "It's a bit flat."

Spencer gagged.

CHAPTER 19

"WOKE US ALL UP."

It was still dark outside when Spencer felt a hand shaking his shoulder. He blinked a few times before his eyes could focus on Penny's face. The young woman was wearing a huge grin.

"I talked him into it," Penny whispered.

"Huh?" Spencer glanced at the clock on the wall. "It's six o'clock in the morning. Why are you waking me up?"

"Shh!" Penny pulled him up from the couch. The team had slept in the teacher's lounge at Woodbury Elementary. There were enough couches and armchairs for everyone except Walter and Penny, who'd volunteered to stay down in the janitor's closet with the Glopified gear.

Penny led Spencer into the hallway, silently shutting the door to the teacher's lounge. "What about the others?" Spencer asked. "Where are we going?"

130

"I thought you should be here for this," Penny said. "Operation Vortex. I talked Uncle Walter into using the leaf blower!"

Spencer paused in the hallway, his feet suddenly too numb to move. Operation Vortex! Spencer was fully awake now. Walter was about to rescue Marv!

Penny grabbed his arm, infusing Spencer with anticipation as they continued down the hallway.

"I convinced Uncle Walter that we needed one more janitor on this mission," Penny explained. "Marv's the best Toxite fighter I've ever met. I'd feel a lot better with him by our side."

Spencer could barely contain his excitement. He'd been waiting months for this day. It was Spencer's fault that Marv was trapped in the vacuum bag. A few months ago, they'd learned for sure that Marv was alive. Penny had captured an audio clip from inside the Vortex. It was Marv's voice booming out, "Haha! Gutter ball!" So, not only was the big janitor alive, but Marv seemed to think he was bowling inside the vacuum bag.

Walter turned as Penny and Spencer entered the janitor's closet. The Glopified leaf blower was on the table and the overcharged Vortex vacuum bag was resting in the crook of Walter's arm.

"Penny?" He made a disapproving face.

She shrugged. "Come on, Uncle. You know Spencer should be here for this."

"I make no guarantees," Walter said. "I have no idea if this will work."

"Of course it will," said Penny. "Now get in there before the others wake up."

Walter lifted the leaf blower from the table and crossed the room. He opened a small door, and Spencer saw that the area beyond was a tight concrete chamber. Everything had been removed, leaving the walls and ceiling bare.

"I'll give you two minutes to tape me in," Walter said. "When you hear the leaf blower start, you'll know I'm about to begin."

"Hold on tight." Penny closed her uncle into the small, dark room. She lifted a roll of duct tape from a nearby shelf. Tearing off long strips, she taped along the seam of the door.

"Glopified tape will keep the door from imploding," Penny said. Spencer was familiar with the tape. It was fingerprint sensitive and unbreakable. The only fingers authorized to peel it off would be the same ones that taped it down.

Penny stepped away from the door, a huge X crisscrossing the frame. No sooner had she finished than the leaf blower's motor roared to life on the other side of the door. The sound that followed was a hundred times louder as Walter pierced a hole into the Vortex vacuum bag.

Spencer clamped his hands over his ears as the janitor's closet filled with deafening suction. The walls shook and the shelves rattled. Even through the taped door, Spencer could feel the pull. He looked down to see his shoelaces standing straight out, stretching toward the door. Spencer leaned back, bracing himself against Penny.

In a moment, it was over. And the silence that followed

seemed almost deafening in its own way. Penny raced forward, ripping strips of duct tape from the door. She crumpled the tape together and cast it aside, a silvery wad of stickiness.

Spencer hung back, his throat so tight with anxiety that it seemed he'd never be able to swallow again. Penny jerked open the door, and Walter Jamison collapsed into her arms. Spencer noticed the papery Vortex bag in his hand as she lowered him to the floor.

Unable to resist, Spencer leapt through the doorway and into the small concrete room. It was dark and, if possible, even barer than before. Spencer felt the smooth walls, noticing how chips of concrete had been stripped away by the suction force.

The room was empty. There was not even a speck of dust, let alone a big, burly janitor.

"I'm sorry," Walter whispered.

"What happened?" asked Penny. "Why didn't it work?"

"The leaf blower was ripped from my hand," he said. "The Vortex sucked the air out of it before I could take aim. The blower wasn't strong enough."

But the leaf blower was powerful! Spencer had seen it blast the jaw off a giant Filth. Why hadn't it worked?

"Nothing can match the Vortex," Walter muttered, as close to despair as Spencer had ever seen him.

Footsteps in the janitor's closet brought Penny and Walter to their feet.

"There you are!" Alan said, rushing to Spencer. The rest

of the team was filing in behind him, still rubbing sleep from their eyes.

"Did you feel the earthquake?" Daisy asked. "Woke us all up!" Spencer decided he could tell her about Operation Vortex later. For now, he let her think the shaking was an earthquake.

"I woke up and you were gone," Alan said. "What are you doing down here?"

The boy stared at his dad. Spencer had done his own thing for so long, why should he have to report to his dad now?

"He was helping us," Penny answered for him. "We're getting the gear together. Thought we should do a little training with the new equipment before we head into the danger zone."

"Make it quick," Alan said. "We should get on the road." After finally opening that mysterious package, he was anxious to find Alsbury High School.

"Hold your horses!" Bernard said. "We're not going anywhere till I make some repairs on the garbage truck. That Extension Grime shattered my window and ripped off the back hopper cover. It'll be several hours at best."

"Let's just take the truck as it is," Alan said. "It's still drivable."

"It doesn't meet regulations," said Bernard. "I'm not gonna risk getting pulled over. My extended cab is meant to hold four people. We're going to be packing six. We don't have seat belts for everybody."

"We can duct tape ourselves down," Daisy said.

"Duct tape, really?" Bernard tugged on the flaps of his aviator cap in frustration.

"Forget it, Bernie," Alan said. "The truck is fine. We leave within the hour."

The garbologist sighed in defeat. He opened his tweed coat to reveal an assortment of vending machine treats tucked into his overalls. "Can't we at least have breakfast first?"

CHAPTER 20

"VANILLA SCENTED."

Penny was so excited to explain the weaponry that she didn't even join in the breakfast of cookies and candy bars. She waited until everyone was seated at the table before taking a janitorial belt from a hook on the wall.

"Everybody gets a belt," she said. "Ultra lightweight, one size fits all." She strapped it around her waist.

"No offense," Bernard said through a mouthful of Snickers. "But shouldn't the warlock explain the gear?"

"Penny's my weapons specialist," Walter said. "Whenever I Glopify something new, I give it to her. She learns how to use it and gives me feedback on how to improve."

"I'm the guinea pig," Penny said. Then she was back to the training.

She pointed to a pouch near the buckle. "On this side,

you've got vacuum dust. The back pouches have a latex glove, chalkboard erasers, and duct tape. This other pouch has a razorblade." She pulled the little blade from the belt. "Flip the button and you've got a sword."

Daisy jumped as the razorblade extended. Penny held it out for everyone to see before closing the blade and dropping it back into the pouch. "If you've got a sword, you'll need a shield."

Penny reached for one of the U clips on the belt. The clips held anything with a handle, making it invisible and intangible while it was on the belt. Penny unclipped a short handle, and a dustpan shimmered into view. With a twist of the handle, the pan fanned out, metal pieces clicking together and expanding to form a circular shield. Penny thumped her fist against the dustpan shield.

"Nearly indestructible," Penny said. "Good for scooping up little piles of dust, too."

She twisted the handle again, and the shield reverted to an ordinary dustpan. When she snapped the handle into the U clip, the dustpan disappeared. "These other U clips are for the usual gear." Penny pointed at the handles in her belt. "Broom, mop, pushbroom, and toilet plunger."

"And all of it's Glopified?" Spencer asked, remembering how he and Daisy had stuck a regular toilet plunger to Walter's back.

"Of course," Penny said. She turned so everyone could see the other side of the belt. There were several nylon loops with plastic spray bottles dangling from their triggers.

"Orange one heals practically any injury," Penny said.

"I remember that one," remarked Bernard.

"Green one causes deep sleep and erases your recent memory of the person who sprayed you."

"I *don't* remember that one," Walter said.

Penny unclipped a bottle of blue spray and held it out for demonstration.

"Looks like Windex," Daisy said.

"You're right," said Penny. "But what does magic Windex do?"

She aimed the spray bottle at the table and gave a few shots. The blue solution hit the wooden tabletop and shimmered briefly with an azure light. Spencer leaned forward, anxious to see the effect it would have.

The wet area of the tabletop changed almost instantly to glass! Spencer could see straight through to the floor.

"We believe this is the spray that was used to rescue Director Garcia from the dumpster," Walter said. "Mr. Clean developed the Glop formula. He sprayed the side of the dumpster, it turned to glass, and he shattered it to free his warlock partner."

Spencer had wondered how Garcia had managed to escape the dumpster. He'd seen the director in visions enough times to know that he was back at New Forest Academy, overseeing the education of his handpicked elite students.

"The Windex will temporarily turn anything to glass," said Penny. "Once the spray dries, the surface will return to its original material."

She hooked the spray bottle back into the belt and withdrew one more item from the nylon loops. It wasn't a plastic spray bottle, like the others. This one was a slender aerosol can.

"Air freshener," Penny said. "Vanilla scented." She held out the can for everyone to see. "Uncle Walter made this for the kids."

"Really?" Daisy said. "I didn't think we were *that* stinky." She lifted her arm and gave a sniff.

"Not for your smell," Penny said with a grin. "For your minds."

"You think our minds need freshening?" Spencer asked.

Walter finally cut in. "The air freshener will temporarily counteract the effects of Toxite breath. If you kids are going to fight alongside us, then we can't have you getting distracted, falling asleep, and losing interest. A quick spritz of air freshener will help you stay focused in the middle of battle."

"Thanks," Spencer said to the warlock. Since adults weren't affected by Toxite breath, the air freshener was truly an invention just for Spencer and Daisy.

"With the BEM Pluggers riding those giant Extension Toxites," Penny said, "we'll need all the weaponry we can carry." She pointed to a row of belts on the wall. There was one for everybody, and each belt was heavily loaded and ready for use.

"The Extension Toxites are tough," Penny said, "but they have a weakness. The Pluggers control the beasts with battery packs and extension cords. Cut the cord and the Toxites go free."

"Free is good?" Bernard asked.

"We got an Extension Rubbish to turn on its rider," Penny explained. "Cut the creatures free and they don't know BEM from Rebel. They just want to kill."

"I think we can stay ahead of the Pluggers," Alan said. "It's been over twenty-four hours since we've seen them. Alsbury High School isn't a Rebel school, so they have no idea where we're headed next."

"Good point," Walter said. "If we keep up our momentum, we have a better chance at shaking them off our trail forever."

There were nods of agreement around the table, and Spencer knew it was time to break the news. "We can't shake them," he finally said. Everyone turned to him, curious about his sudden pessimism.

"The reason we haven't seen the Pluggers for a while is because they stopped by New Forest Academy," Spencer said. "Mr. Clean is outfitting the Extension Toxites for war."

"What does that mean?" Daisy asked. "What kind of outfits do Toxites wear?"

"I don't want to find out," said Bernard. "If we hit the road soon, those Pluggers will never find us. They're a day behind and two states over."

"It doesn't matter how far behind they are. Believe me," Spencer looked at his dad. "They're coming."

"How can you say that?" Alan asked. "You don't know for sure . . ."

"It's *you*, Dad." Spencer cut him off. "You're leading the Pluggers right to us."

"Now, wait a minute!" Alan leaned across the table.

"Are you accusing me of treason? You think I'm telling the Pluggers where to find us?"

"You might as well!" Spencer said. Old anger about his dad's absence was resurfacing, and for once, Spencer decided to let it flow. "Being with you puts all of us in danger!"

"Oh?" Alan stood up. "Is that what you think? Since you seem to have all the answers, why don't *you* lead the mission?"

"Okay!" Spencer shouted. "We'll start by fixing Bernard's garbage truck. We'll start by listening to other people's ideas."

Walter reached out and grabbed Spencer's arm. The contact reminded Spencer that he and his father were not alone in the room.

"Why do you think your dad is leading the Pluggers to us?" Penny asked.

Spencer took a deep breath. "Leslie's Filth is baited." He relaxed his fists. "Mr. Clean had a scrap of my dad's shirt, and he fed it to the Extension Filth. Now it's tracking us and it won't stop until it finds *him*." Spencer pointed at his dad.

Alan ran a hand through his beard in momentary thought. Then he pushed back his chair and headed for the door.

"Where you going?" Bernard asked.

Alan paused at the threshold. "Spencer's right. If the Pluggers have my scent, then it's too dangerous for me to stay with you. I can lead them away from Alsbury High School and give you a better chance of finding the map."

"This is lunacy!" Walter shouted. "We can't send you out there alone with a pack of overgrown Toxites on your trail!"

"I'll go with him," Penny said, tightening the strap on her janitorial belt.

"We stay together!" Walter insisted.

Alan put his hands into his pockets. "Let Spencer decide," he said. "What do you say, Son? Do I stay or go?"

Emotion tightened Spencer's throat as he stared across the room. It wasn't supposed to be like this. He and his dad were supposed to be sharing grand adventures, not bickering and threatening. It wasn't a question, really. Spencer knew he could never send his dad off to be hunted by the Pluggers.

"You stay with us."

Bernard leaned forward and whispered urgently, "But we're going to fix the garbage truck."

Spencer nodded. "But we're going to fix the garbage truck."

CHAPTER 21

"A PAINT SPILL."

It was well past midnight when the garbage truck pulled into the parking lot of Alsbury High School. Repairing Bernard's vehicle had taken longer than anticipated, and the rest of the day was lost in travel to Austin, Texas.

The cab was crowded and uncomfortable with all six team members. And despite the car fresheners dangling from the mirror, the vehicle now smelled like onions from their late-night dinner from a food truck.

Bernard had dug through his steel briefcases of strange trash collections. He had a whole assortment of jewelry that he'd recovered from the garbage. A thin gold chain fit perfectly through the tiny dispenser key, and Alan had it hanging safely around his neck.

Bernard parked the garbage truck next to a dumpster. The headlights turned off, plunging the parking area into darkness. The school looked very old, the main entrance framed in a weathered stone archway. A twenty-four-hour security light flickered above the front doors, giving the whole place the appearance of a haunted mansion rather than a high school.

Penny popped open the truck door, and everyone filed outside. The weather was strange to Spencer. They had traveled far enough south that the air seemed unseasonably warm. It was like winter was behind them. Spencer didn't even need a jacket.

"What's the plan?" Spencer asked as everyone started gearing up.

"Simple," said Alan. "We find the paper-towel dispenser and get out alive."

The answer made Spencer feel like he'd asked a dumb question. Of course he knew that part of the plan. Instead of making a comeback, Spencer focused on strapping down his janitorial belt.

"We stay together," answered Walter. "Search the bathrooms until we find it."

"No." Everyone turned to Alan. "If the Aurans were trying to hide this dispenser, then the bathroom's too obvious. It won't be out in the open. Remember, we've got the key, which means that the dispenser hasn't been opened for at least twenty years—since Rico Chavez."

"And who knows if Rico even made it that far," Walter added.

"So where do we look?" Bernard said, locking the doors to the garbage truck.

Penny, who had been stretching her legs and doing a few simple gymnastic warm-ups, gave another idea. "Let's just get inside and see what we find. I hate standing around like this."

As Penny led the team across the parking lot, Spencer turned back, searching for Daisy. She had fallen behind the others, struggling to keep up while trying to jam something into her janitorial belt.

"Are you okay?" Spencer asked, letting the team pass ahead.

"Yeah," she said, barely glancing up at him. "It just won't fit in this pouch."

"What won't fit?"

Daisy gave up on the belt with a sigh. She turned to show Spencer what she was working on. He almost laughed when he saw it in Daisy's outstretched hand.

"You're bringing *Baybee?*" Spencer cried.

She gave him a look like her decision was obvious. "We're going into another school. We might need a hall pass."

"It's the middle of the night, Daisy! No one's checking hall passes! Besides, Baybee's a . . . baby. I thought we'd been over this!"

She looked up at him, her eyes wide and glinting in the flickering light from the school's entryway. "This isn't Welcher Elementary School," she said.

Spencer nodded slowly. "That's exactly what I'm trying to say."

"I'm scared, Spencer." Her voice was soft. "Running

around strange hallways in dark schools isn't really my thing." She held up Baybee. "But when I'm carrying Mrs. Natcher's hall pass, at least *something* makes me feel like I'm home."

Spencer reached out and plucked Baybee from her grasp. "We'll be okay, Daisy." He tucked back the doll's arms and legs. "I stuffed a gigantic Grime into a belt pouch once," he said. "I'm pretty sure we can fit a baby doll."

The look of fear on Daisy's face melted a bit, and she turned so Spencer could slide Baybee into the pouch.

Just as the doll's head tucked out of sight, Alan's voice sounded behind Spencer. "What are you doing?" His dad grabbed him by the elbow. "Don't you know how dangerous it is to fall behind?" Walter, Penny, and Bernard were already crowded around the school's front door.

"What if something happened to you?" Alan continued, hauling his son toward the others. Daisy jogged to keep up. "Being on this mission means you stay with the team. Got it?"

Spencer pulled away. He didn't have to answer. He was tired of his dad bossing him around, acting like Spencer had never done anything dangerous before.

Penny was crouched in front of the school door with her bottle of Windex. She adjusted the nozzle and gave a small, concentrated spray directly at the lock. The wet area shimmered with a magical blue light.

The rest of the team stepped back to give her some room as she extended a long razorblade. With great precision,

Penny thrust the sharp tip forward, shattering the glass lock and popping the door open.

In a moment, they were inside Alsbury High School, moving carefully down the hallway. Spencer reached for his razorblade. He didn't open it, but he felt safer with the weapon resting in his sweaty palm.

Bernard stopped suddenly, Spencer and Daisy almost bumping into him. The garbologist had his headlamp down-turned, the light illuminating part of the hard floor in the middle of the hallway.

"Pst! I think I found something!" Bernard whispered. Walter and Alan crowded around. Penny reluctantly gave up the lead, doubling back to see what Bernard was so excited about.

Bernard pointed a finger to a brownish stain on the floor.

"Is it dried blood?" Daisy's voice was small in the large hallway.

"Looks like an old paint spill," Walter answered.

"Big whoop," Penny shrugged. "A paint spill."

"It's not the spill, so much as the *shape* of the spill, that matters," said Bernard. "It's a perfect semicircle. Soda pop makes this shape when it runs down the side of a garbage can and pools on the floor."

"What does that have to do with the paper-towel dispenser?" Alan asked.

"It's the middle of the hallway," Bernard said. "Not a logical place to put a trash can." He cast his headlamp down the hallway, spotlighting every garbage can within range. Then he raced off, inspecting each one from top to bottom.

Spencer was mostly grossed out as Bernard ran his hands along the garbage cans. But Daisy seemed wholly intrigued by the garbologist's methods.

In a flash, Bernard was back, carrying a large trash can. He set it down carefully, adjusting it over the crescent of dried paint. "Aha!" He raised a victorious fist. "Perfect match!" Spencer could see a dried drip of matching brown paint on the side of the garbage can.

"What does this have to do with the paper-towel dispenser?" Alan asked again, this time with a hint of impatience in his voice.

"I don't know yet," Bernard said, yanking the plastic liner out of the can. "I'm just reading the trash." Then he threw down the sack of garbage and dove headfirst into the empty trash can. Daisy giggled, but Spencer had to look away. Walter checked his watch.

"Seriously?" Penny said, stomping her foot impatiently. "Can we just go on without him? I thought we were looking for a towel dispenser, not Oscar the Grouch."

"Look no further!" Bernard called, emerging from the trash can. He straightened his duct-tape tie and cleared his throat. "I'm fairly certain that we'll find the dispenser behind this brick wall." He pointed across the hallway.

Penny laughed out loud. "That's the most ridiculous thing I've heard since high school!"

"We're in a high school," Daisy pointed out.

Bernard drew his bottle of Windex, twisted the nozzle

for maximum spray, and began misting the brick wall. The hallway was momentarily illuminated in a sapphire glow. Then the iridescence faded as the brick wall turned entirely to glass.

On the other side of the transparent wall, Spencer saw a hidden, narrow bathroom. There were stalls on both sides, the metal doors securely closed. An old lightbulb cast the secret bathroom in a yellowish haze. And mounted on the far wall, looking isolated and innocent, was the paper-towel dispenser.

CHAPTER 22

"EVERYONE KNOWS THE ANSWER."

W ow," Daisy said, staring through the glass wall at the hidden bathroom. She turned to Bernard. "How'd you know it was there?"

"The trash can told me," answered the garbologist.

Penny scoffed. "Which is another way of saying that you made a lucky guess."

"The middle of the hallway is an unlikely place for a garbage can, which means someone put it there for a special purpose," Bernard explained. "The paint, dripping down the can and pooling on the floor, must have dried before anyone had a chance to clean it up, which means that the job was done in a hurry. Probably during the middle of the night, so as to not block student walkways in the hall. Lastly, there are dried bits of mortar in the bottom of the trash can, which means that someone stood here." Bernard moved in front of the glass wall. "And they scraped their trowel into the garbage can while repairing this wall."

"You're amazing!" Daisy gawked.

Bernard closed his eyes and smiled. "And you're a sweetheart."

"Why would Rico Chavez repair this wall?" Spencer asked, never taking his eyes from the hidden bathroom.

"No," Alan said. "Rico didn't repair the wall. He probably got curious and blew it open. But since he didn't retrieve the map, the Aurans had to hide the paper-towel dispenser again by patching the wall."

"Well," Penny cut in, "we can stand here and hypothesize about which little piggy built this brick wall, but that's not going to help us get to that dispenser."

"Penny's right." Walter checked his watch. "We need to get in there."

Without further discussion, Penny drew a pushbroom from her belt. She twirled it around like a fighting staff and then thrust it against the formerly brick wall. The sound caused everyone to cringe as huge fragments of glass shattered to the floor.

Then it was utterly quiet. The distinctive smell of a public bathroom wafted through the open passageway. Spencer wrinkled his nose.

Penny stepped across the broken entryway. Her hand hovered at her side, ready to draw the best weapon from her belt. Alan and Walter were less than a step behind her, glass crunching under the soles of their shoes.

Spencer glanced at Daisy. She was nervously chewing

her pinkie nail, eyes unblinking. Bernard put a hand on her shoulder and ushered her in alongside Spencer.

The team stood huddled in the bathroom's secret entrance. Alan had his arms out, holding everyone back as he silently studied the area for traps.

"I'm guessing this is where the Toxites were trapped," Alan said.

"So Rico Chavez got suspicious about what was behind the wall," Walter hypothesized. "When he broke it open, the Toxites saw their chance for escape, and poor Rico couldn't get out of the way fast enough."

"We can thank him later," Bernard said. "Those Toxites would be coming out on us right now if it weren't for Rico."

"How can we thank him later?" Daisy muttered. "He's dead."

Spencer peered around Walter and shuddered at the state of the restroom. It was an unusually long bathroom, with about twenty stalls on either side, metal doors tightly closed. Sloppy graffiti covered the ceiling and walls in streaks of red and black. Most of it looked like meaningless lines and scribbles, hardened drips of paint hanging like stalactites.

"There's something seriously wrong with this bathroom," Spencer said after a quick survey.

"Very observant," Bernard muttered. "Do you think it has something to do with the lovely artwork?"

Then Spencer realized why it felt so off. "There aren't any sinks!" He balled his hands into fists, making a mental commitment not to touch anything. What kind of bathroom didn't have sinks? How were people supposed to wash their hands?

"I don't like the look of that," Alan said, drawing a Glopified flashlight from his belt. The flashlight would shine brightly to reveal any magical item in the room.

Spencer and Daisy squeezed through the group of adults as Alan flicked the switch. A white beam shot from his flashlight, illuminating an object in the center of the bathroom.

It was a yellow cone. The words *Caution: Wet Floor* were clearly visible above the symbol of a man slipping. And, judging by the flashlight's attention, this caution cone was definitely Glopified. Then the light beam skipped from the cone to the back wall, illuminating the dispenser. The light seemed to taunt Alan, so easily reaching his end goal.

He flicked off the flashlight and clipped it back into his belt. "Probably some kind of defensive barrier." Alan gestured to the caution cone.

"So what does it do?" asked Bernard.

"It warns you." Everyone turned to Daisy. She shrugged like it was obvious. "Don't slip on the wet floor."

"Our best chance is to approach slowly," Alan said, getting right back to business. "I'll try to move or disable it."

"Let me do it." Penny stepped past him. "If something happens to me, at least we won't lose the team leader."

Alan shook his head. "I'm the only one with experience in disabling Auran traps."

"Relax," Penny said, taking a cautious step toward the cone. "You can coach me from the sidelines."

Penny moved painstakingly slowly, carefully reaching out a foot to probe each step. Her breathing was steady while everyone else in the bathroom seemed to stop breathing altogether. Alan couldn't help but inch forward, giving occasional words of encouragement.

Penny was about halfway there when Daisy spoke up, her voice echoing loudly after so much silence.

"Why did the Toxites cross the road?"

Walter and Bernard glanced at the girl, giving her less than a second before turning their attention back to Penny's perilous approach.

Spencer rolled his eyes. "Seriously?" He turned to her. "Now's not a great time for jokes, Daisy."

"I'm not joking." She pointed to the nearest bathroom stall. "I'm reading."

Written in sloppy paint at the top of the stall door was the joke.

Q: Why did the Toxites cross the road?

"Well?" Daisy said. "Why did they? What do you think?"

"That's a dumb joke," Spencer muttered. "Everyone knows the answer." Somewhat bothered by the cryptic writing on the stall, Spencer turned back to check Penny's progress. She had arrived at the yellow cone and stood motionless before it.

"Okay! Stop right there!" Alan called. "Whatever you do, don't go past the cone!" In his anxiety, Alan had crept forward until he stood about halfway between Penny and the rest of the team. "I need you to inspect the base," he instructed. "See if the cone is somehow anchored to the floor." Penny lifted her foot to take another delicate step.

"Whoa!" Alan shouted. "Freeze! Don't move!"

Penny paused, one foot in the air. A clumsier person might have tipped forward, but not Penny. She was the state champion on the balance beam. Standing like a flamingo in the middle of the bathroom was no trouble at all. But as Penny cast a glance over her shoulder to hear Alan's instructions, she wavered.

It was as though the floor became wildly slippery. Penny's arms shot out for balance, but it wasn't enough. With a shout of disbelief, she went into an uncontrollable fall. Her feet jerked out, passing the caution cone as she went down on her backside.

As soon as Penny's feet broke the invisible barrier, the caution cone released a ripple of magic. Daisy grabbed Spencer's sleeve as he shielded his face from the blast. When he lowered his hands, Spencer saw what had happened.

The floor around the caution cone had changed. It didn't make sense, but Penny was buried in it! The floor, totally solid only seconds ago, had swallowed Penny to the waist. She squirmed in its grasp, sending ripples across the tile and liquefying everything in its wake.

"Get back!" Alan shouted, waving his arms at the rest of the team. When Alan didn't follow, Spencer looked down. His dad had also been caught in the wet quicksand floor.

Alan's feet were completely out of sight, and the tiles were creeping slowly up his shins.

Bernard tried reaching out for him, but Alan shook his head. "It's spreading!" he shouted. Walter pulled Spencer and Daisy back against the graffiti-covered stall door.

Daisy was breathing heavily. "They weren't kidding about the wet floor."

"Get a broom!" Alan was holding still, but the tiles were almost to his knees now. Bernard instantly clipped out a broom and extended the handle toward Alan.

"Not for me." Alan waved off the broom. "I need you to fly to the dispenser. I'll throw you the key once you get over there. Get the map and get out before this whole room sinks."

"Righto, chief," Bernard said. He took aim and tapped his bristles against the floor. The broom pulled him at an upward angle, barely clearing Alan's head. But he hadn't even reached the caution cone when his broom suddenly changed course.

He shouted, the broom pitching downward as though drawn in by the caution cone. Bernard landed with a squelch between Alan and Penny, his broom sticking into the wet floor uselessly. Bernard's rubber boots instantly disappeared as the garbologist sank thigh-deep into the liquefied tiles.

"At least it was a soft landing!" Bernard forced a grin.

With only her neck and head above the floor, Penny had stopped thrashing. Spencer felt a rush of urgency. If they didn't reach the dispenser soon, she'd be gone. They had to get to the other side!

Then it hit him. "The joke, Daisy! The joke!"

She whirled around to read the writing on the stall door behind them. "Why did the Toxites cross the road?"

"To get to the other side!" Spencer answered. "We have to get to the other side of the bathroom!"

The rippling liquid floor was almost to their feet. The only safe path was a retreat back into the hallway.

"We're trying!" Walter said. "I don't see how a joke is going to help you reach the dispenser."

"Not that side," Spencer said. "We've got to get over *there!*" He pointed, not to the far wall with the dispenser, but across the bathroom to the opposite stall. The joke's answer was crudely painted.

A: To get to the other side

"There's got to be something over there," Spencer said. "Something in that stall that will help get us out of here!"

"There's no time!" Alan said. "You have to leave or we'll all be trapped."

"I have to get over there—" Spencer said, but his dad cut him off.

"It's a joke, Spence! A dumb joke! It's not going to save anybody!"

It was silent for a moment, and then Walter spoke softly at Spencer's side. "I think your father's right. We need to regroup in the hallway."

Spencer quickly bent down and untied his shoelaces. "Come on, Daisy." She stepped forward, always a willing accomplice to Spencer's half-baked plans.

Spencer drew his toilet plunger and handed it to Daisy. "You know," he said to Walter, "you would have helped me if it weren't for my dad." Then he pulled up his shirt and turned his bare back to Daisy.

"Plunge me."

"Are you sure?" Daisy said. "I thought you hated these things."

"Just do it! If I think about it too long I'm going to get grossed out." Instantly, he felt the rubber suction cup clamp onto his back. "Now throw me as hard as you can!"

Alan shouted something in protest. Walter reached out for him. But Daisy obeyed. She pulled back and hurled Spencer across the bathroom, detaching the plunger with a twist of the handle.

An involuntary shout left his lips as he sailed through the air. His cry was cut short as he slammed into the stall door, giving him an instant headache. He slid down the door, feeling his feet squish into the quicksand floor.

"Sorry!" Daisy shouted. "You said as hard as I could!"

The liquefied tiles were swallowing his shoes. The loose laces gave him one extra second to slide out before his shoes were completely overtaken by the wet floor. He threw his weight against the stall door, but it wouldn't budge. Spencer felt his feet sink deeper into the floor, and he was grateful to be wearing tall socks.

"Use the Windex!" Bernard shouted. The garbologist

was anchored at the waist, but twisted around to watch the action.

In a flash, the blue bottle was unclipped from his belt. Spencer gave a spray, watching part of the metal door turn to glass. When the transition was complete, Spencer slammed his elbow through the glass, popping out the lock on the inside.

The door swung open. Spencer tugged free of his sunken socks and stepped onto the solid tile in the stall.

It looked like any bathroom stall: a single toilet and a roll of TP. Spencer scanned the walls for more writing, hoping desperately for some instructions on how to save his friends. What if his dad were right? What if it was nothing more than a dumb joke?

Then his eyes fell to the ceramic toilet seat, and he saw the writing. Four words were scribbled out in the same hand that had painted the joke.

Flow shot toy lit

Spencer stared unblinking at the gibberish phrase. He muttered the words aloud, but couldn't make sense of them. "Flow shot toy lit."

"Penny!" Bernard's voice rang through the bathroom. "She's going under!"

Spencer felt a surge of panic take him. This was the strangest riddle he'd ever seen. Toy? In the bathroom stall? He dropped to his knees but couldn't see anything that would help.

Maybe the others knew something he didn't. Scrambling onto his bare feet, Spencer shouted the four words. "Flow shot toy lit!"

"What was that?" Walter called back.

"Flow shot toy lit!" Spencer strung the words together in desperation.

"You're speaking mumbo-jumbo, kid!" Bernard shouted.

There was a moment of silence, and Spencer feared he would never solve it soon enough to save Penny.

Then Daisy burst out, her voice an excited squeal. "Flush a toilet! It's a Mad Gab! Flush a toilet!"

Spencer looked once more at the words on the seat. He mumbled them aloud, "Flow shot toy lit." He heard it clearly now and was upset that he hadn't realized it sooner.

"What are you waiting for?" Daisy shrieked, her voice echoing in the restroom. "Flush it!"

So that was exactly what he did.

CHAPTER 23

"TO GET TO THE OTHER SIDE."

The toilet flushed normally at first. The water swirled upward, filling the bowl. But as the water began to recede down the pipes, things got a little weird. Spencer felt an inescapable pull that caused him to bend toward the toilet. In a heartbeat, he was closer than he ever wanted to be, his head lowering past the rim.

As a desperate last resort, Spencer grabbed the toilet seat, pushing away from the churning water with all his strength. His eyes were clenched tightly and he was holding his breath against the smell and germs of the toilet bowl.

In that unfortunate position, with his head in the toilet, Spencer couldn't help but think of Dez Rylie. If the bully were here, he would be screaming with delight. After escaping all of Dez's swirly threats, it seemed as though Spencer was about to get one after all.

Spencer's hands slipped from the rim of the toilet, and he plunged face-first into the cold water. But to Spencer's great surprise, it didn't end there. His head, clearly too large to fit down the pipe, seemed to compress. Either that, or the pipe suddenly expanded. Whichever was the case, Spencer's whole body was instantly flushed down the toilet.

It was too dark to see where he was going. Spencer shot through the pipes with his arms stretched above his head. Water swirled around him and the bumps and turns nearly forced the air out of his lungs. It was like being in the world's tiniest waterslide, going somewhere that humans were never meant to go.

Spencer's panic was just turning to hysteria when he saw a light at the end of the pipe. He forced his lungs to hold the last wisp of air as he streamed upward toward the exit.

Finally, Spencer erupted from the plumbing. The momentum shot him straight into the air, high enough that he almost hit the ceiling. He crashed painfully to the hard floor, maintaining just enough consciousness to get his bearings.

He was in another bathroom stall. The toilet next to him was still erupting like Mount Saint Helens, shooting water ten feet high. Spencer hauled himself to his feet, spitting toilet water and trying not to throw up. He put a hand to his throbbing head.

"Spencer?" It was Daisy's voice. "Are you okay?"

"Where am I?" he mumbled.

"You're in the bathroom," she answered.

Daisy wasn't telling him anything he didn't already know, and Spencer didn't care for bathroom stall conversations. He found the lock, slid it aside, and pulled back the door.

He was indeed in the same hidden bathroom, just as Daisy had mentioned. But his quick trip through the plumbing had brought him to the farthest toilet. Here, the floor was still firm. And not five feet away was the paper-towel dispenser.

Dripping wet, Spencer stepped out of the stall. Every eye turned from the first stall, widening in surprise at his emergence from the last stall.

"How'd you get over there?" Daisy asked.

"In one toilet and out the other," said Spencer.

"It worked!" Alan cried, his voice ripe with astonishment. He was still thigh-deep in the tile, but he thumped his fist on the hardened floor. Flushing that toilet had not only transported Spencer, it had also disabled the caution cone!

"Just in time, too," Bernard said. "There's nothing left of Penny but a breathing tube."

Spencer glanced at the spot near the caution cone where Penny had been sinking. She was nowhere in sight! In her place was the cardboard paper-towel tube that had been part of the clue package. The tube was sticking straight up, about four inches out of the liquid floor.

"It was hard enough to get that tube into Penny's mouth," Bernard went on. "And in case you didn't notice, I'm fresh out of snorkels."

Walter and Daisy stepped away from the stall as Alan unclasped the golden chain around his neck and handed the key to the warlock. "Get that dispenser open," Alan said. "I'll work on chipping us out of the floor." He drew his bottle of Windex and adjusted the nozzle.

Spencer scanned the room for his shoes and socks, but not even a shoelace was visible anymore. Daisy appeared at his side, handing him the plunger she'd used.

"Thanks for trusting me," he whispered, clipping the plunger into place. "We'd all be in the floor if you hadn't figured out that Mad Gab."

"We play that game at my house all the time," Daisy said. "But it's the first joke I don't get." She scrunched her eyebrows together. "Why did the Toxites cross the road?"

"To get to the other side."

"Toxites." She shook her head. "It doesn't make sense."

"Yeah. It never made sense when it was the chicken, either," Spencer said.

Walter had finally reached the paper-towel dispenser. He ran his fingers across the top until he felt the keyhole. Reaching up, he slid the tiny silver key into place. There was a soft click, and the plastic cover dropped on its hinges.

The dispenser was open.

CHAPTER 24

"DON'T TELL HER I DID THAT, OKAY?"

Spencer took a step toward the warlock, his eyes fixing on the roll of paper towels in the dispenser. Instead of the standard brownish-white paper of most rolls, Spencer saw a design printed on the paper towel. Intersecting lines, each labeled in miniscule writing, covered the roll.

The map wasn't just hidden in the dispenser. The map was actually the roll of paper towels! One of the roads on the map was highlighted, surely marking the route they should travel to find the Aurans' secret landfill.

Walter grabbed the paper-towel roll with both hands and pulled. With surprising ease, the roll came free. "Got it!" the warlock said, a victorious grin across his face.

Daisy dropped to her hands and knees. "These tiles are fascinating! They're so . . . square!"

Spencer had just begun to wonder what Daisy was

talking about when a wave of intense fatigue slammed into him. He staggered a few steps, trying to remain upright. Through the sleepiness, he heard Bernard shout a warning. Spencer's eyes flicked once more to the empty paper-towel dispenser.

There was a hole in the wall. He hadn't noticed it before because the roll of paper towels had blocked it. Now the way was open, and there was movement coming from within the dark hole.

Walter Jamison fired a stream of air freshener from his aerosol can just as the Toxites erupted from their entrapment. Spencer's body was finally giving in to exhaustion when Walter's vanilla-scented freshener wafted past his nose. The haze of Toxite fatigue cleared around him, leaving his mind fresh and alert.

An avalanche of angry Toxites poured out of the hole. Filths hissed, exposing their savage buckteeth. Grimes slithered in every direction along the wall, and a flock of Rubbishes cut through the air.

Rico Chavez may have given his life by releasing the first wave of angry Toxites, but the Aurans had set a double trap!

The bathroom was swarming with deadly creatures, an endless stream entering through the hole in the dispenser. Spencer felt a Grime sear his bare foot with its venomous grip. He kicked it away and leapt up, drawing a mop from his belt.

Spencer spun the mop handle, sending the strings forward in a wide attack. He jumped toward the dispenser, feeling the creatures bite and tear. A group of Rubbishes swooped down, seizing the mop handle in their talons. The weapon was jerked from Spencer's grasp, leaving him vulnerable against the onslaught.

In a flash, Daisy was at his side. The girl blocked with her dustpan shield, giving Spencer time to lunge forward and grab the dispenser cover. Instantly, his arms were crawling with Grimes. A Filth leapt onto his chest, sharp claws digging as it raked downward.

Spencer cried out, heaving the plastic cover of the dispenser and slamming it closed. He felt the latch click and knew that the dispenser could not be opened again without Alan's key.

Spencer threw himself against the wall, shaking free of the Toxites that still clung to him. Closing the dispenser had stopped the flow of creatures, but the bathroom was still under attack by those that had escaped.

Walter slid forward, plunging a Grime to the wall with a splatter of slime. Following Daisy's example, Spencer drew his dustpan. As he twisted the handle, the metal fanned out, forming a circular shield. And just in time! Two Toxites pinged off his defense and fell dazed to the floor.

Spencer's razorblade rang out as it extended from the small handle. With one swing of the blade, both monsters were gone.

"I feel like a sitting duck!" Bernard shouted, still pinned to his waist in the bathroom floor. The garbologist was blocking with his shield, but the Filths were swarming him in a spiky mass of dusty quills.

"Bern!" Walter threw himself forward. He failed to dodge, and Rubbish talons rent his bald head, leaving streaks of red.

Spencer had never fought with such focus before. In the past, he had always struggled against the Toxite breath. But the vanilla air freshener made him more deadly than ever. He hacked and sliced with his razorblade, carving a path across the room.

Without a twinge of distraction in her fight, Daisy was also more deadly than Spencer had ever seen her. She took up a defensive position beside Bernard and Walter.

At least Penny was safe, completely submerged in the floor. Spencer scanned the tiles for her breathing tube. One of the Grimes seemed to notice it at the same moment. The little monster scuttled forward, gripped the cardboard tube, and slid its slimy body inside.

Spencer couldn't see the other end of the tube, but he knew where it led. The thought was horrific! The Grime was slithering down into Penny's open mouth! She would be helpless against the attack.

Spencer raced for the breathing tube, but Daisy beat him there. Throwing aside her shield and plunger, Daisy dove. The wind was knocked from her lungs as she struck the floor. Sliding forward, she grabbed the final inch of the Grime's tail and jerked it out of the cardboard tube. Daisy flung the pale creature across the bathroom and turned back to Penny's breathing tube.

"That was too close," she muttered, reaching into her janitorial belt. There was a silvery flash as Daisy ripped off a piece of Glopified duct tape. "This should do the trick." With a look of success on her face, Daisy placed the piece of tape securely over the top of Penny's tube.

"What are you doing?" Spencer shouted.

"I'm trying to keep the Grimes out!" Daisy replied.

"That's her breathing tube!" Spencer said. "You're keeping the *air* out!"

Daisy's expression changed to sudden sheepishness and she ripped away the Glopified duct tape. "Don't tell her I did that, okay?"

But Spencer didn't have time to answer. There were still too many Toxites, and the air freshener was beginning to fade.

Daisy started giggling uncontrollably. "This tube is snoring!" She had her head twisted sideways, listening into Penny's breathing tube.

"No!" Spencer shouted, mentally pushing past the Toxite breath. He clipped out his can of air freshener and released a long hiss.

"Vac dust!" Walter cried above the chaos. "Everyone use vac dust!"

Slipping his razorblade into the belt pouch, Spencer drew a large fist of vacuum dust. Daisy, crouching low over Penny's tube, did the same.

"Now!" Walter shouted. Spencer, Daisy, Bernard, Alan, and Walter simultaneously released their Palm Blasts of vacuum dust. For a moment, the bathroom was hazy with gritty dust. Then the sound of suction resonated as the Toxites were pulled down against the tile floor.

As the action lulled, Walter quickly dropped to Alan's side, using Glopified Windex to turn the tiles to glass. With precise blows, he used his razorblade sword to chip away until Alan was free.

Seeing the warlock's method, Spencer and Daisy instantly went to work on Bernard. The garbologist pulled free of the ground just as the vacuum suction on the Toxites subsided.

The angry creatures were up and shrieking once more. But the Rebels quickly ducked into one of the bathroom stalls as the relocated Toxites made their way out of the secret bathroom, seeking open air and the brain waves of a younger school.

The Rebels stepped out of the stall, amazed at how quiet the bathroom now seemed. Daisy drew the orange healing spray from her belt and sprayed the top of Walter's bald head. The bloody scratches fizzed as the healing spray took effect.

"How do we get Penny out?" Spencer asked as everyone huddled around her cardboard breathing tube.

"Same way we got out," Alan said, drawing his Windex. "We just have to be careful or we might accidentally turn her to glass."

"I don't think she'd like that," Daisy said.

"Did somebody grab the map?" Bernard asked.

"It's over here," Spencer crossed to where Walter had dropped the roll when the Toxites attacked. "A highlighted route is printed on the paper towel." Spencer picked it up.

Walter squinted at the item in Spencer's hands. "Looks

like a standard roll: eight-inch width, six hundred feet long."

"Whoa," Bernard said. "You're telling me that we've got to follow a six-hundred-foot map?"

Spencer peeled up the end and noticed something else. "Double sided." He held out the paper towel so everyone could see that the map was printed on both sides.

"We'd better rescue Penny so we can get started," Daisy said. "This might take a while."

There was a sudden snarl and the sound of rubble grinding underfoot. The Rebel team whirled around to face the crumpled brick wall, fearful that the relocated Toxites were returning. But it was worse than that. Much worse.

A massive Extension Filth blocked the exit to the hallway. In the dim light from the bathroom, Spencer could see the rider as the beast lumbered into the secret bathroom.

Leslie Sharmelle.

"HOLD YOUR BREATH."

Leslie Sharmelle looked haggard and unkempt. Her blonde hair, once so tidy, was frizzy and dirty. Seeing her in the vision with Mr. Clean had been one thing. But now she was here, still clad in her orange prison jumpsuit, a dangerous sneer on her face.

Daisy gasped as she recognized Mrs. Natcher's substitute teacher. Leslie and Daisy had survived the Vortex together, struggling in a vent above the classroom. The memory was unpleasant, and Daisy slipped to the rear of the group.

And if the convict substitute weren't bad enough, Spencer saw the improvements that Mr. Clean had made to Leslie's beast.

The Extension Filth was outfitted for war in deadly looking armor. Strips of metal, carefully crafted from steel trash cans, covered the Filth's most vulnerable areas. A galvanized helmet sat on the creature's broad head, sharp spikes protruding from the mask like rhinoceros horns. Metal trash-can lids had been shaped to cover the Filth's shoulders, the handles of the lids sharpened into deadly razor edges.

"Alan Zumbro." Leslie's voice was pinched with excitement at having him cornered at last.

Alan, upon hearing his name, stepped forward. The Filth barked, stringy spit swinging from its strong jaws as it sensed its prey. Leslie adjusted the dial on her battery pack, doing everything possible to hold back the Extension Filth.

"My Pluggers are swarming the hallways," Leslie explained. "Things will turn ugly if you run."

The Extension Filth leapt forward, Leslie reigning back as hard as she could. Spencer saw that the bludgeoning tail of the beast was also covered in durable metal, with steel spikes glinting like a flail.

"What happens if I don't run?" Alan said.

"I've come to take you away," Leslie answered. "Once we're gone, your friends can go free."

Alan cast a quick glance over his shoulder, eyes falling on Spencer. The look on his dad's face caused Spencer's throat to tighten. It was bravery, strong and undeniable. But the edges were tainted with fear and burden. It was the look of a troubled parent. And for the first time, Spencer knew that beneath it all his dad cared most about him.

Alan looked away, stepping even closer to the Extension Filth. He stared at Leslie and lifted his hands in defeat. "You will not harm them?" Alan gestured to his son and friends.

"You have my word." Leslie's voice was a whisper, her face shining with deranged excitement. Her task was coming to a close.

Spencer remembered how anxious Leslie was to prove her worth to Mr. Clean. And he remembered the warlock's frightful orders. Alan was wanted dead or alive. It was a long way to Washington, DC. Too many chances for escape. Spencer could tell from the glint in Leslie's eye—his dad would not make it to Mr. Clean in one piece.

Alan hung his head. "Let's go."

"Wait!" Spencer burst to the front of the group. The sudden movement startled the Filth, and it roared at the Rebel team. "Don't you want to know *why* we're here?" Spencer challenged.

"Get back, Son," Alan said. But Spencer had to shift the attention away from his dad.

"The whole point in capturing my dad was to stop us from finding this!" Spencer held up the paper-towel map. "But now you're too late. We found the map to the Auran landfill! We're going there next. And when we get there, the Aurans are going to help us!"

Revealing their whole plan probably wasn't a good idea, but Spencer needed to make Leslie realize that the map was more important than his dad. He swallowed hard and decided to make a risky gamble.

"So, go ahead and take him." Spencer pointed at his dad. "We don't need him now that we've got this." He waved the map roll in front of her.

In one swift movement, Leslie's Extension Filth swept

forward. The creature's metal helmet bucked into Alan, sending him sprawling. Spencer ducked into the nearest bathroom stall. Daisy leapt in beside him, pulling the metal door closed.

The armored horns of the Extension Filth suddenly burst into the stall, puncturing the door like knives through paper. Daisy shrieked and jumped onto the toilet seat.

"Hold your breath!" Spencer said. Grabbing Daisy's hand, he reached over and flushed the toilet.

He was ready for it this time. As the churning water receded, Spencer and Daisy were pulled into the sewage pipes. At the same moment, Leslie's Extension Filth barreled into the stall, crushing the walls and shattering the ceramic toilet.

Spencer's return journey through the plumbing was much like his first one, except that this time, Daisy streamed along behind him. They took corners at impossible speeds, borne along by a violent rush of cold water. It was a nightmare waterpark, and Spencer tried hard not to think of what had preceded him through the pipes.

Straining his eyes upward, Spencer saw the exit light. They'd have to act fast once they emerged. They would have the element of surprise, but not much else.

Spencer and Daisy burst into the air with an aquatic blast that rivaled the Bellagio fountains. Just as predicted, they were back in the first bathroom stall, close to the hallway exit.

Spencer checked the paper-towel map under his arm. It should have been a sopping mess, but the Glopified roll seemed unaffected by the water. Yanking Daisy to her feet, Spencer kicked open the stall door and staggered out.

Leslie and her Extension Filth were a safe distance away. The creature was still rooting around in the far stall, searching for the escapees. A second Plugger had arrived, riding an Extension Grime. He sat high in the saddle, cornering Alan, Walter, and Bernard against the far bathroom wall.

The Rebels were trapped, but Spencer was counting on the hope that Leslie wouldn't leave until she got the paper-towel map. That might give him and Daisy enough time to mount a rescue—if they didn't get captured too.

Without a word, the two kids slipped out of the bathroom and raced down the hall. They were almost to the front doors when an Extension Rubbish swept around the corner.

Its beak and talons were covered in plates of metal armor, looking harder and deadlier than ever. The bird's chest and head were also reinforced with scraps of metal trash can. The top sides of its black, leathery wings had been edged with sharpened steel.

Apparently, Mr. Clean's improvements were not just for Leslie's beast.

"Back!" Spencer cried, pulling Daisy away from the swooping monster. They sprinted around a corner, winding their way deeper into the large high school. Behind them, the Extension Rubbish cawed, probably calling other Pluggers toward the action.

Drawing brooms, the kids flew up a stairwell in one bound. No sooner had they reached the top than an

Extension Grime scuttled across the ceiling and dropped to cut them off. The rider, strapped tightly to the floor-mat saddle, had a mop in his hands. But Spencer was fairly sure that the Grime would eat them before the Plugger even had a chance to use it.

The Grime's armor was the strangest. Like the others, it was made of metal scraps. Strips of steel had been layered across the creature like dragon scales. They covered the Grime's whole body, from head to tail. The armor design was flexible and clever, allowing the monster to move freely.

The Extension Grime's tongue lashed out in hunger, but Spencer and Daisy were already in full retreat, flying backward down the stairwell. They fled, haphazard and reckless on their brooms.

They turned into a dim hallway and Spencer paused, gasping for breath. The kids were hopelessly lost in the heart of Alsbury High School with sounds of pursuit coming from all directions.

Spencer glanced over his shoulder. A shadow flickered, followed by the nearby croak of an Extension Rubbish. Suddenly, Daisy shoved into him.

"What are you doing?" Spencer whispered. Daisy pushed him against the wall of lockers. One of the tall metal doors was slightly ajar, and Daisy dug her fingers in, popping it wide open. She hastily guided Spencer into the opening, sounds of the Extension Toxites drawing nearer by the second.

The locker was tight, and Spencer fit only with his arms

pinned at both sides. There would be no chance to defend himself if the creatures found him hiding in the darkness.

If it was a tight fit alone, it suddenly got even tighter as Daisy grabbed the locker handle and squeezed in beside him. The hinge squeaked, and Daisy slammed the metal door.

Then the hallway was overrun by Pluggers.

CHAPTER 26

"AND THAT'S A LOOSE END."

Through the tiny vent slots, Spencer watched an Extension Grime and a Rubbish pace the hallway. It didn't matter how well concealed he was in the locker, Spencer held perfectly still, not even daring to breathe.

"Where'd they go?" one of the Pluggers said. "I was right behind them."

"They can't be far," said the other. "Let the monsters sniff them out."

Spencer felt his legs begin to quiver. The last thing he needed was for his knees to knock against the metal locker. From his limited viewpoint, Spencer saw the Extension Grime leap across the hallway. There was a resonant *clang* as the monster's sticky fingertips latched onto the bank of lockers.

Daisy's heavy breathing suddenly changed to a faintly

hummed tune—a Disney princess song, to be exact. The Extension Grime was too close. Its breath was distracting Daisy! Spencer reached for his can of air freshener, but the locker was too small, pinning his hands at his sides.

Then his view was blocked entirely as the Grime's huge head slid across the locker. Spencer pinched his eyes closed, waiting for the massive Extension Toxite to rip open the lockers and eat him and Daisy in one gulp.

The locker door rattled. Spencer opened one eye and instantly wished that he hadn't. The Grime's snakelike tongue had slithered through the vent slot. Daisy was getting louder as her humming neared the chorus. The forked tip of the monster's tongue brushed her cheek, and she giggled.

"Where have you morons been?" asked a new voice from the hallway. The Grime's tongue withdrew, and the rider directed it away from the lockers.

Spencer, trying not to let his panting breath betray him, leaned his head forward and peeked through the vents to see an Extension Filth sauntering down the hallway. The man on its back looked annoyed to find his companions.

"We were searching for the Rebels," answered the Rubbish Plugger.

"We already *caught* the Rebels," said the Filth Plugger. "Leslie's holding them in a classroom on the main floor. Wants everyone there."

The Extension Grime cast a final hungry look toward the lockers, but the Plugger twisted the dial and steered the monster away. Daisy's humming came to an abrupt stop, and the dim hallway was totally silent.

Spencer finally sighed, the muscles in his shoulders relaxing a bit. "Daisy?" he whispered, his lips less than an inch from her ear.

"Yeah?"

"I think you locked us in."

"That's okay," she said. "We can Windex the door and break out."

"Except," Spencer strained again to reach the items on his belt, "my arms are pinned."

"Here," she said. "Maybe I can reach yours."

Spencer's heart was still hammering. Luck had saved them this time. Another moment and the Extension Grime would have alerted its master. If it hadn't been for that Filth Plugger calling them back . . .

Leslie's patience was no doubt wearing thin. Spencer didn't know how long he could keep her interest on the paper-towel map before she decided to take Alan and leave.

Spencer needed to figure out what classroom the Rebels were being held in so he could lead a rescue. While Daisy managed to grab his bottle of Windex, Spencer squirmed his hand into his pocket. The bronze medallion was still there. If he could reach it, Spencer might be able to see through Walter and find out exactly where the others were.

The darkness of the locker dissolved into white light as Spencer's fingers brushed the medal. As the light cleared, he got an instant fix on Walter's location. He was on the main floor of Alsbury High School, room 18.

Looking through the warlock's eyes, Spencer saw Leslie Sharmelle dismounting her armored Filth. Half a dozen Pluggers were perched around the room, making any kind of escape impossible.

Leslie approached the Rebels with a plunger in hand. The extension cord stretched between her and the beast, its orange color matching her prison jumpsuit. She reached to her belt and unclipped a walkie-talkie. Lifting the device to her lips, she pressed the button.

"We have them, Mr. Clean," Leslie said.

"Mr. Clean." Bernard scoffed. "Kind of a cheesy name for the arch villain—"

Before he could finish, Leslie brought the wooden handle of her plunger across his face. Bernard slumped forward, blood on his cheek.

The walkie-talkie made some noise, and Spencer recognized the voice of the third warlock. "Eliminate them all."

Leslie pressed down the button to respond, but Alan shouted, his voice carrying through the device. "Hey! Leslie made me an agreement! You've got me now, so let my friends go free."

Mr. Clean's voice came through again. "Leslie isn't in a position to make agreements. Besides, there's been a complication."

"What complication?" Alan asked as Leslie pressed down the button.

"Leslie was supposed to stop you *before* you solved that thirteenth clue. I don't like loose ends," he said. "Your kid has the map to the landfill. And that's a loose end."

Alan grunted in frustration. He beckoned for Leslie, and she held the button on the radio once more. "Why don't you do this yourself?" Alan taunted. "Why send Leslie? Too comfortable in your office to come down and get your hands dirty? Why don't you show your face, coward?"

The response was laughter, so loud that the speakers crackled. "Once you are out of the equation, everyone will know my face."

There was a flash of white light, and Spencer stumbled out into the hallway. He almost collapsed to the floor, but Daisy threw her arms around him for support. While he had been swept up in the vision, Daisy had Windexed the locker and shattered the doors.

Spencer groaned in pain as his bare feet scuffed across the floor. Looking down, he saw a streak of blood on the tile and felt the sting of broken glass in his heel. In no time, Daisy had him seated on the floor. She squinted one eye shut as she pulled out the glass fragment. Her orange healing spray misted over his foot, and Spencer felt the wound seal instantly.

"I just checked on Walter," Spencer said. "Mr. Clean doesn't want us getting away with the map." He held out the paper-towel roll. "Leslie's going to kill the others."

"Everybody?"

Then Spencer realized who had been missing from his warlock vision. "Not everybody."

It took longer than Spencer wanted to find the secret bathroom. The hallways were clear, which meant that the

Pluggers were still in room 18 with Leslie. But there was no way of knowing how long that would last.

Spencer and Daisy entered through the broken brick wall. The hidden bathroom was a mess! Leslie's Extension Filth had destroyed several stalls, and there were deep claw marks in the tile. But one thing remained untouched. In the middle of the bathroom, an inch of cardboard tube jutted up from the floor.

Penny was still under there.

It wouldn't be easy to free Penny from the hard floor. Spencer remembered his dad's warning. If they weren't careful, the Windex might accidentally turn Penny to glass.

They started with a gentle mist. The floor shimmered in iridescence before turning transparent. Penny was lying several inches under the surface, her eyes closed tightly and her body stuck in a tensed position.

Spencer used his razorblade to smash out the first layer of glass. Then, with the Windex nozzle set to a fine stream, he and Daisy targeted the floor around Penny's body.

Spencer had broken out a few more pieces when, suddenly, Penny's hand burst free. She twisted sideways, the transparent floor around her cracking like ice. At last, she sat up and spat out the cardboard breathing tube.

"I was beginning to think that you guys had left me," Penny said, shaking bits of tile from her short red hair.

"We did," said Daisy. "But then we came back."

Penny blew a chunk of floor from her nose and rose on shaky legs. "What happened? Where's everyone else?"

"Leslie's here," Daisy explained. "And she's got a gang

of Pluggers with her. Their Extension Toxites are covered in armor!"

"They captured Walter, Bernard, and my dad," Spencer said. "I hope you've got a plan, because I'm fresh out."

Penny checked her janitorial belt. "I've been lying under the floor for the past half hour, brainstorming worst-case scenarios." She nodded. "I've got a plan. But Bernard's not going to like it."

CHAPTER 27

"REST IN PEACE."

Spencer and Daisy crept down the hallway, staying close to the wall. Spencer checked his watch and realized that Penny was probably in position by now.

"Are you sure this is the right wall?" Daisy asked.

Spencer held a finger to his lips and nodded. On the other side of that wall was room 18. Leslie and her gang of Pluggers were still brooding over the captives. If Spencer listened closely, he could hear Leslie's voice demanding more answers from his dad.

"Ready?" Spencer whispered.

Daisy nodded and held up two bottles of Windex. Spencer drew his as well, noticing that all three bottles were nearly empty. They had turned so many walls to glass, Spencer was amazed they had any blue spray left.

Spencer glanced over his shoulder at their handiwork.

Instead of solid brick, the wall across the hallway was transparent glass, giving him a clear view into an empty classroom. And his view did not stop there. The far wall of that classroom was also glass, as well as the wall after that, and the wall after that. Spencer and Daisy stood at the center of the high school, looking directly through a dozen glass walls and out into the parking lot.

A hundred yards away, vehicle headlights flashed, and Spencer knew that Penny was in position. Spencer nodded at Daisy, and they both opened fire on the last solid wall—the entrance to room 18.

The wall turned a magical blue, but Spencer didn't even wait for it to become transparent. He grabbed Daisy's arm, pulling her down the hallway and away from the glass walls.

There was a horrific crunching and crashing that grew louder with each passing second. A safe distance away, Spencer and Daisy flung themselves to the floor and covered their heads.

At the same moment, the garbage truck burst through the hallway and shattered the wall of room 18. Penny was gritting her teeth behind the wheel. Bernard's truck was hammered, having just plowed through a dozen glass walls. The leg of a desk was wedged in the truck's grill, and a broken bookshelf stuck through the windshield.

For added effect, Penny slammed on the truck horn, filling the hallway with an obnoxious blast of noise. She stepped on the brake, and the truck lurched to a halt. The front of the vehicle was embedded into room 18, leaving the body of the truck straddling the hallway.

All manner of chaotic noise was coming from the classroom. Toxites were shrieking and roaring while their BEM riders screamed commands. Spencer and Daisy sprinted back toward the action. If the plan worked, then Penny wouldn't be parked in the hallway for long. Spencer and Daisy had to get on that truck before it departed!

Penny threw the garbage truck into reverse and stepped on the gas. The large vehicle heaved through the rubble and began a backward retreat. The cab was in the hallway now. Spencer and Daisy drew their brooms and flew forward. The passenger door swung open, and Spencer saw that Walter, Bernard, and his dad were already inside with Penny.

Alan reached out, pulling his son into the crowded cab. The paper-towel map tumbled from Spencer's grasp and into Walter's lap.

Daisy's broom, only a split second behind Spencer's, went off course as an Extension Rubbish swooped into the hallway. Daisy collided with the side of the garbage truck, her broom getting pulled under the dangerous wheels and crushed to bits.

"Daisy!" Spencer leaned out the open door and grasped the girl's hands. Her feet found the bottom step of the truck, and she dangled off balance for a moment.

Snarling and barking, an Extension Filth pounced from room 18. Leslie's arms shot out, and she caught hold of Daisy's long braid. Daisy screamed as her head whiplashed back. Spencer struggled to hold her with the garbage truck crawling backward.

One of Daisy's hands slipped from Spencer's. But

instead of trying to hold on, Daisy reached back and drew something from the pouch of her janitorial belt.

Of all the weapons, Daisy chose that?

Baybee flashed into view, held by one leg like a war club. Daisy brought the doll down, slamming the plastic head into Leslie's face. She struck again and again, battering back the substitute teacher with Mrs. Natcher's hall pass.

At last, Leslie's grip failed. Spencer yanked Daisy into the safety of the cab just as the passenger door snapped off against the wall.

Bernard pulled his leather aviator cap over his eyes, muttering in despair about the damage to his truck. Penny's backward bulldoze was reckless. Desks, computers, filing cabinets . . . anything in the truck's path was scattered or crushed. But still, Leslie and her gang of Pluggers were advancing faster than the garbage truck's retreat.

"Wait a minute," Spencer said, glancing at the hall pass in Daisy's hands. "Why is Baybee's diaper smoking?"

Daisy looked down, her eyes widening. A wisp of white dust was floating up from the doll's cloth covering. But that wasn't all. Baybee's head was starting to expand, the plastic stretching tightly, like a balloon threatening to pop at any second.

"I think I forgot to take the chalkboard eraser out of her," Daisy said.

"She's gonna blow!" Spencer snatched the doll from Daisy's hand. Without a moment's hesitation, he hurled Baybee through the broken windshield of the garbage truck.

The doll sailed through the air on a final kamikaze

mission. Baybee struck the armored face of Leslie's Filth and exploded with a loud *pop*. The chalk dust, which had been billowing and brewing inside the hall pass, formed an immediate cloud that engulfed the oncoming Pluggers.

"Drive faster!" Walter shouted at his niece. The chalk cloud was sweeping toward them. Penny picked up the pace, and Bernard moaned in defeat.

Scraping and bumping, the garbage truck rolled into the parking lot. The white cloud spread into the open air, consuming the side of the school but giving Penny a moment to turn the garbage truck around. In no time, the vehicle was limping away from Alsbury High School forever.

Daisy turned to Spencer, her eyes unblinking since the doll's demise. "You killed Baybee!"

Spencer shrugged unconvincingly. "She might have survived."

Alan reached forward and plucked something off the truck's dashboard. It was a severed doll's leg, charred and smoldering. It must have shot back into the truck when Baybee exploded.

Daisy snatched the doll leg and held it close. "Rest in peace, Baybee. Rest in peace."

CHAPTER 28

"SO, THAT'S IT?"

Penny paused in the parking lot, the damaged truck idling noisily.

"Which way do I go?" she asked.

Spencer glanced back at the high school. None of the Pluggers had emerged from the chalk explosion, but waiting for directions made him uncomfortable.

Walter had the paper-towel map resting on his knees. The warlock had unrolled a foot or two and was trying to make sense of the directions.

"If this is Alsbury High School," he pointed at the map, "then we need to go left." He dragged his finger along the highlighted route. Penny turned the wheel and pulled out.

"You're supposed to stop for the crosswalk," Daisy said.

Penny shrugged as she drove over it. "Forget the crosswalks. Not many pedestrians out before dawn."

Walter quickly counted the streets on the map. "In four blocks, you need to turn right."

"Well," Bernard said, emerging from under his cap. "You sound like a genuine GPS."

Penny halted at the stop sign and followed her uncle's directions. "What next?"

Walter traced the highlighted route, his eyebrows bushing together. "Hmm. The trail runs off the edge of the map."

"So, that's it?" Daisy asked.

"Six hundred feet of map and we're there in four blocks?" Bernard pulled a face.

Walter unrolled another length of paper towel. "The route continues farther on," he said. "But it seems like we're missing a portion."

Penny stopped at a red light. "Can't we just skip ahead?"

"I don't think so," Alan said. "The Auran clues are hard to decipher, but once you figure them out, they're usually quite specific. We might miss something important if we don't follow the route."

"There is no route," Bernard said.

"What about the other side?" Spencer suggested. "It's got to be double sided for a reason."

Walter flipped over the paper towel and found another fragment of the highlighted route. "This side's no better."

"Wait a minute," Alan said, his voice a dawning of realization. "You've got to fold it. Fold the paper towel so that the route on the front connects with the route on the back."

The stoplight turned green, and Penny inched the truck through the intersection. Walter folded the paper on an

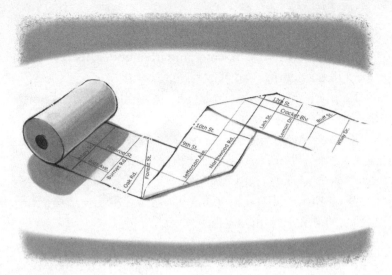

angle and, sure enough, the routes from the front and back connected.

"TURN LEFT!" Walter and Alan shouted in unison. Penny slammed on the brakes and cranked the wheel, catching the curb as she redirected the garbage truck.

Alan and Walter worked together now, one unrolling the paper towels while the other folded to connect the highlighted route.

"Might as well get comfy, kids," Bernard said, reclining in his seat. "Only about five hundred and ninety feet of map to go."

CHAPTER 29

"STRAIGHT ON TILL MORNING!"

Spencer didn't remember falling asleep, but he awoke with the morning sunlight on his face. Wind came through the truck's shattered windshield, but it hadn't been enough to keep him awake.

Spencer wiggled his toes, warm in a new pair of shoes from the duffel bag. Bernard and Daisy were still snoring softly, but Penny was hunched over the steering wheel, her eyes looking hollow and sleep deprived. Walter and Alan looked no better.

The cab of the truck was full of paper towels. The map filled the space around their legs and covered everyone's laps. Hundreds of folds and creases whipped in the wind as the two men continued to unroll and match the route.

"Merge into the left lane," Walter muttered. The enthusiasm was gone from his voice. Spencer glanced at the

Mickey Mouse clock on the dash. It was a little after six. They'd been following the map for over two hours.

Spencer looked at the roll in his dad's hands. There wasn't much paper left on the tube. They had to be getting close. Glancing through the broken windows, Spencer noticed that there was no sign of civilization anywhere.

"Where are we?" he finally asked. The last thing he remembered was a series of pointless turns through the suburbs of Austin. Now they were on a highway, moving at a decent speed.

"Somewhere in the Texas wilderness," his dad answered. "After taking a tedious tour of schools in the Lone Star State."

"What do you mean?" Spencer said.

"Dumb map led us in circles for a long time," Penny answered. "I bet we drove past twenty schools."

"Were we supposed to stop?" Spencer asked. "What if there was something at the schools that we were supposed to pick up?"

"We're *supposed* to follow this map," Walter said. "And in about ten more feet, we'll know why."

Penny suddenly let off the gas pedal, and the big truck gradually began to slow. "What are these yahoos up to?" she muttered, squinting at the road ahead. Walter, Spencer, and his dad looked up from the map.

There were two white vans parked broadside across the road ahead. They blocked both lanes of traffic and appeared to be in no hurry to move. Penny continued to slow down, and the change of pace awoke Bernard and Daisy.

"There hasn't been a single car on this road," Walter said, "and then two white vans decide to park in the middle?" He shook his bald head. "Everything about this is suspicious."

Bernard dug through the unraveled paper towels and reached under the seat. He withdrew a pair of dusty binoculars and squinted his beady eyes through the lenses.

"Definitely BEM vans." The garbologist passed the binoculars to Walter. "Dummies didn't even bother to cover the Bureau seal."

"Hold on," Penny said, accelerating once more. "We're bigger than they are. We'll just bash through 'em."

"I think not!" Bernard said. "You already bashed through a school. I'm not sure how much more bashing this baby can take!" He reached up and patted the dashboard.

"Can you swerve around them?" Daisy asked.

"The ditch is too deep," Penny said. "We'll roll."

"Take a left!" Alan shouted, making a crease in the paper towel.

"There isn't a road!" Penny yelled back.

"The map says to turn left!" Alan pointed ahead. "There! By that tree!"

Not far ahead, just yards from the BEM vans, Spencer saw a gnarled mesquite tree. Jutting off the side of the highway, narrow and inconspicuous in the tree's shadow, was a dirt road. It didn't seem to lead anywhere, and Spencer couldn't help but question the map.

Penny had to slow down to make the tight corner. Even

still, she grated against the mesquite tree, snapping off a few of the thinner branches.

Spencer glanced back at the white vans. The drivers were fumbling with the keys, desperate to overtake the garbage truck.

"Bet they're feeling sheepish!" Bernard said. "Set up the roadblock on the wrong road."

"They're as clueless to where we're going as we are," Walter replied.

The garbage truck jarred and bounced along the washboards of the dry dirt road. Dust billowed out behind them like a dingy cloud. Without the truck's windshield gone, a strong breeze whipped the dirt into their faces, and they choked for a breath of fresh air.

The white vans handled far better on the bumpy road. In no time, they were nudging in behind the Rebel garbage truck.

"Low fuel light just clicked on!" Penny announced. "Don't know how much farther we can run."

"We're almost there!" Alan shouted, unrolling the last length of map. The paper towel slipped off the bare cardboard tube, and Alan stretched the directions tight. "Straight on till morning!"

The garbage truck clipped past another scraggly mesquite tree and the dirt road rose up a steady hill. Penny pressed the gas pedal to the floor, the vehicle feeling like it might shake apart at any minute.

"I think I can, I think I can," Bernard chanted as they

lost speed up the incline. Spencer was clutching his seat belt with both hands, and Daisy's grip was sweaty on his arm.

The white BEM vans were gaining.

Then the garbage truck crested the ridge, and the road sloped downward. At the top of the ridge, the Rebels could see what had been hidden before.

Straight ahead was a wide and deep gorge. The impossible chasm stretched out of sight on both sides, encircling the largest pile of trash Spencer had ever seen.

This was the secret landfill! The paper-towel map had actually led them right! But the veritable mountain of garbage was unreachable, surrounded completely by the intimidating gorge. They would be forced to stop at the edge. If they did that, the BEM vans would catch up for sure.

The speed that was lost driving uphill quickly returned on the downward slope. The garbage truck thundered ahead, bucking so violently that Spencer wouldn't have been surprised to see the wheels fly off. Penny was hunched over the steering wheel with no apparent inclination to slow down.

"I don't mean to be a backseat driver," Bernard said, "but in case you didn't notice, we're doing sixty toward the edge of the Grand Canyon!"

"I thought the Grand Canyon was in Arizona!" Daisy said.

"Then this must be its little brother!" Bernard called back.

Walter, somehow remaining calm, squinted through the binoculars. "I think there's a bridge!"

Spencer peered ahead, but the truck was bouncing so much he couldn't see anything.

Walter lowered the binoculars. "The bridge should take us over the gorge and into the landfill!"

Like a madwoman behind the wheel, Penny continued to accelerate toward the drop-off. All hope for survival was riding on what Walter thought he saw through the dust and binoculars.

"Get your brooms ready!" Alan shouted at the kids. "In case we don't make it, maybe you can still fly out of this mess."

Daisy reached down to her belt, eyes widening. "My broom got crushed at the high school! Anybody got an extra? I'll give it right back when I'm done."

A strong gust of wind crossed the road. For a moment the dust cleared. Not ten yards ahead, just as Walter had described, a strong paved bridge stretched across the deep gorge. It was flat, with an arch of supportive steel beams underneath.

What Walter hadn't seen was the metal gate, chained and locked to prevent anyone from entering the bridge. A huge white sign hung on the metal gate, its bold red lettering easy to read:

WARNING: NO TRESPASSING
AUTHORIZED VEHICLES ONLY
BEYOND THIS POINT

And in tiny letters across the bottom, Spencer caught a glimpse of the last sentence:

VIOLATORS WILL FALL TO THEIR DOOM

He didn't have time to shout a warning. No sooner had he read the sign than Penny smashed through the metal gate. Bernard winced and put both hands on his head. Daisy screamed. Spencer suddenly felt his dad's hand slide onto his shoulder. Alan gave it a firm squeeze, like he wouldn't let go of his son no matter what happened.

The garbage truck rolled out onto the bridge. After the rough dirt road, the pavement felt so smooth that Spencer thought for sure they were free-falling. His dad's grip lightened a bit, and Daisy stopped screaming. Penny took advantage of the level bridge by accelerating to even more dangerous speeds.

The garbage truck was more than halfway across when the white BEM vans swerved through the wrecked gate and pulled onto the bridge.

There was a sudden groan from the steel supports under the bridge. The terrible grating sound resonated in the dry gorge. There was a sharp metallic *clang*, and Spencer saw one of the steel beams break away. Bent like a boomerang, it whirled through the dusty air, plummeting the unfathomable depth of the gorge.

Immediately, the bridge tilted. The garbage truck lurched, and Penny corrected with the steering wheel, nearly sending them over the edge. There was another sound, this one louder than before, as the steel supports buckled together.

The asphalt cracked, and the edge of the road crumbled like a stale cookie. The bridge was sagging in the middle, and the garbage truck puttered as it climbed upward.

They were so close to the other side! Spencer realized that he was holding his breath, both hands gripping the dashboard. Daisy had her eyes closed, mumbling something incoherent.

The bridge gave a final shriek as steel folded on steel. The rear wheels of the garbage truck had just touched solid ground when the bridge collapsed completely. Both BEM vans were caught in the free fall, spiraling downward until they looked no bigger than Matchbox cars.

CHAPTER 30

"FASCINATING PLACE!"

Penny slammed on the brake, but the garbage truck had too much momentum. With tremendous force, it burrowed into a loose pile of trash.

Stinky garbage filled the cab, the odor causing Spencer to choke. The truck rocked back, finally coming to a halt.

"Is everyone all right?" Walter asked, unbuckling his seat belt.

"I've never been better," Bernard said. His head was barely visible above the trash heap. "I think I've died and gone to trash heaven."

With the passenger door missing, everyone climbed out that way. Slithering over smelly piles of old plastic sacks and decomposing gunk, the Rebels soon stood next to the truck.

Bernard rubbed a hand along his vehicle. "Poor beauty."

He shook his head. "Remind me why we let the teenager drive?"

Penny scowled at him. "I got us here, didn't I? Besides, I'm actually twenty."

Alan and Walter were standing at the edge of the gorge surveying the damage far below. Spencer didn't need to look to know that the BEM vans were demolished, with no chance of survivors.

"Look at this place," Spencer said, staring off into the heaps of garbage. They stretched far beyond his sight, like rolling hills of trash.

"Never been to the dump?" Bernard asked.

"It's a landfill," Penny corrected.

Bernard, ignoring the comment, bent down and picked up a scrap of plastic. "Fascinating place! Think about it, garbage from far and wide gathers here, forgotten and undisturbed."

Penny chuckled. "The way you talk makes it sound like the trash has a mind of its own."

All at once, without any warning, a pile of garbage exploded next to Spencer. The trash plowed forward, bowling Spencer into Daisy and sending both kids sprawling on the ground.

The attacking trash loomed above them, stretching to a height of nearly seven feet. It took Spencer a moment to decipher what he was seeing.

It was garbage, no doubt about that. But the trash was fused together, forming a crude humanoid shape. Stout legs supported a dense torso made of rotting groceries and dented cans. Long arms dangled apelike, with springs and scrap wires jutting akimbo. The head, if it could be called such, was formed of an old cereal box.

The garbage figure roared, a crunching, grating sound that was unlike anything Spencer had heard before. Then it leaned forward, dropping onto its knuckles like a gorilla, as its head seemed to examine Spencer and Daisy.

The trash creature lifted one arm, pieces of old soda cans jutting out of its hand. It remained poised above Spencer, like a cat that wanted to toy with a mouse. Spencer was petrified, Daisy whimpering at his side.

The other Rebels were already moving to attack, but help suddenly came from an unexpected source.

"Back off, you worthless lump of garbage!"

The Rebels whirled around, scanning the heaps of trash for whoever had spoken. Spencer saw a figure crouched at the top of a garbage pile. It was a girl, silhouetted in a halo of sunlight so he couldn't make out her features. Her hair was silvery white, its shimmer enhanced by the lighting around her.

She skipped down the trash pile with agility and precision, sliding and jumping until she reached the Rebel garbage truck.

"I said, back off!" the girl shouted at the trash figure. "I could take you down with one blow, you weak, pitiful little trash heap!"

At this, the garbage figure righted itself again, roaring at the girl as she strode past Spencer and Daisy. She stood face-to-face with the creature and shouted once more.

"Get out of here, you lazy pile of junk!" She stomped forward for intimidation. "I've seen moldy leftovers that looked scarier than you! Begone!" The girl flung her hand in a dismissive gesture.

The big garbage figure crawled backward, still growling but unwilling to stick around. The thing slunk away, falling into pieces of junk as it reached the pile and melted into the garbage.

"Sorry about that," the girl said. "Not the best way to welcome you to the landfill."

"Who are you?" Alan asked.

But as the girl finally stepped into plain view, Spencer went rigid. A petrifying chill started in his toes and rapidly worked its way up his spine. It was as though his mind refused to register the face he was seeing. But then she smiled, and Spencer knew for sure who it was.

"Jenna?"

"IT'S RHO."

It was purely inexplicable. What was Jenna doing at the hidden Auran landfill? There was only one explanation, but Spencer's mind kept refusing it. Jenna was too perfectly normal. That was what he'd liked about her at New Forest Academy. Was it all a lie? Was Jenna actually one of the . . .

Jenna nodded. "I'm an Auran, Spencer."

"What!" Daisy shrieked. "You? But . . . why'd your hair turn white?"

Jenna suppressed a grin. "It was always white. It's an attribute that all the Aurans share. I had to dye my hair every morning at New Forest Academy just to make it blonde."

Well, at least Spencer had missed out on that side effect. His hand instinctively raised to touch his own brown hair. He wasn't ready to go gray.

"I didn't know there were girl Aurans," Daisy said, a hint of awe in her voice.

"Ten girls, three boys," Jenna said. "That's the way the Founding Witches wanted it."

If Spencer had been thinking clearly, it might have bothered him that the girl Aurans outnumbered the boys more than three to one. But before he could ponder it, his mouth was spouting another question for Jenna. "What were you doing at New Forest Academy?"

"I was there to keep an eye on Director Carlos Garcia," she said. "He's one of the warlocks."

"Yeah," Alan said. "We figured that out the hard way."

Jenna walked past the group and peered over the edge of the gorge. "Looks like your friends weren't so lucky."

"They weren't our friends," Penny said. "It was the BEM. They were trying to stop us from reaching you."

Jenna shook her head. "They should have read the sign on the gate. This is a limited access area. Authorized vehicles only."

There was something different about Jenna. The way she moved and talked. She showed an air of wisdom and maturity that contradicted the youthful person that Spencer had met at New Forest Academy. Walter had explained that the Aurans were more than three hundred years old, trapped forever in juvenile bodies. Still, Jenna had played quite a convincing thirteen-year-old back at the Academy.

"Are you saying that my garbage truck *was* authorized?" Bernard asked.

Jenna strode over to the vehicle and inspected the tires. "How did you find this place?" she asked.

"We solved the thirteen clues," Alan said. "We followed the map that led us here."

"Did you follow the map closely?" Jenna asked. "Made every turn and drove every inch of the highlighted route?"

Alan nodded.

"Then, yes," she replied. "Your vehicle *is* authorized."

"I don't get it," Bernard said.

"The route on the map took you past twenty-seven schools," Jenna said. "Each school had a crosswalk painted over the road. The paint for those crosswalks was Glopified. As your vehicle passed over the crosswalks, a magical residue adhered to your tires. All twenty-seven lines, when driven over in the proper order, create an authorization code. That bridge," Jenna pointed to the wreckage, "was designed to recognize the crosswalk code, allowing your vehicle to pass over safely."

"But we barely made it over!" Daisy said. "It wasn't safe at all!"

"The BEM vans," Walter muttered. "They hadn't followed the map route, so their tires weren't properly coded."

"Like I said," Jenna cut in. "Only authorized vehicles are allowed over here. The bridge is rigged to collapse under non-coded tires. It's a strict policy. Violators fall to their doom."

Spencer could barely follow the conversation. The fact that Jenna was there, welcoming them to the landfill, was too much to take in.

"So you lied?" he finally managed.

She turned to him. "Pardon?"

"At New Forest Academy," Spencer said. "You lied about everything?"

"No," Jenna said. "Not everything. Remember when you flew that school bus off the edge of a cliff? I trusted my life into the hands of a twelve-year-old boy. I was genuinely terrified. No lies there." She chuckled, but her expression changed when she saw the stony look on Spencer's face.

"I'm sorry," she finally apologized. "I couldn't tell you I was an Auran. The time wasn't right. But it is right now." She smiled at him. "I hope you can trust me."

Something popped into Spencer's mind. He thought of the note Jenna had given him when she left New Forest Academy. He'd read it so many times that he had the thing memorized. The last line stuck in his mind. *"Next time we meet, I hope U can trust me 2."*

Spencer took a deep breath. Jenna wasn't who she'd said she was. But she had only lied to protect him. If she was ready to deal the truth now, Spencer was all in.

"Okay, Jenna. What now?" he asked.

"One more thing," she said. "My name's not Jenna. It's Rho."

Daisy shrugged. "I think I like Jenna better."

"It's Rho," the girl repeated. "And that's what you'll call me." She kicked a piece of trash back onto a pile and strode off, dangerously near the edge of the gorge.

"Where are you going?" Alan called.

"The other Aurans will be excited that you've arrived," she answered. "We must call them home. Follow me!"

"Rho." Spencer whispered the name to himself. In a way, he was grateful to call her something different. Jenna was gone. Never existed, really. She was Rho now. An Auran.

CHAPTER 32

"JUST LIKE CAMELOT?"

Daisy took a few quick steps to catch up to Spencer. "Where's Jenna taking us?" she whispered.

"It's Rho," he corrected. Then he answered her question with a shrug. "How should I know where we're going?"

"I just thought maybe you'd have an idea," Daisy said. "Since you're one of them."

"Shh," Spencer said. Learning how much Jenna had kept secret from him at the Academy made Spencer want to keep his own secrets. He wondered if Rho suspected his powers. Whatever the case, it didn't seem right to tell her that he was an Auran. The Rebels had agreed when the mission had started not to reveal Spencer's abilities to anyone. He assumed they would keep that strategy going here. Alan had been adamant about it.

As they passed the pile of garbage that had exploded on them, Penny voiced the question they were all wondering.

"What was that . . . garbage thing?"

Rho glanced over her shoulder. "We call them Thinga-majunks," she said. "The landfill is full of them. There's too much Glop in the trash here. It takes on a life of its own."

"So," Daisy said, "they're bad guys?"

Rho laughed. "I've never met a Thingamajunk that didn't want to eat me. They're wild, untamable. Like animals."

"How did you scare it off so easily?" Alan asked.

"Trash talk," Rho said. "It's the only thing they understand. I've spent years perfecting just the right insults for the right occasions. You can't let them see any fear. You have to stand up and talk trash right in their faces. If you're convincing enough, the Thingamajunks will usually back away without a fight."

They followed Rho for several hundred yards before she turned away from the cliff's edge and cut between two massive heaps of garbage. As the Rebels followed, jumping over decomposing lumps of trash, Spencer saw their destination.

It was a large cinderblock building, hidden from outside view by the heaps of garbage all around. Rho led them around the side of the building and onto a flat slab of concrete. Here, roughly a dozen dumpsters sat with lidless openings tilted skyward. Trash brimmed, overflowing the dumpsters and strewing the concrete pad with icky garbage.

"So the other Aurans are inside?" Alan gestured toward the building.

Rho shook her head, white hair swaying. "They're out on assignments right now." She stepped across the scattered garbage and approached the line of dumpsters. Rho reached around the side of the first bin, her hand grasping something out of sight. As she stepped away, she held a boxy walkie-talkie, its rubbery antennae standing straight from the top.

She pressed a button, lifted the device to her lips, and spoke. "This is Landfill, calling all Aurans. We have a Code One. I repeat, Code One. This is not a drill."

As Rho spoke, the walkie-talkie hummed slightly, shimmering with a magical glow that could mean only one thing.

"That's a Glopified radio," said Alan. "Similar to the ones we were using before we found the package. It's a simple device, but it has unlimited range."

"What's she thinking?" Daisy whispered. "Doesn't she know we're supposed to be off the grid?"

"I'm more concerned about Code One," Penny said, still untrusting. "What do you think it means?"

"Relax." Rho lowered the two-way radio. "By crossing that bridge, you've earned every right to be here. And believe me, we're just as excited as you are. We've waited a long time for this day."

Spencer had just opened his mouth to ask what that meant when movement from the nearest dumpster caught his eye. He staggered an involuntary step back, shocked by what appeared to be happening.

A hand thrust through the trash and gripped the rim of the dumpster. A head appeared next, with brilliant white hair to match Rho's. It was another girl, and she didn't appear to be distressed at all by the fact that she was climb-ing out of a dumpster.

The Rebel team spun around as, one by one, the Aurans emerged from the row of trash bins. They pulled themselves over the edge of the dumpsters and climbed onto the con-crete pad.

Another girl followed. And then another. Within a minute, there were ten Aurans, Rho included, standing alongside the dumpsters. One detail seemed to unite their appearance—each had a head of silvery white hair. They wore the hair in a range of lengths and styles, but the dis-tinctive feature made them easily recognizable.

"Ten girls," Penny whispered.

It was sinking in for Spencer now. "Where are the three boys?"

One of the girls stepped forward. She was tall and slen-der, and her white hair flowed around her in incredibly long, thick waves. She studied the Rebels silently for a moment, her gaze a mixture of excitement and surprise.

"Welcome to the landfill." She smiled broadly, her eyes lingering on Spencer for an extra moment. "My name is V. I'm sure you have questions, and you've definitely earned some answers. Let's head inside where we can talk."

The Aurans moved forward, opening a personnel door on the side of the building as V led the Rebels inside. After the midmorning sun, the building's interior seemed dim. The group headed down a windowless hallway and around a corner. Finally, V directed them into a large room that had a vaulted ceiling pocked with skylights.

In the center of the space was a wooden table, vast and round, with thirteen carved chairs tucked around it. The Aurans quietly slipped into their seats, leaving three chairs conspicuously empty.

Bernard smirked as he touched the edge of the table. "Just like Camelot?"

V shrugged. "It worked for King Arthur."

"Until Sir Lancelot came along," Bernard pointed out.

V's eyes dropped to the three empty chairs. "We've already had our share of Lancelots."

The Rebels stood awkwardly behind the chairs until V gestured for them to take a seat. Clearly, there weren't enough chairs for everyone, but Walter and Alan were the obvious choice. Spencer was surprised when the third chair was pulled out and Penny sat him down in it. Bernard, Penny, and Daisy stood behind them like bodyguards.

"Let's have a proper introduction." V placed her hand on the table. "I'm V, named for Virginia."

The girl next to her placed a hand on the table. "I'm Jersey, named for New Jersey."

The introductions proceeded in the same manner around the table. "I'm Lina, named for South Carolina."

"I'm Netty, named for Connecticut."

"I'm Yorkie, named for New York."

"I'm Dela, named for Delaware."

"I'm Sylva, named for Pennsylvania."

"I'm Shirley, named for New Hampshire."

"I'm Gia, named for Georgia."

Then finally, Jenna spoke. "I'm Rho, named for Rhode Island."

"Phew," Bernard said. "That's a lot of names. I hope there's not a quiz at the end."

Daisy nudged Spencer in the arm and whispered, "Does that make you Ida, named for Idaho?"

"As you can see," V explained, "we get our names from the original thirteen colonies. A long time ago, those were the regions that we served. America has grown a bit. Now we're all over the place."

"What about the other three?" Spencer asked. He wasn't quick enough to deduce which three colonies were missing, but Rho had said there were three boys.

The table grew somber at the question. The Aurans glanced furtively at one another. Then V answered. "Three hundred years is a long time to survive. The others are dead. There are only ten Aurans now."

Spencer felt a pit in his stomach. The boys were dead? He wanted to find out more, but his dad was already moving the conversation forward.

"Thank you for welcoming us here," Alan said. "My team has sacrificed a lot to reach you. But I believe it will all be worth it if we can stop what the BEM is doing."

"Do you have a plan?" V asked.

Alan paused for only a moment, seeming to wonder if honesty was the right answer. Then he went ahead with the truth. "My old associate, Rod Grush, and I discovered that Toxites are being born out of Glop. If we can find the Glop source, and destroy it . . ." He trailed off, but V finished for him.

"Then you destroy all Toxites forever."

The Auran girls were glancing at one another. Spencer looked to Rho, but she was studying her fingernails in thought.

"So," Alan prompted. "Do you know where the source is?"

V took a moment to make eye contact with each girl. Then she slowly nodded her head. "We do."

More silence. Then, "Will you take us there?"

Again, V nodded slowly. "We will take you to the Glop source," she said deliberately. "And we will help you destroy it."

Alan couldn't hold back his grin. Spencer could see the joy and relief etched on every feature of his father's face. This was the quest he'd started over two years ago. This was what Rod Grush had died for.

"It's the least we can offer," V said, "after all your efforts to solve the thirteen clues."

"Where is the Glop source?" Walter asked.

"It's here at the landfill. Quite far, though," V said. "We're looking at a two-day hike to get there."

"Hiking through trash . . ." Bernard smiled. "Sounds thrilling!"

Thrilling wasn't the word Spencer would have used, but he saw the importance. They had come a long way to learn about the Glop source. Now they would be there in two more days and a whole lot of trash.

"When do we leave?" Alan asked.

V smiled. "Right away."

CHAPTER 33

"THEY LEFT US NO CHOICE."

The landfill was rugged terrain. The deeper they hiked, the more things changed. Heat increased beyond the warmth of the Texas afternoon. The very earth seemed to radiate stifling waves of heat, and before long everyone was bathed in sweat. The smell increased with the heat, the only relief coming as a light wind whipped across the trash-heaped landscape.

They had separated into two groups. V and Rho stayed back with the Rebels, while the other eight Aurans hiked about an hour ahead, scouting for traps and enemies.

"Enemies?" Daisy had asked. "More Thingamajunks?"

"Or worse," V had answered. Then she instructed everyone to meet by nightfall in a place called the Valley of Tires.

Spencer paused to tighten the straps on his backpack,

feeling his water bottle glug sideways. His dad was suddenly there, hoisting up the pack in an attempt to be helpful.

"I got it, Dad." Spencer stepped away and checked the buckle on his janitorial belt. He moved over to Daisy, annoyed at himself for ignoring his dad again. Maybe when this was all over he and his dad would see eye to eye.

V strode past, and Spencer looked again at the strange object she had brought from the building. It was an old-fashioned shovel. The long handle was wrapped in rawhide, and the wide end was made of shiny black metal, tapering to a dangerous point. She swung it over her shoulder and glanced out over the endless piles of trash before them.

"What's with the shovel?" Spencer finally asked her as they began skirting along a deep, garbage-filled ravine.

V wiped the sweat from her forehead and hefted the item. "It's called the Spade. We'll need it to reach where we're going."

"We have to dig to get to the source?" Alan asked.

"If that's the case, then shouldn't we all have shovels?" Bernard pointed out.

"It's not digging in the traditional way," V answered. "Think of this whole landfill like a giant treadmill. Right now, we're hiking across, from the southern gorge that you crossed this morning to a similar gorge on the north side. When we get there, it might look like we're out of land. That's when the Spade comes in."

Spencer slipped on a piece of trash, but Penny caught his arm and steadied him. "I'm guessing the shovel's Glopified?"

"When we reach the other gorge," V said, "I'll stick the Spade into the ground, and the whole landfill will rotate. Like someone started the treadmill. New ground will come up from below, and we'll be carried back to the other side of the landfill, where we continue our journey."

"I've never heard of a Glopified tool powerful enough to do something like that," Penny said. "Where did it come from?"

"The boys," V answered. "I don't remember which one created it."

The answer caused Spencer to pause in his tracks. "You mean the boy Aurans? They created the Spade? But I thought only warlocks could use Glop . . ."

"Those boys were special," V said. "They had *unique* powers."

Spencer felt all eyes boring down on him. He wanted to reveal it then, to tell V that he was an Auran. Maybe he had hidden powers that she could help him discover.

"You see," Rho cut in, "all of us have the ability to see through the warlocks' eyes when we touch bronze. That's a standard power. It's how we make raw Glop deliveries to the warlocks."

"But the boys," Alan pressed. "They had powers that the rest of you didn't have?"

"Too much power," V said. "That's what got them into trouble. The boys weren't like the rest of us. Their powers changed them. Their hearts were consumed by selfish darkness and evil. We called them the Dark Aurans, and eventually, they betrayed us."

"What did they do?" Daisy asked.

"They got out of control," said V. "They stopped us from making a very important decision."

"How did they die?" Spencer finally asked.

"We destroyed them, of course," V said, with remarkably little feeling. "They left us no choice."

The Rebels fell completely silent, and Spencer was sure that each of his friends was renewing their pact not to reveal his identity as an Auran. But that wasn't the only thing bothering him.

Spencer paused to drink from his water bottle. He let the distance widen between him and V, trying not to think too hard about the Dark Aurans. He had only minimal powers, not like the boys V was talking about. Being an Auran was hard enough. Being an evil Auran would be far worse.

CHAPTER 34

"I COULDN'T BE HONEST ABOUT ANYTHING."

T he Valley of Tires was a sight unlike anything Spencer had ever seen. V and Rho led the team of Rebels in, cresting a giant mound of trash as the sun finally set. In the dusk light, Spencer looked into the valley head, trying to comprehend how such a thing was even possible.

The valley was made of thousands, maybe millions, of old car tires. They were stacked unbelievably high on both sides, with a deep and narrow ravine cutting down the middle. Some tires were set vertically, others horizontally, as if some great architect had carefully placed each one. The result was stunning, with purplish red hues from the sunset shining through uncountable holes.

As they drew nearer, descending into the valley, Spencer noticed an even more stunning feature. The tires, so carefully placed, seemed fused together, as if the rubber had melted and rejoined. Every size and diameter of tire was present, and Spencer saw several brands that he recognized—Michelin, Goodyear, Firestone.

Wind whistled through the gaps in the tires, creating an eerie hum of varying pitches. As V led them deeper into the valley, the tires on both sides seemed to radiate unnatural warmth.

"Who built this place?" Spencer whispered to Rho. She hadn't said much to him as they'd hiked along. So different from the Jenna he knew. Now she merely laughed.

"No one built it," Rho said. "This is the Valley of Tires. The edge of the landfill." She pointed ahead, and Spencer sensed, more than saw, another deep gorge at the far side of the valley.

"So we reached the other side already?" Spencer was puzzled. He could envision the landfill, ringed by a deep gorge to keep out trespassers. But if they'd already traversed the whole place . . . "Then where's the Glop source?"

Rho glanced at Spencer. Shadowy rings from the tires fell across her face in the dim twilight. "Tomorrow V will use the Spade to uncover more ground. You'll see."

At the heart of the valley, V stopped. She slipped out of her backpack, shoulders marked with sweat from the straps.

"We sleep here tonight," V said.

The other Aurans had already arrived, breaking out a minimal camp and getting a fire going with scraps of garbage that let off plumes of stinky smoke. As the last trace of daylight faded, the Aurans settled into the walls of the valley, searching for comfortable tires to curl up in while the Rebels huddled alone near the fire.

"Listen," Walter whispered, when he saw they were alone. "This probably goes without saying, but we have to keep Spencer a secret."

Penny nodded in agreement. "V was pretty shifty about the Dark Aurans. I don't think she'd like to find out that there was another boy Auran around."

"We can't risk anything," Walter said. "We need to make sure they never suspect."

"What about your friend from the Academy?" Alan said. "Jenna. Does she know?"

"Her name is Rho now," Daisy corrected. "Confusing, I know."

"I don't think she knows," Spencer said. "I've been trying hard to remember our time together and I'm pretty sure it never came up . . ."

Spencer trailed off as Rho approached, rolling a loose truck tire near the fire and sitting down next to the Rebels. It was awkwardly silent for a moment. The kind of silence that seemed to scream, "We were talking about you!" Then Walter broke out with a question.

"The Spade," he said. "V mentioned that she'll need to use it to reach the Glop source?"

Rho tore open a granola bar and bit into it. "This land-fill is a lot bigger than what we can see," she said. "The surface is just the normal part."

Spencer cast his eyes around, but he didn't feel like anything he'd seen today was too normal.

"How much do you know about landfills?" Rho asked.

"I did a report on them in high school," Penny said. "By the way, is this a landfill or a dump?"

Rho shrugged. "What's the difference?"

Bernard gave a soft chuckle of victory and folded his hands behind his head.

"Anyway," Rho said. "In a common landfill, trash is dumped into a big hole. As liquid trickles down through the garbage, it collects pollutants and dangerous chemicals. It settles at the bottom—a nasty, sludgy substance called leachate."

Rho threw her wrapper onto the ground. It didn't matter since the whole place was covered in trash already. "This landfill's a little different. Old Glopified supplies have been dumped here for hundreds of years. As liquid trickles down through the garbage, it gets tainted with Glop instead of normal pollutants. The Glop pools at the bottom of the landfill and causes some strange side effects."

She gestured up both sides of the Valley of Tires. "It's only going to get weirder, the deeper we go. When V uses the Spade to turn the landfill, we never know exactly what might surface."

"This place just keeps getting crazier," Spencer said. He sat quietly upon the hard ground, his head tilted back so he could watch the stars wink overhead. The Rebels were silent again, each lost in thought about their strange location.

"I wish I would have known who you really were," Spencer finally said. He didn't care that the others were listening. He needed to get it off his chest. "At the Academy. I could have used your help. Instead, you just . . . pretended."

He was thinking about the heart picture she'd drawn in art class. He was thinking about the attention she'd given him, and the conversations they'd had at lunch. He was thinking about the note.

"I had to pretend," Rho admitted. "I was there for a very specific reason, and I couldn't let you know about it. I couldn't be honest about anything."

"What about chicken tenders?" he asked.

"Huh?"

"You said you liked chicken tenders dipped in ranch," Spencer said. "Was that true?" It was a dumb question, and now he felt embarrassed to be speaking in front of his dad and friends. But Spencer needed something from their time together at New Forest Academy to be real.

She smiled then, a Jenna smile. It made Spencer feel ridiculous. Of course Rho didn't feel anything special for him. He was twelve. She was three hundred. He'd spent months hoping to get another letter from her. Now he knew why she never wrote.

"The truth is," Rho said, "you didn't need my help at the Academy. I needed yours. I was there to spy on Garcia, but things were a lot worse than we expected. I'd probably still be trapped at the Academy, with giant Toxites rotting my brain, if you and Daisy hadn't saved me."

Spencer felt his face go red at the praise. He was about to say something more when Penny slipped quietly to her feet, holding out a hand that demanded silence. She was tensely poised, her head tilted attentively to one side.

Rho and the Rebels rose next to her, their eyes following Penny's gaze past the fire into the deep blackness of the valley. Their alertness had gained the attention of the Aurans now. The girls approached slowly and silently, their ears to the wind and their hearts racing.

Something was drawing nearer, moving swiftly toward them through the Valley of Tires. The firelight glinted and flickered, hinting at a frightening number of advancing figures. The wind howled through the tires, rising in dissonant harmonies. But floating among the eerie wind tones was the distinctive grunting and growling of a host of wild Thingamajunks.

CHAPTER 35

"WHO'S BEHIND THIS?"

Spencer saw them approaching in the moonlight, a stampede of Thingamajunks entering the valley. Their garbage arms flailed and their legs milled old trash as they came forward in a rush of noise.

Daisy staggered backward, tripping into Rho and Spencer. The Rebels and Aurans came together, everyone holding a deep breath of anticipation.

"What's going on?" Spencer finally asked. The stampede was obvious. But the reason for the Thingamajunk charge was less so.

"Should we trash-talk them?" Penny asked.

V glanced over her shoulder toward the deep darkness of the gorge at the end of the Valley of Tires. "They're moving too fast. We wouldn't get a word out before they trampled us," she said. "Get to the tires! Stay out of their way and they'll run themselves right off the edge of the cliff."

"Really?" Bernard shouted. "That's the plan? Hide on the sides and hope the Thingamajunks run over the edge?"

"They're dimwitted on the best of days," V said. "Something's really gotten them into a frenzy. They can't think straight. Not that they ever can."

"What scared them?" Spencer couldn't help but ask. Was there something in the landfill that struck fear into Thingamajunks? "What are they running from?"

V froze, her face paling. "Oh, no," she muttered. "They're not running away from something. They're running *toward* it."

Right then, something came hurtling through the air. It was a bundle of some sort, a large tarp. It came slinging over the wall of tires as though it had been launched from a catapult.

"RUN!" V shouted, but it was too late. The bundle hit the ground only a few feet from where the group stood. The tarp exploded like a water balloon on impact. And it was indeed full of liquid, though definitely not water.

The tarp was full of something black and gooey. It splattered everywhere, splashing onto the Rebels and the Aurans, causing them to gag and choke at the smell.

Spencer fell to his knees, trying to hold his breath while the contents of his stomach almost came up.

"What . . ." He gagged. "What was that?"

"Stink bomb," Rho said, her voice hoarse. "Old scraps

of food, wrapped up tight and left in the sun until the whole thing turns to smelly mush."

"That's disgusting!" Spencer was on the verge of panic. As if the stampeding Thingamajunks weren't bad enough, now he was covered in shrapnel from an organic stink bomb.

"Why do Thingamajunks throw stink bombs?" Daisy asked.

"They don't," Rho said. "Thingamajunks are attracted to this kind of garbage. The smellier, the better. And now we smell like dinner."

"If the Thingamajunks didn't throw the stink bomb," Spencer said, "then who did?"

V was shouting again. "Prepare for battle!"

Like well-trained soldiers, the Aurans fell into a defensive formation. Glopified pushbrooms and mops bristled, ready for action. The Rebels moved in next to them, but as Spencer drew a razorblade from his belt, his dad pushed him back, forcing him to the middle of the defensive ring.

"Dad!" Spencer protested. "I can fight!"

But Alan wouldn't hear it. He grabbed Daisy and directed her over to Spencer. "The two of you keep your heads down and stay out of the way."

Crouching next to the dying fire, Spencer clenched his teeth in frustration.

"He's only trying to protect you," Daisy whispered.

Spencer knew she was right, but it still felt like an insult. Hadn't he proven to his dad that he could take care of himself? Spencer extended the razorblade from its little handle and waited for the stampede of Thingamajunks to strike.

V was barking out a game plan to the other girls, brandishing a fancy, double-sided mop with heads at both ends of the handle. "We mop tie the first wave of Thingamajunks. Once they are down, we stand our ground as long as possible. If the formation breaks, then we retreat to the tires!"

The Aurans pulled back their arms, Glopified mops ready to extend. They acted with such confidence and unity that the Rebels followed their example.

V held up her hand, waiting for the precise moment when the stampeding Thingamajunks would come into range. They could probably take down almost a dozen with the first strike, but Spencer wondered if that would be enough.

"Now!" V screamed, her face flushed in the flickering light of the dying fire. Like a volley of arrows, the Glopified mop strings stretched out, an impenetrable network of ropes streaming toward the wild Thingamajunks.

Suddenly, there was a sound like a giant guitar string being plucked. A line stretched tight across the ground, throwing a puff of dirt into the air. It was a strand of barbed wire, carefully buried so no one had noticed it in the dim light.

The barbed wire snapped up, catching the Glopified mop strings in midair and tying them into useless knots. Then the line went slack again, dropping to the ground and pulling the tangled mops out of the defenders' hands.

"No," V cursed softly. "He thought of everything . . ."

Spencer didn't have time to ask who was the architect of this attack. The Thingamajunks weren't intelligent enough to do this alone. Clearly, someone was calling the shots from a safe distance away. And, like a true mastermind, the mysterious person was about to defeat the Aurans without ever being seen.

There was a terrible, breathless moment before the impact, and then suddenly, the stampede of wild Thingamajunks was tearing into the defensive line of Rebels and Aurans, driven mad by the smell of the stink bomb that clung to their clothing.

Weapons flashed in the moonlight. The closest Thingamajunk went careening away, struck by Sylva's push-broom.

A long arm, comprised mostly of old tin cans, thrust through the ring of Aurans. Spencer rolled aside just as the hand snatched at the air where he'd been. Penny's backup mop tangled around the extended arm. She jerked upward, bending the tin cans until they ripped apart under the pressure.

The action quickly proved too much for Dela. She let out a scream, slammed her broom against the ground, and rocketed upward and away from the fight.

Lina shifted sideways, desperately trying to fill the hole that the deserter Auran had created. But the Thingamajunks were too swift. One of the garbage figures sprang into the gap, a broken cafeteria tray forming a shovel-like hand.

"Look out!" Daisy pushed into Spencer, knocking him aside as the broken tray cut a gouge in the dry earth.

Spencer leapt back, swinging his razorblade and severing the Thingamajunk's hand.

The disruption from within the circle broke the defensive formation. In a matter of seconds, they were scattered across the valley floor, each Rebel and Auran fighting alone.

Spencer reeled, trying to find an ally. Daisy had been right beside him a moment ago. Now she was nowhere to be seen. He glimpsed Walter Jamison, but the warlock was too far away. Then, out of nowhere, Rho grabbed Spencer's arm, leading him toward the shelter of the tires, dodging Thingamajunks as they ran.

"Who launched that stink bomb?" Spencer called. "Who's behind this?"

"I have a guess," Rho answered. "And if I'm right, we'll never even see him."

One of the Thingamajunks rolled forward, its legs comprised of old bike wheels. Atop the wheels was a huge, tattered suitcase snapping open and shut like jaws. Unseen eyes sensed Spencer and Rho making a desperate retreat, and the Thingamajunk moved to intercept. Rho's foot caught in a loose tire and she went down. Immediately, the Thingamajunk closed on her, suitcase maw opening wide.

"Spencer!"

He whirled around and saw the danger. In desperation, he dropped his open razorblade to the dirt and drew a mop from his belt. With one swift motion, the mop strings went swirling outward, snaring the Thingamajunk by the wheel axle. Spencer pulled on the mop, jerking the garbage figure away from Rho just as the suitcase snapped shut.

Rho was safe, but trying to pull a Thingamajunk on wheels was not the best idea. It rolled backward far faster than Spencer could anticipate. In an instant, it swiveled, ripping the mop from Spencer's hands. Then the suitcase opened, assaulting him with the strong smell of mothballs. The Thingamajunk stooped forward, and by the time Spencer yelled for help, he'd already been swallowed.

CHAPTER 36

"NOW I'M YOUR PRISONER?"

Spencer bumped painfully along. The inside of the Thingamajunk suitcase smelled like his grandma's closet, but the stench of his own clothes, splattered with the contents of the stink bomb, overpowered anything else.

Spencer grasped at the lid of his prison, trying desperately to wedge the suitcase open. The Thingamajunk seemed to be running around with a mouthful of Spencer, but at least he wasn't being digested.

Abruptly, the bouncing stopped. Spencer pounded against the lid of the suitcase, and, to his surprise, it popped open. Before he could even gasp a breath of fresh air, someone had seized him around the middle and yanked him out of the Thingamajunk's mouth.

Surrounded by darkness, he saw a flash of stars overhead. Then he was plunging headfirst into cold water. Somehow he held his breath as his head went under. He thrashed, feeling the brush of human hands as they shoved his head down.

What was happening? Was someone trying to drown him? Then Spencer was hauled upward, lifted over the edge of a great tub of water, and dropped onto the hard ground.

He gasped once and ran a hand across his dripping face. Sounds from the wild Thingamajunks echoed upward from where the creatures were still locked in combat with the Aurans and Rebels. Spencer knew he was still in the Valley of Tires, but he seemed a safe distance away from the action, snug against one of the tire walls.

Spencer shivered against the water in his clothes. Then he finally looked up to see his captor. It was a boy, short and stocky, though looking to be about Spencer's age. Details were impossible to make out in the darkness, and on top of that, the boy was shrouded, wearing some kind of black cloak, deep hood shadowing his face.

"Sorry about that, mate," the boy whispered. He extended a hand, wearing a glove with the fingers cut out. He had a strange accent, and Spencer couldn't tell if it was real.

"Had to dunk you," the boy said, helping Spencer to his feet. "Had to get the stink off you or the Thingamajunks would smell you out and get hungry."

"Who are you?" Spencer asked.

"Oh, right," the boy said. "Forgetting my manners. Name's Aryl." The boy gestured up to the towering wall of tires beside them. "Now start climbing."

Spencer staggered to his feet. He looked up at the wall,

but in the darkness, he couldn't even glimpse the top. "Climb?" Spencer repeated. "Are you serious?"

"Deadly serious," Aryl said. "Got to get somewhere private so we can talk a bit."

"But . . ." Spencer stammered. "What about the others? Shouldn't we help them?"

"Help them?" Aryl snorted. "I just set this up so I could get you away from them!"

Spencer shivered again, but it wasn't from the chill of his clothes this time. "It was you, then?" Spencer stared at the shadowy figure. "The stink bomb and the barbed wire?"

Aryl grinned, his broad jaw tightening. "The Aurans are so predictable," he said. "Boring, really. Stopping in the Valley of Tires? Please! V's losing her touch."

"So you led the Thingamajunks on that stampede, knowing we were down there?"

"All it took was a well-placed stink bomb to start them running. A second bomb splattered the Aurans, making them the target. A little hidden barbed wire to take out the mops. Then I trash-talked one of the Thingamajunks into swallowing you and bringing you to me. I painted myself the perfect opportunity to get you alone." He shrugged as though this elaborately premeditated plan was just an ordinary day's work.

"Now I'm your prisoner?" Spencer said.

Aryl raised his eyebrows. "Bit gloomy, but if you want to think like that, then sure. You're my prisoner for the next half hour. Just let me tell you about your Auran powers and then you're free to go."

Spencer went rigid. How did Aryl know he was an Auran? The Rebels had been trying hard to keep it a secret, but this boy pointed it out like it was common knowledge.

Aryl gestured once more at the wall of tires. "Let's climb."

The stout boy leapt past Spencer and clutched onto one of the tires. With surprising agility he started the ascent, not even looking back to see if Spencer would follow. But the boy was too intriguing not to follow. He somehow knew that Spencer was an Auran. He seemed to have a lot of information, and he was willing to part with it. But for some reason he wanted to do it hundreds of feet up.

Spencer cast one last glance toward the sounds where the others fought on. He wasn't really leaving them. He would just find out what Aryl had to say and be right back. Spencer grabbed the first tire and pulled himself upward.

The climb was strenuous and dizzying. After a few moments, Spencer felt the muscles of his arms and legs begin to shake. He didn't know how Aryl managed, so swift and confident.

About halfway up, Spencer made the mistake of looking down. From such a terrifying height, the moonlit earth seemed to reel.

"Keep up!" Aryl shouted over his shoulder. But Spencer, suddenly aware of the dangerous fall, seemed to freeze. He wanted to climb higher, but his legs and arms locked up. Trying to forget about the unsteadying elevation, Spencer began focusing on his next move.

Above him was an oversized tractor tire with thick,

deep treads. It jutted out from the other tires, making an impassible overhang. The only way Spencer could reach Aryl would be to squeeze through the middle of the big tire and pull himself through. The wind howled past him, tousling his hair and causing him to tremble.

Gripping with both hands, Spencer pulled himself up. He was halfway through the huge tire, his head rising through its center like a rabbit emerging from its hole, when the tire suddenly shifted, its weld to the wall straining under the boy's weight. A shout escaped his lips, and Aryl turned back for him.

Spencer was stuck now, feeling the tire gradually breaking free, ready to plummet the unfathomable distance.

Aryl backtracked, dropping nimbly toward him. He paused above the tractor tire, reaching down for him.

Spencer risked letting go just long enough to reach for Aryl's gloved hand. But the distance between them was too far, and if Aryl got any closer, his weight would surely detach the unstable tire.

"Don't you have a mop on your belt?" Aryl called.

Spencer fumbled for the handles. He'd lost one mop against the Thingamajunk, but Penny always stocked the belts with a backup. He drew the weapon from its U clip and extended the handle toward Aryl. Just as he got a solid grip, the tractor tire groaned and broke away. Spencer's hand slipped from the mop shaft, and he found himself in a heart-stopping free fall atop the tire.

His hands gripped the dirty tread of the tractor tire like it was some kind of life preserver, his eyes clamped

shut. Then his fall came to a jarring halt, nearly throwing Spencer from the tire. He thought for sure he had struck the ground until he opened his eyes.

Aryl had used the mop to lasso the falling tractor tire. He struggled to hold on as Spencer dangled from the world's largest, most deadly tire swing.

He gasped for breath, unable to believe that Aryl had managed to catch him. Then he screamed again, nearly slipping once more as the tire swing began to sway back and forth. Aryl was whiplashing the tire swing from side to side in an attempt to reconnect Spencer with the wall. He was gathering speed, swinging faster and farther with every move Aryl made.

Then, at the peak of his swing, Aryl jerked the handle just as the mop strings retracted. Spencer was flung upward, as though launched from a slingshot. His grip failed and he separated from the tractor tire.

Had anyone else executed the stunt, Spencer might have died. But Aryl's move was precise and calculated, perfectly landing Spencer at the very top of the tire wall.

Spencer lay back, closing his eyes and trying to get his head on straight. His clothes and hands were now filthy black from the tire tread, and he wondered when he might get the chance to wash himself clean.

"How's that for a shortcut?" Aryl's voice startled Spencer, and his eyes snapped open to find the other boy just summiting.

"I thought I was dead." Spencer was still panting as he sat up.

The height was staggering. Here, above the howling wind and grunting Thingamajunks, the night was almost serene. Rising moonlight touched the land, and Spencer felt as though he could see forever in any direction.

At such a distance, the moonlit Aurans and Rebels battling below looked no bigger than toy action figures. He hated leaving them behind and convinced himself that he wouldn't stay long with Aryl. Spencer would get the information he needed and get back to help his friends.

Aryl let him linger in the moment, settling down into a tire beside Spencer. The movement seemed to cause the whole tire mountain to sway beneath them, and Spencer reached out to steady himself.

"Well," Spencer finally said. "We're up here now. You want to start by telling me who you are?"

"I'm not that different from you, Spencer," Aryl said. "Yes, I know your name." He said it before Spencer realized that he'd never introduced himself to Aryl. "And I know a lot more than that."

Aryl's gloved hands reached up, and he cast off the deep hood of his cloak. His hair was trimmed short. In the moonlight, it shimmered as white as the driven snow.

"That's right, Spencer." Aryl nodded. "I'm an Auran too. But you probably know me by a different name. They call me a Dark Auran."

CHAPTER 37

"HOW MUCH CAN YOU TRUST HER?"

Spencer lurched sideways in an attempt to get to his feet. The tire mountain wobbled, and he suddenly felt dizzy.

"Where're you going to go?" Aryl said. "We're quite alone up here."

Spencer scolded himself for being so rash in his decision to follow Aryl without even really knowing who he was. "That's why you brought me up here? So I'd have no place to run when I found out what you are?"

"Precisely." Aryl nodded. "I needed a few undisturbed minutes with a captive audience so I could try to set you straight."

"I don't understand," Spencer said. "V told me that the Dark Aurans were . . . dead."

"Lie number one," said Aryl, "since I'm clearly alive."

"But why would V lie about that?"

"She lies about a lot of things. Where are they leading you?"

"None of your business," Spencer said. "You're trying to fool me. Trying to turn me against them. I fell for this with Garth Hadley. I'm not falling for it again. You're the dark one. The Aurans said your powers made you evil."

Aryl clicked his tongue. "That's a bit harsh. You haven't heard my side of the story."

They stared at each other for a moment. When Aryl didn't go on, Spencer followed up with another question. "What did you do?"

"We stole something from the Aurans," he said. "Important information that we didn't think they could be trusted with."

"So you're a thief," Spencer said. "This isn't helping your cause."

"When the Aurans found out what we'd done, they took us by surprise and dragged us out into the middle of the landfill. To an ancient place called the Broomstaff," Aryl said.

"Broomstaff?"

"It's an Old English word, mostly obsolete now," said Aryl. "The modern term is *broomstick*."

"The Aurans took you to a broomstick?" Spencer said. If Aryl was making this up, he should have thought through it a little better.

"Not just any broomstick. The Broomstaff was built by the Founding Witches long ago. It has more power than the Dark Aurans combined." Aryl grimaced at an old memory.

"The girls led us there, one hundred and ninety-two years ago. They destroyed us."

"What did they do to you?" Spencer had to know. "What happened at the Broomstaff?"

Aryl leaned forward. In the moonlight, Spencer saw a glint of metal around the boy's neck. Aryl tugged at the collar of his cloak to fully expose what was there. A thin sheet of bronze was bent across his shoulders and fused together just beneath his chin. It was rectangular in shape, and when the boy turned, Spencer could see that there was a smooth handle jutting out the back, like a single spike raised along his spine.

At first, Spencer couldn't make any sense of it. Why did this strange Auran boy have a sheet of metal welded tightly around him? Spencer took a moment to mentally unfold the piece of metal, trying to envision its original shape before it bent around Aryl's form. Then it clicked. It wasn't just an ordinary sheet of metal. It was a dustpan!

"They call it the Pan," Aryl said, his voice soft and intense. Ancient and weathered, the metal around Aryl's neck bore countless dents and scratches, each seeming to hold some untold story.

"What does the Pan do?" Spencer didn't want to ask, but he needed to know. Obviously, the girls had lied about a few things. Spencer still hadn't decided to trust Aryl, but at least the Dark Auran was giving answers.

"The Pan mutes our powers." Aryl flicked the metal around his neck, and it echoed in the darkness with a resounding ping. "Makes it so we can't use any of our Dark Auran abilities unless the other Aurans order us to do so."

"So, the other boys," Spencer said. "The other Dark Aurans are still alive too?"

"They're just like me," Aryl said with a bitter smile. "Reduced to hapless puppets. We're no more than slaves to the other Aurans. The Pan makes us do whatever they command, no questions asked."

Aryl made it sound terrible, and it was. For him. But perhaps it was for the better. If the Dark Aurans really were evil, if they'd really stolen something that didn't belong to them, then maybe the girl Aurans had done this to keep the boys in control.

"Why don't you run?" Spencer asked. "Leave this place forever, so the other Aurans can't find you?"

Aryl grimaced. "Can't leave. That's part of the Panning. We're trapped here, doomed to wander this landfill forever."

"And you've been like this for . . ."

"One hundred and ninety-two years," Aryl said without hesitation. "But who's counting?"

There was one thing Spencer didn't understand. "Down in the Valley of Tires," he said. "I think the other Aurans knew you were behind the attack. Why didn't they just order you to stop the Thingamajunks?"

"The Aurans can only give me orders when they are holding onto the handle of my Pan." He grinned rakishly. "I've spent one hundred and ninety-two years making it right near impossible for them to reach me." He leaned closer to Spencer. "They can take away my powers, but I won't let them use me to do their bidding."

"What exactly are your powers?" He was tired of hearing people mention such things without knowing what the Dark Aurans were capable of.

"Same as yours, I imagine," Aryl answered, "since you're a boy Auran."

"I don't really have powers," Spencer said. "I'm just the basic-package Auran."

Aryl chuckled. "You just haven't figured it all out yet. I could help you. I could teach you all I know and set you down the path that I walked over a hundred years ago."

Spencer drew back at this. What was Aryl's path? V had said the Dark Aurans had turned corrupt and used their powers for evil. "I'd rather not know," Spencer finally said. "Whatever powers you guys had led to that." He pointed to the Pan around Aryl's neck. "I'm here for another reason."

"You still don't trust me," Aryl said. "You think I'm evil."

"You did lead a stampede of wild Thingamajunks into the Valley of Tires with the intent to trample the Aurans," Spencer pointed out. "That doesn't really seem like something a good guy would do."

Spencer didn't know exactly when it had happened, but he suddenly noticed that the sounds of battle had ceased from below. Now, only the wind howled through the tires.

"I should go back," Spencer said, peering over the steep edge. "The others will be looking for me."

Aryl sighed, his shoulders slumping just slightly in defeat. "I wouldn't take any chances with them."

"What do you mean?"

"If the Aurans find out who you really are, they won't be happy," Aryl said. "They won't wait for you to discover your powers. By then you would be too strong. If they find out you're an Auran, they'll lead you to the Broomstaff, Spencer. And they'll Pan you."

"That's not going to happen," Spencer said. "They don't know I'm an Auran and they're not going to find out."

"I found out," Aryl observed.

Spencer looked at him. "How?"

"It's amazing what kind of evidence was left behind in that garbage truck you drove in on." Aryl reached into the depths of his cloak and pulled out a spiral-bound notebook. "I found Walter's notes. They were quite telling."

Spencer swallowed hard. He wondered what other important information was hidden among Walter's Glop recipes and sketches.

"Don't worry," Aryl said, hiding the notebook away once more. "I took it before the other Aurans had a chance to scour the vehicle."

"No problem, then," Spencer said. "The girls don't know I'm an Auran, and as long as you keep quiet, they're never going to find out."

"Unless they already knew before you came here?" Aryl said.

Spencer scoffed nervously. "That's ridiculous. How would they . . . ?" He trailed off as he thought of a way.

"I guess they could have seen me through Walter's eyes. Maybe heard us talking about me being an Auran."

Aryl shook his head. "The Aurans are far too cautious to trust what they see through warlock visions. They would have sent someone in person to make sure."

The doubt that had been nagging Spencer finally expressed itself as a whisper. "Rho."

"How much can you trust her?" Aryl said.

Spencer sat up like a dog on point as voices drifted up from the valley below. It was the Aurans and his Rebel friends shouting his name.

"They're looking for you, mate," Aryl said. "What's it going to be? Are you going back to the Aurans? Or are you sticking with me so I can teach you about your powers?" He extended a hand.

The voices were rising in unison now. "Spencer? Spencer?"

He felt his gut twist with nerves. He couldn't trust Aryl enough to abandon his friends. Leaving the Aurans was one thing. But Daisy, his dad, Bernard, Walter, Penny?

"I have to go back," Spencer said. "At least for a little while. We didn't come all this way to chicken out now. The minute I think the Aurans are on to me, we'll make our escape."

Aryl shrugged. "Just don't wait too long." He tugged at the collar of his cloak again, as if to give Spencer one final clear look at the Pan.

"Spencer?" the voices called from below. "Spencer?"

"Thanks for your help, Aryl." Spencer shook the Dark Auran's still-outstretched hand.

"You better answer them," Aryl said.

Spencer let go and leaned over the edge of the tires. "I'm up here!" he shouted as loudly as he could.

Spencer sat up again. "Think they heard that?" he asked Aryl. But when he turned, the Dark Auran was gone.

CHAPTER 38

"I DON'T KNOW ANYTHING ABOUT THAT."

Spencer awoke to morning sunlight and acrid smoke. His eyes fluttered a few times and then he sat bolt upright.

They were still in the Valley of Tires, but the place looked quite different than when they'd arrived. There were scattered body parts from ruined Thingamajunks littered around. The Aurans must have set fire to the remains, and the smoldering scraps of trash tainted the air with dark pollutants.

"You woke up with a jump," Rho said, crossing over to him. "Thought you were still up there?" She pointed up the side of the wall of tires. Spencer felt dizzy just looking at it in the daylight. It was much higher than he'd thought.

Spencer had come up with a good story. The girls already suspected that a Dark Auran was behind the Thingamajunk stampede. Lying to the Aurans would only arouse their suspicions. So he went with the truth. A *version* of the truth, anyway.

"So you didn't catch his name?" Rho asked as she passed Spencer a steaming bowl of oatmeal.

"Whose name?"

"That Dark Auran you met last night," Rho said casually.

Spencer shook his head and ladled a spoonful of oatmeal into his mouth. "I told you, he pulled me out of that Thingamajunk's mouth, dunked me in a tub of rainwater, and then made me climb. By the time we reached the top, you were all looking for me. I shouted down, and I guess he didn't want to get caught, so he took off."

He was pretending. And he hoped it was good enough to fool Rho. In a way, it felt satisfying to deceive her. She'd lied to him about being Jenna. And according to Aryl, she might be lying now. He stared into her eyes, trying to see if she knew about his Auran sense.

Spencer took a few more bites of oatmeal. It burned his tongue, and he could just picture his mom saying, "That's what you get for lying." But he couldn't tell the Aurans the truth. He had to be cautious and see what he could learn from them.

Spencer scanned the valley. The Aurans were looking worse for wear, silvery hair disheveled and dirty. The fight against the wild Thingamajunks had been grueling, but all the Aurans had survived. His Rebel friends were helping to untangle mop strings from the barbed-wire trap.

"Why did V tell me that the Dark Aurans were dead?" Spencer asked.

"They are dead to us," Rho answered, unwilling to make eye contact. "They're evil, Spencer. I'm surprised he didn't hurt you."

It was risky, but he probed further. "He was wearing something strange. It looked like a piece of metal around his neck."

Rho shrugged. "I don't know anything about that. I haven't seen the Dark Aurans in years." She swallowed a mouthful of oatmeal and quickly changed subjects.

"So, V's getting ready to use the Spade," Rho said. "She's literally going to rock the earth. The ground is going to peel up out of the gorge in front of us, and the ground behind us is going to get sucked down into the gorge that you crossed yesterday."

"What about your building? The one with the round table?"

"It has a Glopified foundation," Rho said. "It always stays topside, regardless of the rotation."

Spencer paused, thinking about what might happen to Aryl when V used the Spade. It would be suspicious if he asked outright, so Spencer thought of a cover question. "But the Thingamajunks?"

"We're at the north side of the landfill right now, but the Spade will roll us back to the south."

"So all the Thingamajunks behind us will get pulled underground," he said.

Rho nodded. "It takes them a while to crawl out, but they usually find their way topside again."

Thingamajunks were creatures of Glop and garbage, so they could survive underground. Aryl was a human being who needed oxygen. Spencer was surprised to find that he was nervous for the Dark Auran. His anxiety was probably misplaced anyway. If Aryl had been clever enough to set that elaborate stampede to separate Spencer, then he was probably clever enough to stay ahead of the Aurans when V used the Spade.

V strode past, gripping the rawhide handle of the Spade in both hands. "All right!" she called. "Let's get packed up and get a move on!"

Spencer tossed his Styrofoam bowl of oatmeal and stood up. He secured his janitorial belt and pulled on his back-pack. Leaving Rho to follow, he set off after V.

The Aurans and Rebels gathered around V at the edge of the north gorge. "It's been a while since we've trekked this deep into the landfill," V said. "Things kind of get out of proportion from here on. After the ground shifts, we'll break into two groups again. We travel fast and rendezvous at our destination just after dusk."

V lifted the Spade. It looked like an ordinary shovel in her hands. "Brace yourselves," she said. Then, with a mighty thrust, she drove the metal end deep into the hard soil.

A huge crater formed in the ground where the Spade touched down, as if the force of V's thrust had blasted the soil away. At the same time, a shock wave rippled out from the Spade, knocking Spencer onto his back.

There was a tremendous grating sound, and Spencer felt the ground shift beneath him. His fingers dug into the dirt, and he felt like he might fly off the earth at any second. He heard Daisy crying out in surprise at his side.

Something bizarre was happening in the north gorge. The landscape was bending and warping, new formations appearing like cardboard cutouts in a child's pop-up book. The earth seemed to be rolling away from the gorge. Spencer watched the abyss grow smaller and then disappear completely, his view claimed by new, odd trash-scapes.

Then it ended as suddenly as it had begun. The ground came to a ripstop halt, and Spencer's momentum sent him rolling in the dirt.

He sat up, taking stock of his surroundings. The Rebels were still in the Valley of Tires, surrounded by Aurans. But the Valley of Tires, instead of being near the north gorge, was now comfortably situated at the opposite edge of the landfill, near the spot where the bridge had collapsed under Bernard's garbage truck. With the new terrain exposed, another day's worth of hiking lay before them.

"Is everybody all right?" V said, picking herself up off the ground and plucking the Spade out of its newly formed crater.

"I'm a little motion sick," said Daisy, grasping at her head. "That was like a bad roller coaster."

The Aurans seemed less affected. They were on their feet in moments, while the Rebels rose unsteadily, as though the ground might get pulled out from under them again.

"Okay," Bernard said, dusting off his tweed coat. "This place is officially crazy. Enchanted landfill, trash with a mind of its own. What's next, dumpsters that dance the hula?"

CHAPTER 39

"WITH AN ATTACHMENT."

T hey set off, leaving the Valley of Tires behind at last. Gia, Lina, Netty, Dela, Shirley, Sylva, Yorkie, and Jersey had gone ahead to scout, just like yesterday. Rho and V remained behind with the Rebels.

Just as Rho had mentioned, the Valley of Tires was only a foreshadowing of the strange features yet to come. This far into the landfill, the landscape became even more affected by the settling Glop pollutants.

They hiked through huge arches that looked like they'd been chiseled by wind and eroded by water for thousands of years. But instead of natural rock, the twisting archways were formed entirely of garbage. Dirty plastic bags, their contents resilient against decomposition, were knit together by the percolated Glop.

The morning drew on with little conversation and few

breaks. Every time Daisy put down her left foot, she whimpered. When Spencer finally asked what was the matter, she paused just long enough to pull down her dirty sock to reveal a blister the size of a quarter.

"Here," Spencer said, unclipping the orange healing spray from his belt. "This should help for a while." He sprayed the blister and watched it miraculously heal as the liquid foamed up.

"Thanks," she said. "I didn't think of that."

Spencer was growing weary too, and the heat of the day already seemed stronger than yesterday. His thoughts turned once more to his conversation with Aryl. The Dark Auran had warned him about the girls. The Rebels had been tight-lipped about Spencer's secret. But Spencer's thoughts kept straying back to his time with Jenna at the Academy.

He decided to take a risk and try to get Rho talking—see if she suspected anything about him. The conversation would seem harmless, like reminiscing over old times. Especially if he included Daisy.

Spencer waited until the two girls were side by side, and then he jogged a few steps to catch up with them.

"This hike makes P.E. at the Academy seem like a cake walk," Spencer said.

"Actually, I think this is better," Daisy said. "There's no Dez here."

"Dez?" Rho asked.

"He's that annoying kid that came with us to New Forest Academy," Daisy said. "Remember?"

Rho nodded. "What ever happened to him?"

"He stayed there," Spencer answered. "Made a deal with Slick. Now he works for the BEM." They hiked in silence for a moment, but Spencer refused to let the conversation dead-end.

"You know," he said, "we had some pretty good times at the Academy, didn't we?"

Daisy gave him a big-eyed look like he'd gone insane. "Good times? I only remember being chased, kidnapped, attacked, paralyzed, and scared out of my mind!"

Spencer nodded. "There was that. But the Academy had a great library, I remember that."

"Didn't you pass out in the library?" Rho asked. Good, she had taken the bait. Spencer had collapsed in New Forest Academy's library when he had touched the bronze doorknob and unexpectedly gone into a vision.

"How is your fainting problem?" Rho said. "Any idea what causes it?"

Daisy nearly gave him away, but Spencer managed a quick elbow to her ribs.

"I was under a lot of stress," Spencer lied. "I'm better now."

The conversation was frustrating as they danced around the subject. Spencer couldn't tell what Rho was thinking. And he couldn't exactly come right out and say, "By the way, did you know I'm an Auran too?"

Spencer didn't dare probe further. He fell back a few steps and hiked in silence beside Walter Jamison.

They journeyed on into a strange new landscape with high plateaus rising like cliffs on both sides of the trail. V paused before they entered, scanning the narrow slot canyon ahead for any signs of a trap.

"Umm," Bernard said, poking the vertical side of the nearest plateau. "This definitely isn't stone." He poked it again and it compressed, soft and spongy.

"You're right," Rho said. "It's a couple of mattresses. Queens, I'd guess."

Daisy made a surprised face. "Queen of England?"

"Queen size," Rho corrected.

Daisy stared up at the towering mattress. "She must be huge."

"This canyon's only wide enough to enter two at a time," V said. "We should pair up and—"

Suddenly, a huge black hose rose into view like a massive python. The hose was ribbed and flexible, dipping low between the mattresses. The head of the hose was wide like a mouth, with an underworking of spinning bristles.

"That's a vacuum hose," Walter muttered.

"With an attachment," Penny added.

"Why's it so big?" Daisy said.

As they watched, the hose swooped low, an insanely loud suction ripping through the canyon. Trash flew upward into the mouth of the vacuum attachment. The spinning bristles caught the debris, tearing it and sucking it out of sight.

"Everybody hold still," V said. "Maybe it'll go away."

Everyone froze. Spencer slouched into a bulky lump of trash, hoping to conceal himself among the rubble. But the vacuum hose didn't retreat. It dragged its attachment along the trail, sucking up every scrap of garbage on a path toward the travelers.

"I don't think it cares if we're holding still," Bernard said. "This isn't Jurassic Park."

"Why didn't the scout team double back to warn us?" Alan asked.

"The vacuum probably moved in after they passed through," Rho said.

"Or maybe the vacuum already ate the scout team," Bernard said. When his comment was met with disapproving glares, he tried to amend it. "Or maybe they're all happy and safe, having a picnic on the other side."

V turned her attention back to the massive vacuum hose. "I've never seen this thing before. I'm open to suggestions."

"Why don't we find a different path?" Alan said. "Go around the mattresses?"

"That'll add a couple of hours to our journey," Rho said. "We'll never make it to the Glop source by nightfall."

"If it's a vacuum," Walter said, "maybe we can unplug it."

V shook her head. "Things don't really run on electricity around here. That thing's definitely Glopified."

"What we need is a distraction," Penny said. "I bet I can scale one of these walls. I'll climb up on top of the mattress and draw the vacuum after me. The rest of you make a run for it, two by two."

"Like Noah's animals," Daisy pointed out. "Except they had a flood. We have a giant vacuum."

Spencer could see the vacuum hose clearly as it drew even closer. It strafed along the trail, hovering about six feet high. In a heartbeat, the area below the hose was cleared out. Trash flew through the air, catching in the whirring attachment as it whipped hungrily toward them. The hose seemed to be in no hurry, and Spencer was pretty sure that it hadn't spotted them yet. Did it even have eyes?

"It's as good a plan as any, I supposed," V said. "You take one mattress, I'll take the other. Two distractions are always better than one."

Without another word, Penny drew a broom and launched herself straight up. When the broom began to lose its power, she pulled out a plunger and leapt onto the side of the mattress. The plunger clamped on, and she clung like a bedbug as she drew a second plunger. Then, hand over hand, she clamped the plungers and pulled herself higher.

V used the same approach to scale the other wall, and Spencer was amazed at how strong and coordinated she looked. Then again, she'd had almost three hundred years of practice.

As Penny and V finished their climb, Walter turned to the remainder of the group. "Rho and I will lead. Alan and Spencer come next, but wait a few minutes for us to get through. Then Bernard and Daisy will take up the rear. Don't enter the slot canyon unless you're sure the vacuum is distracted. We'll be sitting ducks in there."

Rho stepped up next to Walter at the mouth of the canyon. It wasn't long before they heard Penny's voice rising to a shout. She hurled a piece of trash at the vacuum, causing the attachment end to perk up. The long hose reared back and came sucking down blindly on the top of the mattress.

"Now!" Walter shouted. He and Rho sprinted into the long slot canyon, trying to cover as much ground as possible before the distraction ended. In a moment, they were out of sight.

Spencer and his dad stood ready, their eyes on the vacuum hose. After several long minutes, Alan took his son by the shoulder and said, "Let's go!"

They sprinted into the chute, Spencer bouncing off one of the walls as he grazed against it. Sound seemed muffled between the two oversized mattresses. All the dense foam and fabric held a stifling amount of heat. And the smell was worse than a wet dog.

Spencer's feet pounded. A roaring suction sounded overhead, and his eyes flicked upward. The vacuum hose was right above them, the canister perched on the edge of the mattress. It must have grown tired of groping sightlessly for Penny and decided to return to the windblown scraps of garbage caught between the mattresses.

Spencer shouted a warning to his dad, but his voice was whisked away as the attachment bristles whirred closer.

Then mop strings streamed overhead, lashing out from V's side. The strings whiplashed into the vacuum hose, causing it to rise once more in search of its aggressors.

Spencer and Alan burst out the other side, stumbling in the trash and falling to their knees next to Walter and Rho.

The warlock's eyes were directed up toward the tops of

the mattresses. "Two more to come," he muttered. "Keep it up."

Spencer waited, patiently at first, but growing more anxious as time ticked by with no sign of Daisy or Bernard. V and Penny were growing desperate, throwing every attack they could to keep the vacuum hose from dipping down again.

"Where are they?" Spencer said, trying to peer down the narrow canyon. "They should be here by now!"

"Relax," his dad said. "They're probably just waiting for an opening."

Spencer pointed to the vacuum hose. "It hasn't come down since we came through!" He might have been jumping to conclusions, but he said it anyway. "Something happened to them. We've got to go back."

"They'll be fine," Alan said. "Give them a minute."

His dad's comment seemed insensitive, and that bothered Spencer. Was Alan even worried about Daisy and Bernard? They could be hurt . . . or worse.

Spencer's jaw tightened as he glanced at his dad. Talking got him nowhere. It was better just to act. With that thought, Spencer bolted back into the slot canyon, his dad calling after him.

Spencer was halfway through when he saw the problem. Bernard was slumped in the middle of the pathway, unmoving. Daisy seemed frozen, her Glopified belt in a heap next to Bernard and her back to the mattress. She was weaponless and trembling.

And right before her stood a growling Thingamajunk.

CHAPTER 40

"SAY THE MEANEST THING YOU CAN THINK OF!"

In his panic, Spencer tried to run faster. "Daisy!" he screamed. But his feet were moving too quickly for the rest of him to keep up. His toe caught a length of plastic webbing and he went down hard, stars dancing in his peripheral vision. His leg was tangled and stuck. In his haste, he'd ruined any chance of saving his friend.

The Thingamajunk dropped forward onto its long arms and roared into the girl's face. It looked similar to the other Thingamajunks they'd encountered: hulking scraps of garbage fused together by the Glop that gave them life. This one had a dented lunch box for a head, with a moldy textbook hanging on like a dislocated jaw.

"Daisy!" Spencer shouted. "You have to trash-talk it!"

She glanced sideways at him. "What?"

"Trash-talk!" Spencer said. "Pretend like you're tough!"

Daisy's hands balled into tight fists. She leaned forward slightly and shouted, "Hey there, big guy!"

"No!" Spencer coached. "You have to insult it!"

She took a deep breath. "You're huge and scary!"

"That's not an insult, Daisy," Spencer yelled. "That's what it's going for!" He drew his razorblade and started cutting himself free of the plastic webbing. "Say the meanest thing you can think of!"

Daisy squinted her eyes and screamed at the trash, "You're made of garbage!"

The Thingamajunk reached out with its long arm and knocked her back against the spongy mattress.

"I'm sorry!" Daisy's voice was small and quivering. "But you are."

The Thingamajunk made a series of grunts and grabbed Daisy by the arm. With only words to defend herself, Daisy gathered her courage and made one final attempt.

"Listen here, big buddy. You are big and scary and made of trash. But under all that yucky garbage, I bet there's a really nice guy. Maybe you're upset because you don't have any friends. Maybe you're mad because other people make fun of you. Maybe you feel like there's not a single good thing about you. I've been there, buddy. I've felt like garbage. Dez Rylie made me feel that way every day of fifth grade. But I didn't go around trying to eat people!"

The Thingamajunk paused, its lunch-box head cocked curiously to one side. It snorted once as if in disbelief over Daisy's pathetic resistance. Then the covers of the old textbook peeled back to reveal a crooked line of broken pencils that, more or less, formed teeth. But squirming between the Thingamajunk's jagged teeth were at least a dozen pale worms, munching away on the decomposing paper.

"Bookworms." Daisy shuddered from head to toe. The Thingamajunk continued gnashing its teeth savagely, but Daisy was on a roll now.

"There!" she said. "That's better. At least you're smiling now."

Spencer didn't point out that the Thingamajunk was actually gnashing. Smiling and gnashing were two very different things. Spencer stood, at last free of the webbing. But Daisy didn't seem to need help anymore.

The Thingamajunk dropped the girl to the ground. Its mouth closed and then opened again, stubby pencil teeth jutting awkwardly in an attempted smile.

Daisy cringed at its rotting mouth. But seeing the Thingamajunk's nasty attempt at a smile seemed to spark an idea for Daisy. She dug into her pocket and quickly found the item she was looking for.

It was a pink retainer. The one from Bernard's strange dumpster collection.

"Here." Daisy held it out. "It might be a little small, 'cause you've got a huge mouth. But you seriously need some dental work."

The Thingamajunk leaned forward, examining the small item in Daisy's outstretched palm. It cocked its head to the other side and grunted in thought.

"Take it," Daisy insisted. "It will help your teeth get

straighter. Then maybe there won't be enough room for the worms."

Spencer dropped to his knees next to Bernard. With a shot of orange healing spray, the garbologist began to revive.

"What's she doing?" Bernard muttered, sitting up.

"She's bargaining for her life," Spencer said. "With a retainer." It was absolutely ludicrous!

"One of my dumpster retainers?" Bernard asked. "Those are special edition! Carefully collected in more than forty states!"

The Thingamajunk's hand was hovering just above Daisy's. It seemed frozen, like it was expecting some kind of trick.

"Go ahead," the girl coaxed. "Take it."

The garbage hand closed around the pink retainer. And just like that, the Thingamajunk exploded.

It happened so unexpectedly that Daisy was knocked backward against the wall. Trash fell to the floor around her like shrapnel.

Daisy's eyes were big as she staggered back to her feet. "What happened?"

"He blew up," Spencer pointed out. It didn't make much sense.

"Because I trash-talked him?" Daisy asked.

"You couldn't even insult a pile of garbage!" said Spencer. "I don't know what that was, but it definitely wasn't trash-talking."

"Trash-whispering?" Daisy tried.

"I suggest we finish this debate in a safer location." Bernard pointed upward as the huge vacuum hose dropped into the slot canyon, bored by Penny's and V's distractions.

Bernard led the way, with Spencer and Daisy close behind. The vacuum attachment was bobbing up and down, gobbling trash between gasps of fresh air. The trio paused, trying to time their escape perfectly.

The garbologist went first, diving and rolling through the trash as the vacuum hose lifted. Spencer was right behind him, feeling the suction lift his hair as he barely made it past.

Daisy came last, but her timing was off. She rolled forward just as the vacuum attachment came down. The girl screamed, her braid flying upward as her feet left the ground. Spencer doubled back, calling her name, but he realized that she would be swallowed long before he could reach her.

Abruptly, a pile of garbage directly beneath the vacuum hose sprang to life. It leapt straight into the air, bits of scrap and trash forming together into a Thingamajunk.

The garbage figure caught the neck of the vacuum hose in both apelike arms. It roared, a rustling sound that outmatched the whirling attachment. The vacuum hose bucked under the attack, but the Thingamajunk continued to squeeze, pinching off the hose and stopping the suction.

Daisy dropped to the hard trail as the vacuum hose went slack. The Thingamajunk swung sideways, its garbage feet kicking off the wall and pulling the hose so that it doubled over itself. Then, with a final roar, the Thingamajunk dropped down, tying the vacuum hose into a tight knot.

The vacuum reared back, pulling its knotted hose over the top of the mattress and out of sight. The Thingamajunk dropped onto all fours and lifted Daisy back to her feet.

She stared at the garbage figure, too stunned to say a word. Then the Thingamajunk smiled at her. And there, wedged into the moldy textbook that formed its mouth, was a pink retainer.

CHAPTER 41

"YOU GAVE IT A GIFT?"

R ho, Walter, and Alan came sprinting down the slot canyon. The Auran girl at the lead saw the Thingamajunk and instantly started trash-talking.

"Get out of here, you clumsy pile of scrap! You're a disgrace to garbage!"

The Thingamajunk started growling. The pink retainer, clipped between two stubby pencils, started rattling as the garbage figure drew itself up to full height and roared.

"That's right!" Rho carried on. "I'm not afraid of you or your smelly excuse for a body! You can go—"

"Stop it!" Daisy screamed, stepping between the Auran and the Thingamajunk. Rho backed up, surprised that Daisy would stand so close to the dangerous creature. Daisy reached back and put a steadying hand on the Thingamajunk's arm.

"He's not hurting us," Daisy explained. "Bookworm saved my life."

"Bookworm?" Alan asked.

"That's what I'm calling him," said Daisy. In response, the Thingamajunk bent low and flashed its wormy imitation of a smile. The Rebels all pulled back in disgust.

Just then, Penny and V drifted down from the mattresses, landing skillfully with brooms in hand. Instinctively, V began a strain of loudmouthed trash-talking when she saw the Thingamajunk, but Daisy quickly cut her off.

"What's going on here?" the Auran demanded.

"Looks to me like Daisy made a friend," Bernard said.

V shook her head. "Impossible. You can't make friends with a Thingamajunk. It's got to be a trap. This one must be smarter than the others. It's going to wait until we turn our backs and then attack when we're least prepared. We should destroy it now while it's outnumbered!"

The Thingamajunk began slinking away from V as her voice rose. Daisy reached out a hand for the garbage being.

"Don't listen to them," she said. "Nobody's going to hurt you." Daisy took a step closer. "Do you speak English?"

The Thingamajunk shook its lunch-box head, grunting a few times in response.

"I don't think that was English," Daisy said, looking to her companions for affirmation.

"Definitely not," Bernard said.

Spencer stepped forward to ask Bookworm another question. "Do you understand us when we speak to you?"

The Thingamajunk nodded, grunting something that sounded like "garblar."

"Garblar," Daisy said. "Maybe that means 'yes.'"

"Why did you save Daisy from that vacuum hose?" Spencer asked.

The Thingamajunk reached up to its mouth and plucked out the pink retainer. It held the object for all to see, nodding excitedly.

"You liked my gift?" Daisy asked.

"Oh, please!" V rolled her eyes. "You gave it a gift?"

Bookworm popped the retainer back into its mouth and gave another smile.

"Has anything like this ever happened before with a Thingamajunk?" Walter asked the Aurans.

"Never," Rho answered. "We're always fighting them off. Thingamajunks don't help people."

"Maybe that's because you trash-talk them all the time," Daisy said. "Maybe you hurt their feelings and that makes them mad."

V shrugged incredulously. "They're made of garbage. Garbage doesn't have feelings."

Daisy was going red in the face, trying to mount some defense for her rescuer. Whether Bookworm had feelings or not, Daisy had changed something about the Thingamajunk. She'd shown it a bit of kindness, given it a simple gift, and now the garbage figure was standing behind her like a bodyguard.

"Whatever," Rho said, diffusing the tension. "We should keep moving."

Daisy glared at V and then looked once more at the Thingamajunk. "I have to go now, Bookworm. Thanks for saving me." She held out her hand again, and this time the garbage figure accepted it. The Thingamajunk shook her hand so hard that she nearly came off the ground.

"Will I see you again?" Daisy asked.

"Garblar," grunted Bookworm. Then he leapt backward, his body losing cohesion and falling into loose pieces of trash on the trail.

"Daisy," Spencer said. "Good job."

She looked at him. "What do you mean?"

"I think you just got yourself a guardian Thingamajunk."

"WE'RE GOING UNDER."

It was midafternoon when they finally stopped again, and Spencer was grateful for a break. V's pace had been relentless. They hadn't even stopped for lunch, instead eating their light meal as they hiked along.

V hadn't mentioned the Thingamajunk incident again. She stayed at the head of the group with her eyes on the trail and the Spade over her shoulder. But Daisy talked nonstop. She asked Bernard lots of questions about garbage. Despite her newfound interest, Bernard pointed out that he had never actually worked with living garbage before and couldn't claim to be an expert. But Daisy wasn't going to give up easily. She was convinced that she would see Bookworm again.

When V finally stopped, it was to study the landscape ahead. The area was blackened and charred. For the first time in what seemed like days, Spencer saw bare dirt without garbage. But scattered across the land were hundreds of propane tanks.

The tanks were lying haphazardly across the dirt, some half buried in the blackened soil, others tipped carelessly on their sides. Spencer had seen propane tanks at Aunt Avril's house, hooked up to the fancy grill on the back patio. They were full of gas, and Alice was always telling Max to stay away from them. She said a single spark could ignite the gas and . . . well, the evidence was right in front of Spencer.

The propane tanks were spurting huge columns of yellow fire. They flared up sporadically, jetting flames in any direction at any time.

"We're not going through there?" Walter said as a propane tank launched a twenty-foot streamer of fire straight into the air.

"The propane tanks have been tainted with Glop," Rho explained. "They seem to have an endless fuel source, and they ignite randomly, making it almost impossible to pass through without getting burned to a crisp."

"Which is why we're not passing through," V said, her eyes flicking left and right along the edge of the burn field. "We're going under."

"We're looking for a marker," Rho said. "Something that the Auran scouts would have left behind to show the way into the tunnels."

"There." Bernard pointed away to the left. "That empty water bottle."

The team moved over to a bottle standing upright on

a large rock. "How do you know that's the marker, and not just some old piece of trash bottle?" Penny asked.

"First of all," Bernard said, "it's a twenty-ounce bottle with a narrow base and a heavy lid. The fact that it's standing upright means it was carefully placed here. It couldn't have landed like this coincidentally, since this bottle model is notoriously top-heavy when empty."

That seemed like a reasonable explanation, but Bernard swiped his finger around the rim of the water bottle and continued. "And secondly," he said, "it's still damp, which means someone was drinking out of this less than an hour ago."

Rho picked up the bottle. "He's right," she said. "This is Gia's."

V clipped the Spade into her janitorial belt and drew out a pushbroom. Warning everyone to stand back, she struck the rock. It spiraled skyward, revealing a dark opening into an underground tunnel.

"Everybody in," she said. The Rebels dropped down one by one. Spencer noted how the air felt different below ground. It was dry and cool, a refreshing contrast to the Texas afternoon in the landfill. Quiet, too, though Spencer could still hear an occasional whoosh as one of the propane tanks ignited overhead.

In a moment they were on their way, V moving into the lead once more. The tunnel was surprisingly large. Even Alan, who was the tallest among them, could stand up straight.

"How did the scouts know there would be a tunnel?" Spencer asked.

"It's actually an old garden hose," Rho answered. "Somebody threw it away and, after a while here, the Glop changed it. The hose generally stays in the same area near the propane tanks, but the entrance is in a slightly different place each time."

Spencer expected it to grow unbearably dark, but as they moved deeper into the tunnel, he noticed how portions of the garden hose had rotted away above their heads, letting dusty columns of light into the dark passageway.

The tunnel snaked along, making a number of turns and bends. They had been walking in silence for several minutes when Daisy suddenly spoke out.

"What's that?" she said, pointing toward the roof of the garden hose. There was a skylight hole rotted above them, the biggest Spencer had seen since entering. A glimpse of fire and a ray of natural sunlight filtered through. But the hole wasn't what Daisy was asking about.

Covering the opening was a massive spiderweb, at least a dozen feet across. Like most things in the landfill, there was something very strange about it. Instead of the usual white, cottony fibers of a spider's web, this seemed to be made of . . .

"Bubble gum," Rho said.

A vast amount of prechewed gum had been stretched together to form a complex web. It was multicolored, mostly pink and green and blue. The gum web sagged over the hole in the roof, as if it were waiting for an unsuspecting victim to fall into its sticky snare.

Spencer was disgusted. He could practically see the germs crawling to and fro.

"What kind of spider makes a web out of bubble gum?" Daisy asked.

"Doesn't matter," V said. "The exit isn't far ahead. Let's keep moving."

Spencer took an uneasy step forward. Suddenly, the ground cracked under his feet. He tried to leap backward, but the garden hose was caving in too fast. The floor of the tunnel was collapsing! Everyone was caught in the free fall as the tunnel gave way beneath them.

A loud squelching sound came from overhead, and Spencer saw a strand of gum lash out. He felt the sticky rope latch onto his back. As his friends tumbled down into darkness, Spencer alone was flung upward toward the light.

Spencer stuck to the bubble-gum web, feeling the pre-chewed gum adhere to his clothes and hands. He thrashed wildly, but the action only caused him to get more tangled in the disgusting, chewy mess.

"Spencer!" Walter's voice drifted up from the darkness below. The cave-in had settled, and Spencer knew his friends could see him silhouetted against the midafternoon light like a fly in a web.

"Hang on, Spencer!" his dad shouted. "We're coming for you!"

Then Spencer felt the strands of bubble-gum webbing vibrate around him. Something else was climbing onto the web. Spencer turned his head sideways, putting his cheek dangerously close to a string of Bubblicious.

It wasn't a spider coming for him. It was another person. Agile and strong, the figure maneuvered across the top of the gum web until he was poised behind Spencer. A razorblade flashed in the firelight, cutting Spencer free one strand at a time.

Spencer held still, thinking that he would plummet down to his friends at any moment. But as the last stretchy piece of gum was severed, the stranger seized Spencer by the backpack and hauled him out of the tunnel.

They rolled onto the charred dirt above, where a plume of fire streamed dangerously close to Spencer's head. He was reaching for his weapons, preparing to fight off his assailant, when Spencer finally got a glimpse of him.

It was a thin boy, tall and wiry. He wore a singed pair of jeans and a shirt with the sleeves cut off. His hair was stark white and buzzed almost to his scalp. And around his neck was a bronze dustpan.

It was another Dark Auran.

CHAPTER 43

"BEING AN AURAN JUST GOT GROSS."

The Dark Auran kicked the nearest propane tank, spinning it sideways and launching a stream of fire across the opening. The bubble-gum web was instantly charred and the Rebels' way out was cut off.

Spencer drew a plunger from his belt. The heat was intense here, with random spurts of fire dancing around them. "I'm armed," Spencer said. "You don't want to fight me."

The boy laughed. "Spare me the bravado," he said. "I'm not going to hurt you."

"So that's why you collapsed the tunnel and dragged me up into a burning field?" Spencer said. "Because you don't want to hurt me?"

"It was risky, I'll admit," said the boy. "But Aryl told me you'd be worth it."

"You won't get away with this," Spencer said. "My friends will find me."

"Of course they will," he said. "But in order to reach you, they'll have to go all the way back to the entrance and maneuver their way through the fire bursts. That should give us a bit of time to talk."

The Dark Auran sat cross-legged on the ground, his face sweaty and blackened from working so close to the fire tanks.

"I'm Olin," he said. "Aryl told me that he began a promising conversation with you last night. But unfortunately, you ran out of time." He smiled. "I'm here to finish the chat."

"I had nothing more to say to Aryl," Spencer said. "I've kept it a secret. The girls still don't know what I am."

"And what exactly are you?" Olin said. "Like them? Or like us?"

"I don't have your powers," Spencer said. "And if powers lead me to where you are now, then I never want them."

Olin rolled his eyes. "Of course you do. You're one of us, Spencer. You just haven't explored your abilities."

"And I don't need to," Spencer argued. "I can live out my life just the way I am."

Olin held up a finger. "You're afraid."

"I'm not afraid!"

"Deep inside, you know that the moment you embrace your full powers as an Auran, you give up any chance of living a normal life."

Spencer had no argument to this. Olin had pinpointed

his feelings better than Spencer could in his own heart. He knew it was true. Being an ageless kid was bad enough. Adding more powers to his situation would only increase the responsibilities in his future. Maybe he was afraid of reaching his full potential.

"Don't fight it," Olin said. "You made yourself an Auran, Spencer. Why not be the best Auran you can possibly be?" Olin let him think about it before adding, "The powers within you could turn the tides for your Rebel friends. You would be the secret weapon."

Spencer wanted to go home. He wanted to walk up the stairs of Aunt Avril's house, shut his bedroom door, and sit in his tidy bedroom. Well, he really wanted to take a long, hot shower first.

Spencer hadn't made himself an Auran on purpose. He would gladly give up his position if he could. But there was no backing out. Only moving forward. If his inner powers could help the Rebels overthrow the BEM and save the world, then surely it would be worth it for him to learn about them.

"I know how to use bronze objects to see the warlocks," Spencer said. "But that's all I can do."

"Weak," Olin said. "Every Auran has that power. The girls have been doing it for hundreds of years. I'm asking you to dig deeper. To discover powers that only the Dark Aurans have."

"Like what?"

The Dark Auran rapped gently on the bronze Pan around his neck. "I need you to remove this."

Spencer stared. It looked just the same as Aryl's had, equally dented and likely very uncomfortable. He tried to imagine what life would be like wearing a Pan, cursed to wander the landfill forever powerless.

"But isn't it Glopified?" Spencer asked. "How can I take it off?"

Olin leaned forward, his voice soft and intense. "I want you to de-Glopify it, Spencer."

De-Glopify? He'd never heard of anything like this. Sure, old Glopified weapons got maxed out after too much use, but Olin was talking about something entirely different. He was talking about removing the magic from the Pan.

"I can't de-Glopify," Spencer finally said. "Even if I could, why would I set you free? Didn't they Pan you for a reason? Because you're dangerous or something?"

"They Panned us because we stole something that they weren't worthy to have."

Spencer wondered what could possibly be so important. Whatever the Dark Aurans had stolen had led to almost two hundred years of imprisonment. "Why don't the Aurans just order you to give it back? Isn't that what they do? Boss you around?"

Olin made a disgusted face. "They'd like to have that kind of control, but we're not easy to track down. The only way they could find what we stole would be to get the three of us together. We make sure that never happens." Olin sighed. "They still manage to snag one of us from time to time. They grab onto the Pan and give us orders. 'Glopify this,' they say. 'De-Glopify that.'"

Spencer was curious now. If the Dark Aurans had the power to Glopify and de-Glopify, then that indeed made them powerful. Spencer was already imagining himself with those powers, thinking of all the ways he could aid the Rebels.

"Who do you think made the Spade?" Olin pointed his thumbs at his chest. "I did. And the Glopified foundation for the Auran building, and the traps for the thirteen clues. . . . We did it all, because the other Aurans forced us." He paused, his eyes boring into Spencer. "Who do you think made the Vortex?"

Spencer felt his blood run cold. Olin knew about the Vortex? No, more than that. Olin had *created* the Vortex. "I have a friend who—" Spencer started, but the Dark Auran cut him off.

"Marv," Olin said. "Trapped in the Vortex. I know."

Spencer was going to ask how he knew; then he remembered that Aryl had stolen Walter's notebook of ideas from the truck. There were plenty of sketches about Operation Vortex in there.

"Let me cut you a deal," Olin said. "I'll teach you how to harness your Glopifying powers so you can un-Pan me. Do that, and I'll tell you how to get Marv out of the Vortex."

It was an uncomfortable proposition. Un-Panning a Dark Auran didn't seem like the best idea. "What will you do when you're free?" Spencer asked.

"McDonald's," Olin said. The answer caught Spencer off guard, and Olin chuckled. "I can't tell you how many fast food bags come through the garbage. But I've never had a real hamburger, only scraps I can dig out of the trash. So that's what I'll do." Olin leaned back. "I'll free the other two Dark Aurans and we'll get out of here. We'll find McDonald's and have a burger."

Spencer stared at the boy with a sudden surge of pity. Eating scraps out of the garbage for hundreds of years was a horrible existence. Whatever the Dark Aurans had stolen couldn't be that important.

"Okay," Spencer said, making a quick decision. "Teach me my powers."

Olin scooted across the blackened soil, drawing even closer to Spencer. "When you became an Auran, your body underwent a physiological change. As part of that change, Glop was introduced to your system."

"What system?"

Olin rolled his eyes. "Your body."

The answer surprised Spencer. "There's Glop inside my body?"

"Just trace amounts," he answered, "in all your bodily fluids—blood, tears, sweat, saliva, urine."

Spencer couldn't suppress a chuckled cough. Did Olin just say *urine?*

"Oh, grow up," Olin hissed. But that was oddly funny too, since Spencer was never going to grow up. "Anyway," Olin went on. "The Glop is most concentrated in blood and spit."

Spencer didn't like this topic. "Being an Auran just got gross." He shuddered.

Olin lifted his hand in front of his mouth and spat into the palm. Spencer made a face and scooted away.

"The Glop in your body reacts to friction," Olin said. He rubbed his hands together, smearing the glob of spit between his palms. "Spit's the easiest to use since it's always available." He held out his damp hands. Spencer wanted to throw up. "Of course, it's not working for me because of the Pan," Olin said. "Normally, a bit of friction will activate the Glop, causing your hands to glow with the Aura."

Spencer remembered the Aura. It had surrounded him after he had pounded the nail into the School Board last September.

"This part's very important, so listen up," Olin continued. "Right hand Glopifies. Left hand de-Glopifies."

"Anything I touch?" Spencer asked.

Olin nodded. "Anything janitorial. And the powers of the Dark Aurans are not limited like those of the warlocks."

"Limited?"

"Our stuff doesn't max out." Olin grinned rakishly. "It just gets stronger and stronger."

"Like the Vortex." Spencer nodded. "So how do I get Marv out of the bag?"

Olin stood up and stuck out his neck, eager for Spencer to un-Pan him. "Take this off and I'll tell you how."

Spencer rose awkwardly to his feet beside the Dark Auran. He lifted his hands and looked at the palms. "So," he said, stalling. "I just spit?"

"They sure made it easy, didn't they?" Olin said, his expression anxious as he wondered at the delay. "Any time now." He stepped even closer. "Left hand, remember."

"I . . ." Spencer stammered. His mouth felt dry, and the

prospect of spitting into his hands was growing more and more repulsive.

"Just do it," Olin said.

"But . . . I don't like spit," Spencer finally admitted. "I kind of have a germ thing . . ."

There was a sound behind him. Spencer whirled to see V and Rho leading the Rebels in a dead sprint for their position. They were zigzagging wildly, dodging flames as they erupted from the unstable tanks of propane.

Spencer spun back around, finally committing to do the job and de-Glopify Olin's Pan. But in the brief moment that Spencer had turned, the Dark Auran had disappeared.

Spencer felt a surge of panic. He had wasted his chance to free Olin, his Glopifying power was still undiscovered, and he still didn't know how to rescue Marv from the Vortex.

A small piece of paper fluttered at Spencer's feet, the only piece of trash in the baked wasteland. He hadn't noticed it a moment ago. Hurriedly, Spencer scooped it up and unfolded it.

There was a simple message, written in what must have been Olin's handwriting.

RHO KNOWS ABOUT YOU

"What happened?" V asked. "Where's Olin?"

"I don't know," Spencer said, crumpling the paper into his hand. "He was here one second and gone the next. Must have dropped back into the tunnel."

"What did he tell you?" V asked.

Spencer's eyes moved to Rho, but she was looking down. Olin's note said she knew. Rho already knew that Spencer was an Auran! He had suspected it, feared it, even. But as long as she didn't say anything to the others, then Spencer would be safe.

"What did Olin tell you?" V asked again.

But Spencer was spared from answering as the propane tank right next to him erupted with flame. Walter pulled him aside as the fire singed his backpack. The note tumbled from Spencer's hand and whipped into the hot fire.

"Nothing," Spencer finally answered. "Olin didn't say anything."

Spencer watched the note turn to white ash and scatter on the breeze.

CHAPTER 44

"IT SMELLS LIKE AN AMBUSH IN THERE."

The rest of the journey across the landfill passed slowly for Spencer. The weather grew muggy and the air seemed thick. Spencer saw storm clouds gathering on the horizon.

Spencer had all his trust staked on Rho now. If she revealed his identity as an Auran, the other girls would likely rally against him. According to Aryl, they would take him to the Broomstaff and give him a Pan of his own. But if Rho kept it quiet, everything would play out smoothly.

As the sun began to set, V and Rho led the Rebels over a wide mound of trash, and they found themselves at the edge of a forest. But this was unlike any forest Spencer had ever seen.

Instead of deep green trees, there were huge forks and spoons rising from the littered soil. Most were plastic, with a scattering of bent metal utensils. They stood stock straight by the thousands, some right side up, with the tines in the air, others downturned, digging into the ground as if it were a humongous piece of cake.

"We're almost to the Glop source," V said. "We should eat something before we head in." The storm clouds were overhead now, resulting in a sudden drop in temperature.

"What about staying ahead of the storm?" Alan asked.

V shrugged. "A little rain never hurt anybody."

"I don't have a great feeling about this place," Bernard said, peering into the forest. "It smells like an ambush in there."

Daisy sniffed the air. "What does an ambush smell like?"

"Have you ever smelled a dirty sock?" the garbologist asked. "I mean, really smelled it, with your nose right in there?"

"Yes." Daisy nodded. "Is that what an ambush smells like?"

"Not at all." Bernard cracked a smile. "But why on earth would you smell a dirty sock?"

"I wouldn't worry about it," Rho interrupted. "If there was danger ahead, Gia and the others would have doubled back to warn us."

"No offense," said Penny, "but I don't really have a lot of confidence in your scout team. We've already been through a couple of tight squeezes without a word from them."

"That's the nature of the landfill," V said. "Things are changing all the time. We stay on our toes and we'll be fine."

Something dark swept out of the utensil forest with a rush of leathery wings. Penny dove aside a split second before armored talons closed. The giant Rubbish shrieked, blowing a huge plume of black dust from deep within its throat.

A BEM rider leaned over the edge of his Extension Rubbish and shouted.

"Attack!"

From the depths of the utensil forest sprang a dozen Pluggers. And riding at the front, on a slobbering, vicious Filth, was Leslie Sharmelle.

CHAPTER 45

"WHAT KIND OF SODA?"

There was barely time to react. In a heartbeat, Leslie's gang of Pluggers was everywhere. Spencer reeled away, dropping his backpack and scrambling for his weapons.

"How did they get into the landfill?" Penny screamed as the Pluggers closed in.

"The gorge doesn't keep out Toxites," V answered. "They probably flew, or burrowed, or climbed. What I'm wondering is how they knew you were here?"

Leslie's hungry-eyed Filth was the answer. The creature was still baited with Alan's scent. There was nowhere the Rebels could go that the Extension Filth wouldn't find them.

Alan smashed into the nearest Extension Grime with a pushbroom. The creature's Glopified armor repelled the attack, which barely did enough to knock it back. Its long tongue snaked out, but Spencer's dad batted it away.

As the Grime breath reached her, Daisy turned in distraction to look at the forest. "Whoa! Those are definitely the biggest spoons I've ever seen. Just think about how much cereal I could eat in one bite!"

An Extension Grime paused next to the distracted Daisy. Its neck started to balloon, filling with venomous slime. Walter reached the girl just as the creature expectorated. Walter and Daisy tumbled to the ground inches from a steaming smear of greenish slime.

The Extension Grime doubled for a second attack, but V leapt into the fray. The Spade thrust like a spear and punctured through the Grime's Glopified armor, causing the rider to pull back.

In the wide-open space, the Pluggers had a huge advantage. The Extension Rubbishes were circling like vultures, diving at the Rebels whenever an opportunity presented itself.

"Into the forest!" Walter shouted, dragging Daisy toward the huge utensils. Penny cleared a path, her mop strings woven into a defensive net. An Extension Filth came loping in for Spencer. He felt its breath and swooned with fatigue. Alan shot a stream of air freshener and pulled his son into the safety of the silverware.

At the edge of the forest, one of the Extension Rubbishes went into a steep dive, hoping to pick off Bernard as he slipped into the shelter of the utensils. Wings folded back and armored talons flexed, but Penny screamed a warning.

Bernard flopped down on the ground, covering his head with both hands. Penny's mop strings whipped overhead, lassoing tightly onto the stem of a metal fork. With a grunt, she pulled.

The Glopified strings bent the huge fork, angling the sharp upturned tines just perfectly. The Extension Rubbish, at the steepest part of its dive, was unable to turn aside. There was a crunch as the fork stabbed through the armor. The creature croaked once, impaled high upon the tall fork. Then it disintegrated, leaving its rider perched precariously on the sharp tines.

The Rebels had fought their way into the forest, but Leslie's Extension Filth instantly took off after them, anxious to sink its buckteeth into Alan Zumbro.

There was a low rumble of thunder overhead. The heavy clouds let down a few drops—a mere warning of what was sure to come.

The Rebels were ducking and weaving through the utensils, staying as close together as they could manage. As in a true dense forest, it was dark among the tall silverware. And the blackening clouds only served to block out the last glimmer of daylight.

Spencer felt his heart racing as the sound of Pluggers pursued them through the forest. The Rubbishes flew overhead, waiting for a clearing in the utensils. The Filths bludgeoned their way forward, spiky quills raking through the forks and spoons. But the Grimes were catching up, their

reptilian bodies easily designed to move through tight spaces.

There was a bright flash of lightning overhead, momentarily silhouetting the Extension Rubbishes against the dark sky. Thunder cracked and the clouds opened their full fury. Sheets of rain poured down, causing the dry ground to run with muddy rivulets. There was another flash in the stormy sky.

"This is not a good place to be in a lightning storm!" Alan shouted to his companions. It was true. Nothing could be worse than running through a forest with metal trees. "We need to find shelter!"

"There's a cave over there!" V pointed through the utensils, her long white hair hanging in wet ropes from the rain. "This way!"

Daisy slipped in the mud, but Spencer pulled her back up as they raced for shelter. For a brief moment, Spencer lost sight of V. Then lightning brightened the sky and he saw her standing in the mouth of a black cave. He ran toward her, the utensils thinning until he found himself in the open air once more. Without the cover of the silverware, the rain was more intense than ever. Spencer could barely breathe as the water struck his face.

"Everybody inside!" V shouted. Penny was already in the opening, reaching out for her uncle and pulling Walter through the mouth of the cave and into the shelter. Bernard and Alan ducked through as Spencer helped Daisy find her footing in the threshold.

There was something strange about the cave. The

sound of rain pinging overhead reminded Spencer of BBs on a tin roof. The air was stale, with a peculiar, moldy scent. The pounding rain was almost deafening, but their shelter seemed dry and secure.

Rho and V stood just outside the cave's opening, watching for approaching Pluggers. Walter fumbled in his backpack and produced a flashlight. The bulb flicked on and illuminated the cave.

Their shelter was perfectly smooth and rounded, forming a cylindrical chamber that dead-ended a short way down. Spencer reached out and touched the wall. It was hard, but not stone. It felt more like cold metal.

"Guys," Bernard said. He was crouching at the end of the tunnel, his yellow boot sticking to something that had pooled there. Walter's light shone on the viscous puddle, and the garbologist leaned down and swiped the substance with his finger.

Spencer looked away as Bernard lifted the finger to his mouth and took a quick taste.

"I don't think this is a cave," the garbologist said. "I think it's a giant soda can."

"What kind of soda?" Daisy asked. "

"Going by this residue," said Bernard, "I'd say it's a 7-Up can."

The shape of the cave made sense now. It was an aluminum can, a hundred sizes too large, lying on its side in the mud. The cave's mouth made a perfect oval where the can had been popped open.

"I don't like this," Penny said. "Only one way out."

Alan nodded. "We should get out of here while we can . . ."

Mop strings flicked through the oval opening and seized Spencer around the middle. He was jerked outside, back into the pouring rain.

Spencer skidded on his back in the mud, writhing to see who had attacked him. As he traced the mop strings back to their source, his heart sank.

It was Rho.

Spencer sat up just in time to see V slam her pushbroom into the side of the soda can. The rain-soaked soil gave way into a tremendous landslide; carrying the old aluminum can down a slippery slope.

Spencer watched his friends topple out of sight. He staggered to his feet and lunged at V. But the Auran was too quick. She turned, drawing a green spray bottle from her belt and pulling the trigger. A fine green mist engulfed Spencer. He felt his legs weaken and buckle. Spencer fell backward, and Rho caught him under the arms.

His vision was growing fuzzy, and, try as he might, Spencer couldn't remember who had just sprayed him with the green solution. Then his eyes rolled back in his head and he blacked out completely.

CHAPTER 46

"I LOVE A STORM LIKE THIS."

Spencer awoke to cold water in his face. The rain was still coming down in sheets, forcing him to gasp for air as he sat up.

His brain felt patchy as he tried to piece together the recent events. He remembered fighting Leslie's gang of Pluggers in the utensil forest. He remembered taking shelter in an oversized 7-Up can. He remembered Rho pulling him out and V knocking the can down the hill. But he couldn't remember anything after that.

Where was he? How had he gotten here?

"He's awake!" came a shout from behind him. Spencer turned to find all ten Aurans standing in a wet huddle.

"What's going on?" Spencer said. "What happened?"

"We've arrived," V said, striding to the front of the group. She gestured to her right, and Spencer turned.

A short distance away was a man-made lake. But it was not a friendly lake of flowing crystal water. It was a stagnant lagoon of grayish sludge, radiating a visible energy. Spencer recognized the disgusting substance, even though he'd never seen so much in one place.

It was a lagoon of Glop. It bubbled and roiled, emitting a foul, sulfuric odor.

At the center of the lagoon was an island of scorched, barren soil. And rising from the center of the island was the largest broom Spencer had ever seen. It towered nearly a hundred feet high, planted in the earth like a gnarly tree trunk. The broomstick was coarse wood, twisted and crooked as it rose higher. At the top, the straw bristles splayed heavenward, worn and weathered from hundreds of years of solitude. It was a witch's broom, old-fashioned and frightening.

"This is it?" Spencer muttered. "This is the source of all Glop?"

V laughed. "No, no. In fact, we have no idea where to find the source of all Glop."

"But you said . . ." stammered Spencer. "You were leading us . . ."

"It was a lie," V said flatly. "We needed to get you out here and we knew you'd take the bait."

Spencer glanced back at the Glop lagoon with the gnarled broomstick rising from its heart. If this wasn't the Glop source, then it could mean only one thing. "The Broomstaff," Spencer whispered, feeling a pit of despair open in his stomach.

Rho stepped forward. "I'm sorry, Spencer."

"You . . ." He couldn't find the words. His eyes were stinging and his throat was tightening. "I trusted you!"

"You never would have come here if I'd told you the truth," Rho said.

"Exactly," V interjected. "Rho was critical in making this work. We've known about you for quite some time, Spencer. Ever since Rho was sent to New Forest Academy to spy on you."

"What?" Spencer faced Rho, feeling sick inside. "You said you went to the Academy to spy on Director Garcia."

"Why would I need to do that," Rho asked, "when I can see every move Garcia makes through bronze visions! I was there for *you*. We would have captured you sooner, but we knew you were on the trail to solving the thirteen clues. If you succeeded, you would come to us."

"You've been planning this?" he yelled.

Rho nodded. "For months."

"So now what?" Spencer cried. "Now you're going to Pan me?"

"How did you know about the Pan?" V narrowed her eyes. "So you *did* speak with Olin!"

"Of course I did," answered Spencer. "Aryl, too. They warned me about this. They said you'd try to Pan me like you did the Dark Aurans."

"That's what you are, Spencer," said V. "We have to keep you under control."

It was the most ridiculous thing he'd heard. "I'm not a Dark Auran! I don't even have any special powers."

"It is only a matter of time before you discover the full range of your abilities," V said. "Then you would become just like them. You'd try to stop us from doing what the Founding Witches would want."

"How can you say that?" Spencer yelled. "Haven't you seen what the BEM is doing? I'm trying to stop *them!*"

V took a deep breath. "And I have to stop you before you become a threat to us." She turned back to the Auran girls. "Come on!" she barked. "Let's get this kid Panned!"

Spencer was too sick with despair and regret to mount any kind of defense. He was weaponless, his janitorial belt slung over Rho's shoulder. He let the girls move him along, his mind numb from the sudden turn of events.

It grew warmer and smellier as they approached the lagoon of raw Glop. By the time they reached the bank, the smell was almost unbearable. Spencer watched the lazy bubbles rise and splatter, releasing concentric rings of glowing energy.

V came to a halt and swung the Spade over her shoulder. "Shall we set sail?"

It was fully dark now, and only the grayish glow from the Glop lagoon made it so Spencer could see what she was talking about. A fleet of six blue recycle bins floated and bobbed in the Glop like small boats. They were tethered to the bank by a few rough ropes.

The Aurans were jumping into boats by the pair, and V took Spencer firmly by the arm. "You're coming with me."

V pushed him to the edge of the lagoon. For a frightful second, Spencer thought he might fall into the Glop.

The blue recycle bin bumped against the bank, and Spencer stepped into it, not liking the way it wobbled under his weight.

V lowered herself down, got situated, and pushed off from the bank. The boat drifted aimlessly in the Glop for a moment while V rummaged around in the bottom of the floating recycle bin.

"Here it is," she said, lifting a toilet brush into view. The plastic handle was about a foot and a half long, with a brush of white bristles at the end.

"What's that for?" Spencer asked, defenseless since the Aurans had taken his janitorial belt. If V wanted to attack him, couldn't she at least use a more sanitary weapon?

"I don't want to be floating out here all night." She leaned over the back of the boat and dunked the white bristles into the Glop. Instantly, the brush began to spin, propelling them forward like some kind of motorboat. V held on to the handle of the toilet brush, steering them toward the bare island and the Broomstaff.

Spencer felt the wind in his face, steamy and rotten smelling. The rain was relentless as the dark clouds let down their load.

"I love a storm like this," V said. "Glad to see it still works after all these years."

"What still works?" Spencer said.

"It has to storm, or the Pan won't work," V said. "The Broomstaff is designed to create bad weather whenever we get close."

A bright flash of lightning overhead momentarily

silhouetted the crooked Broomstaff. Thunder cracked and the clouds seemed to drop more torrent. Sheets of rain came down, the water hissing and evaporating as it landed in the steaming Glop lagoon. It was wild to see so much raw Glop in one location. He couldn't believe this wasn't the source.

"You really expect me to believe that you don't know where the Glop source is?" Spencer said.

"I don't care if you believe me," V said. "It's the truth. Do you think I'd still be here if I knew where to find the source? The Broomstaff is all we know. It's a disposal site for all this Glop. See that pump house over there?" V pointed across the lagoon to a decrepit-looking brick building. "When the lagoon gets full, one of us has to come down here and turn that thing on."

"That's how you destroy it?"

"Glop can't be destroyed," V said. "Only the Founding Witches had that kind of power."

"What?" Spencer didn't understand. "Then what happens to all this?" He pointed at the gurgling lagoon around him.

"We pump the Glop down into the earth so it can resurface at the natural source. We don't destroy the Glop, Spencer. We *recycle* it."

Spencer stared at V, her veins of betrayal running even deeper. "You don't destroy it? But . . . but the Toxites are born from Glop!" He pointed to the lagoon. "If you recycle this, then you're just creating more Toxites."

"It's all we can do," V spat. "You've seen the effects the

Glop has on the land around here. We have to get rid of it *somehow*, or the result would be catastrophic."

The blue recycle-bin boat butted up against the island. V lifted the toilet brush from the Glop and dropped it back in the bottom of the boat. Then she stepped up onto the muddy bank, dragging Spencer along.

Visibility was so poor in the rain. Spencer barely noticed that the other Aurans had already arrived and were waiting for him at the base of the Broomstaff. The wooden handle of the giant broom rose above them, rough and wide as the trunk of a large tree.

"This is it!" V shouted above the storm. "Hand me the Pan and strap him to the Broomstaff!"

Gia seized Spencer by the front of his shirt and pushed him against the Broomstaff. Rho stepped up, pulling out long strips of Glopified duct tape and circling the Broomstaff, pinning Spencer securely in place. He saw her rain-streaked face glowing faintly in the shimmer of the Glop lagoon, but she wouldn't make eye contact.

V approached through the downpour, a shiny bronze dustpan in her hands. She reached around Spencer and slid the Pan behind his shoulders. He tried to wriggle free, but his lashing to the Broomstaff was too tight, and the dustpan was pinned.

"What now?" Spencer screamed. Was it finished? The Pan hadn't wrapped around him yet.

"Now we turn on the pump," V said. "The Pan only works when the Glop is draining from the lagoon, pumping back into the earth's core. Then lightning strikes the Broomstaff and *voilà!* You're free to roam the landfill."

V picked up the slender Spade and leapt off the bank into one of the blue recycle boats. The other Aurans followed her, some of them giving Spencer a solemn backward glance, others refusing to look at the doomed boy. Through the blustery wind and slanted rain, Spencer watched them motor away from the Broomstaff island.

CHAPTER 47

"AND I'M SUPPOSED TO LIKE THIS PLAN?"

Spencer's thoughts turned to his terrible predicament, duct taped to the Broomstaff. Once the Pan was in place, he would be forever cursed to wander the landfill, friendless and alone.

"Spencer!"

His heart pounded. Had someone just called his name?

"Spencer!" He recognized that voice. And through the angled rain, he saw a figure climbing out of a boat onto his small island.

It was Rho!

"I wasn't completely honest with you yesterday," she said. Why had she come back to the island?

"Yesterday, I told you that everything I did at New Forest Academy was just pretend," Rho continued. "But I wasn't pretending when I said that you're different than

311

other boys. Good different. I've met a lot of people in the last three hundred years, and I think you're the bravest, most honest boy I've ever known."

Spencer opened his mouth to say something, but rainwater filled it.

"And I'm not going to let you get Panned." Rho's hands tore at the strips of duct tape as she began to rip it away.

Suddenly, the Glop in the lagoon began to roil and froth more violently than before. It swirled around the small Broomstaff island, ripples and waves that sloshed against the shore.

Spencer glanced toward the pump house. He couldn't see it through the rain, but he knew that the pump had been activated. The Glop was draining downward, returning to its unknown source. Returning to create more Toxites in this never-ending chain.

Lightning crackled overhead, brewing ever closer to strike the giant Broomstaff.

"Hurry!" Spencer couldn't help but say it. Rho tore away the final strip of tape just as a jagged bolt of lightning blasted into the top of the Broomstaff.

Electricity shot down the gnarled trunk, infusing heat and power into the bronze dustpan. Rho pulled Spencer away just as the Pan curled, welding itself around the space where Spencer's neck had been only seconds ago. Then it fell to the mud with a clunk.

Rho pushed her wet hair back as the storm seemed to suddenly fizzle out. She bent down and picked up the Pan.

Without hesitation, she hurled it into the churning Glop lagoon.

Spencer stared at Rho in grateful disbelief. "Thanks."

"You have to get going," Rho said. "Your friends are trapped in that soda can. Mud caved in around them, but they're digging themselves out."

"That's good, right?" Why did she look upset?

Rho shook her head. "Leslie Sharmelle is waiting for your dad. She's set a trap, and I'm afraid she's going to get him this time."

Spencer started toward the edge of the island, where he presumed Rho's blue recycle boat was tethered. Rho grabbed his arm, her head shaking.

"We can't take the boat back," she said. "Too dangerous while the pump is turned on."

"Then how do we get across?" he asked, desperate to save his dad. "Brooms?"

"The broom won't carry you far enough." She paused. "Unless . . ." Rho pulled a pushbroom from her janitorial belt. "I'm going to hit you as hard as I can."

"And I'm supposed to like this plan?"

"The pushbroom should launch you about halfway across the lagoon," Rho said. "You can use your regular broom to take the rest of the way." She unclipped the janitorial belt she was wearing and handed it to him.

"I'll be in midair," Spencer said. "What do I tap the broom against?"

"Your foot, your knee," said Rho. "Anything to activate

the magic." She leveled the pushbroom toward Spencer. "Ready?"

He had barely finished cinching the janitorial belt around his waist when Rho slammed her pushbroom into his back as hard as she could. It knocked the wind out of him, and Spencer found himself gasping for breath as he soared out over the Glop lagoon. Just as Rho had predicted, he was about halfway across when his flight began to descend.

His fingers clutched at a broom handle and he pulled it from his janitorial belt. Angling the bristles, he tapped it against his foot. The magic activated and pulled him back upward, arching quickly toward the shore.

He sailed over the white heads of the Aurans, who waited at the edge of the lagoon in somber formation. Spencer couldn't tell if they'd spotted him in flight, and he didn't care to wait and find out.

Spencer touched down running, his shoes sloshing through the thick mud. With only a mist in the air, Spencer could see much better than before. Straight ahead was a mound of mud, the corner of the oversized soda can jutting out.

There was a flicker of lightning, an afterthought for the breaking storm. But in the flash, Spencer saw a glint of metal. It was the armored Filth, Leslie Sharmelle astride its prickly back. Rho was right about the trap. The creature was already in position to kill Alan Zumbro, crouched above the soda can's opening like a cat waiting to pounce on an unsuspecting mouse.

Spencer was sprinting, his breath coming in desperate gasps. He knew he was probably too far away, but he refused to give up. In his anxiety, Spencer tripped and went down, sliding painfully in the mud. His broom tapped the ground and shot off in the wrong direction.

Spencer pushed himself up. A dark opening formed in the mud, and Alan was the first to slide out of the giant 7-Up can. Spencer's dad stood up, scanning the dark landscape.

Spencer had just opened his mouth to shout when the Extension Filth pounced, Leslie Sharmelle twisting in the saddle to hurl a Palm Blast of vacuum dust at Alan. Spencer's dad went down, helplessly pinned by the suction.

Leslie reached down and turned the dial on her battery pack, letting the angry Filth feed its hunger at last. Slavering jaws stretched wide as the Filth's spiky tail whipped around, as fast as a striking snake.

But then, out of the darkness, a lone figure appeared. There was a glint of metal and a resounding clang, knocking the Filth's bludgeoning tail away from Alan. The beast toppled, pulling Leslie under its bulk and pinning her with a grunt.

The Extension Filth snarled and righted itself. Leslie's orange prison jumpsuit was caked in dark mud, her hair disheveled and as wild as the look in her eye. A razorblade flashed in her hand, and she urged the hungry Filth after Alan.

The mysterious figure acted fast. Mop strings whipped out from his hand, entangling the Filth's armored legs. For the second time, the creature went down. This time Leslie was thrown from the saddle, still linked to her beast by the extension cord at her waist.

The stranger leapt forward, a razorblade gleaming in the damp night, and sliced through Leslie Sharmelle's extension cord. There was a shower of sparks, and then the beast was free.

The Filth's giant head perked up, nostrils flaring. Leslie was no longer in charge, no longer restraining its desire to feed on Alan Zumbro. The beast roared like a bear. It ducked into a quivering hunch and then released a shower of quills, blocking the Rebels from exiting the soda can.

Alan and the stranger threw themselves down as the sharp projectiles sank deep into the mud around them. Then the Filth charged, its body looking strange and frightening with the absence of its quills. Already, new spikes were rising through its mottled fur, pressing through the flesh and glinting sharply in the moonlight.

"Here!" the stranger cried as the beast came for Alan. The figure closed the razorblade and hurled the handle at Spencer's dad. Alan dove for it just as the monster pounced, tackling him into the mud.

There was a sound of ringing metal as Alan's thumb slid along the handle of the razorblade. The sword extended, deadly blade piercing through the Filth's flesh and fur. The Filth grunted and rolled aside, its soft underbelly beginning to disintegrate.

Alan rose to his feet, jerking the blade out of the creature's gut. With its remaining strength, the Filth snapped at him, buckteeth closing just short of Alan's legs. Then the razorblade came down once more, severing head from body. Instantly, the Filth was gone, turned to dust and caught up on the wind.

Spencer pushed himself up from the mud, barely believing that his dad had just defeated the Filth that had tried so many times to eat him. In the still of the moment, Spencer had all but forgotten about Leslie Sharmelle.

Then he saw her, climbing atop the soda can to the place where she had first lain in wait to spring on Alan. This time she had no Toxite, but with her razorblade drawn, she was every bit as much of a threat.

Before Spencer could shout another warning, Leslie Sharmelle leapt from the top of the can, razorblade clutched in both hands above her head, ready to bring it down on her victim.

It was the stranger who reacted, swift and accurate. A blue spray bottle of Windex streamed from his hand, catching Leslie midflight in a cloud of mist.

The woman shimmered with an azure glow, a final scream escaping her lips. In less than a second, Leslie Sharmelle had turned to glass. Then, with a terrible sound, she hit the ground, shattering into countless pieces.

It was utterly silent. Only the drip-drip of the rainstorm dared make a sound. Then Bernard and Daisy stepped out of the can.

"What happened?" Bernard said. "Did we miss the fun?"

Daisy bent down and picked up a shard of glass that looked strangely like a finger. "Looks like something broke."

CHAPTER 48

"IT DOESN'T MATTER, SPENCE."

Spencer pulled himself up in the mud, scrambling the final distance to meet his friends. "Dad!" Spencer threw both arms around the man. Daisy touched his back, as if reminding him that she was also there, even though Spencer hadn't said anything to her yet.

The quiet moment didn't last long, as soft radio static filled the air. Spencer looked down, surprised to see that Leslie Sharmelle's Glopified walkie-talkie had survived the Windex. It lay in the mud, half buried and forgotten as the voice of Mr. Clean drifted out.

"Leslie. Leslie, do you hear me?"

The stranger who had rescued Alan stooped down and retrieved the walkie-talkie. He took a step forward, pulling a baseball hat off his head to expose a shock of white hair.

"Who . . . ?" Walter started, but Spencer knew exactly who it was.

Spencer pushed past his dad and came face-to-face with the boy stranger. "You're the third one," he said. "You're a Dark Auran."

In response, the boy pulled down his collar to show Spencer the Pan. It meant more to Spencer now that he'd been within a second of wearing one of his own.

"Name's Sach," the boy said. "I heard you might be in a spot of trouble. Thought I'd stop by to help." He glanced at the muddy walkie-talkie in his hand as Mr. Clean's voice came through again.

"Leslie Sharmelle! Leslie, do you copy?"

Sach held the radio out to Alan. "I think it's for you."

Alan accepted the walkie-talkie. Pressing the button, he lifted it to his lips. "Hello, Mr. Clean."

It was silent for a moment, and then the BEM warlock spoke.

"Alan."

"Leslie's dead, Clean. But I'm still here. Just goes to prove that if you want a job done right, you should do it yourself."

"You can't escape my wrath, Zumbro!"

"I'm not trying to," Alan said with a smirk. "Come on, Mr. Clean. No more henchmen. No more bodyguards. No more hiding. Why don't you come out and meet me face-to-face?"

The radio was silent for a moment. Then Mr. Clean's

answer was low and slow. "You should hope it never comes to that."

Just then, the entire gang of Pluggers came careening over the edge of the slope in a vicious downward charge. They must have been waiting at the edge of the utensil forest, and when they saw that their leader's surprise plan to take Alan had failed, they rode hard to finish the job.

Alan dropped the walkie-talkie into the mud and brought his heel down hard, smashing the device into ruined pieces.

"This way!" Sach shouted, racing back toward the Glop lagoon. Walter pulled Daisy away from the shattered form of Leslie Sharmelle as Bernard and Penny followed closely behind. Spencer stood beside his dad, who lingered for only a moment at the site where Leslie and her Filth had met their demise, a look of unmasked relief on his face. Then they were sprinting after the others, making a hasty retreat before the Pluggers reached them.

"Where are we going?" Spencer shouted at Sach. The Dark Auran appeared to be leading them right back to the Broomstaff. Spencer could see the group of Aurans gathered at the shore of the lagoon.

"We need to join forces," Sach said.

"With the Aurans?" It didn't seem like a good plan, but Sach was set on it.

The Aurans fanned out when they saw the Rebels coming in. Janitorial belts were at the ready and weapons were in hand. Spencer almost laughed at the astonished look on V's face when she saw Sach leading the Rebels in.

"You!" V shouted. "I should have known."

"One of us had to interfere," Sach said, "since none of you seemed interested in saving Spencer's dad."

"What about Aryl and Olin?" V said. "I assume they're nearby."

"Oh, we know you'd love to have all three of us together," Sach said. "Which is why I'm here alone." He held out his hand. "Lower your weapons. We're not here to fight."

"Speak for yourself," V said. "I'm always ready for a fight."

"Well, good," Sach said. "Because we're going to have one in less than a moment. But it's going to be against them." He pointed behind him to where the gang of Pluggers was closing fast.

"They're after the Rebels," V said. "They're not our enemies."

"Maybe not," answered Sach. "But they're too close now. You can't hope to get away before the Toxite breath overpowers you. And when it does, you'll be helpless against them."

"What are you suggesting?" V tilted her head.

Sach reached over and unclipped the vanilla air freshener from Daisy's janitorial belt. "This nullifies the effects of Toxite breath," he said. "Stay close and we all have a chance of surviving."

V hesitated for only a moment. "This doesn't make us comrades," she muttered, squaring her shoulders for battle.

Spencer didn't know who to trust anymore. The Aurans

had tried to Pan him, and Sach was supposedly evil. But bygones had to be bygones—at least for a while. The Rebels had a much better chance of survival by joining with ten more fighters. Then Spencer realized that there were only nine Aurans on the shore of the lagoon.

Spencer glanced back toward the towering Broomstaff. Rho was the only Auran worthy of trust, but she was trapped on the island with no way off while the Glop was being pumped into the earth.

Seeing the churning mixture caused Spencer another wave of despair. He had to tell his dad that this wasn't the Glop source. He had to tell him that there was no way to destroy the Glop, and that everything they saw in the lagoon was being recycled to make more Toxites.

"This isn't the source, Dad. They're pumping the Glop . . ." He started to explain, but his dad suddenly pulled him into a tight hug.

"It doesn't matter, Spence." And for a moment, it didn't. The impending attack of the Pluggers, the trickery and deception of the Aurans, the Glop lagoon . . . for a moment, as he was held in his dad's arms, none of it mattered.

For the first time in his recent life, Spencer felt at peace with his dad. Here beside the gurgling lagoon, he realized that although the quest into the landfill had not brought them to the source, as they'd hoped, it had brought him and his father together. And that was more than either of them could have hoped for.

Then the illusion of safety was broken as Spencer saw the gang of Pluggers drawing into an offensive line. He pulled away from his dad, renewed to face the dangers ahead.

The riders twisted the dials on their battery packs, reining back their creatures at a distance of about forty yards. The monsters stamped and hissed, but they were far enough away that the Toxite breath did not reach the Rebels or Aurans yet.

Spencer tried to count them, thinking it might be a good idea to know how many Pluggers they were up against. Then he decided that counting was only cause for despair. There were maybe a dozen Extension Filths, and almost as many Grimes. Overhead, a handful of Extension Rubbishes went into a dive, landing heavily in the mud to form an impassable line.

"Ready!" shouted one of the Pluggers, who had obviously taken charge in Leslie Sharmelle's absence. The rider reached down through his Filth's bristling fur and lifted a bucket from the saddle. He ripped off the lid with one hand, and Spencer saw bristling wings, tails, and quills, confined in the bucket by an unseen force.

An Agitation Bucket.

Spencer hadn't seen once since his time at New Forest Academy. The buckets held small Toxites against their will, causing them such anger that, once released, the Toxites would attack with unmatched fury.

Spencer didn't know if the Aurans understood the danger. He didn't even have time to shout a warning before the man on the Extension Filth upended his Agitation Bucket and let the creatures stream forward unbridled.

Spencer felt a wave of sleepiness hit him as the agitated Toxites came tearing across the dark earth, their bodies twitching with anger.

"Freshener!" Walter shouted, releasing a hiss of aerosol. The other Rebels joined the spray, instantly purifying the air around them and the Aurans.

The Plugger seemed dismayed by the defensive air freshener. "Release another bucket!" he shouted. The rider at his left popped open the lid of a second Agitation Bucket and heaved the contents forward. Then the gang of Pluggers charged in a line of beasts and Glopified weapons.

The small, agitated Toxites struck first, rending and biting in a hiss of claws and teeth. Spencer fell back, his hand closing around the dustpan at his belt. With a twist of the handle, the metal dustpan fanned outward, forming into a round shield. Diving Rubbishes pinged off his defense, streaks of black in the glow of the Glop lagoon.

Spencer found the pouch containing his razorblade and flicked the button. The blade leapt out, skewering a little Grime and reducing it to a splatter of yellowish slime. Daisy was pulling him up, her pushbroom angling past his head and taking out a Rubbish midflight.

There was nowhere to retreat. The agitated Toxites were as thick as a swarm of gnats, and the larger, more deadly Extension Toxites were circling around to flank them.

Penny's short-handled mops looked more lethal than ever. She spun them around like nunchucks, the strings extending and retracting to snuff out the agitated Toxites.

An Extension Filth sprang for Walter, but Bernard and

Alan moved to block its path. The creature reared on its hind legs, bellowing, as the spiked tail thumped the sodden earth.

Sach and the Aurans were carving out a defensive ring, their countless years of combat training coming in useful. One of the Extension Grimes spat a chug of venomous slime. V sidestepped the steaming liquid and delivered a well-placed blow from her two-headed mop to the Grime's neck. The Glopified armor turned the mop strings aside, but the creature withdrew.

As long as the air freshener lingered around the Aurans, they would have a fighting chance. But Spencer knew that, with so many Toxites, the monster breath would win out soon. He released another shot of air freshener from behind his shield, hoping it would be enough.

The Auran defenses were breaking down. Spencer was moving to fill the gap when an Extension Filth charged through. It loped toward Daisy, rearing back on its hind legs before the rider spurred it to attack.

The beast's hairy jaws were opening, sharp claws descending, when something miraculous happened. The scraps of garbage at Daisy's feet suddenly moved. In a heartbeat, the trash sprang to life, forming quickly into a familiar Thingamajunk.

Bookworm met the Filth head-on, wrestling the creature back with his strong arms. They were an equal match for only a moment before Bookworm tossed the Filth aside. The Thingamajunk's foot came down in a solid kick, cracking the Toxite's helmet and leaving a dusty gash across its face. The rider retreated instantly, coaxing his injured beast to the sidelines of the battle.

"Bookworm!" Daisy cried. "You came back!"

The Thingamajunk dropped onto all fours and gave a snarling grin, covers of the textbook folding back. The pink retainer was still there, and this time, there seemed to be fewer worms.

Daisy was still reveling in the reunion when an overhead attack, unexpected and accurate, came from an Extension Rubbish.

The beast opened its massive beak and blew a stream of thick black dust like a ribbon of fire. The cloud settled around the Aurans, obscuring their vision and causing them to gasp for fresh air. In the chaos, huge talons closed around Spencer and Daisy, lifting them into the darkness.

But as Daisy screamed out, Bookworm flung into action. The Thingamajunk leapt high into the air, seizing the Extension Rubbish by the beak and pulling it into a headlock.

The huge Rubbish squawked, dropping its prey as it spiraled off into the darkness with Bookworm still clinging around its neck.

Spencer landed face downward in the mud, dangerously close to the edge of the lagoon. He heard Daisy grunt as she struck the ground. Glancing up, he saw her slide past, momentum causing her to tumble across the slick earth.

"Daisy!" Spencer threw aside his shield and reached for her, but it was too late. Daisy Gates slipped off the edge of the muddy bank and fell, out of sight, into the roiling lagoon of Glop.

CHAPTER 49

"I HAVE TO SHUT THIS DOWN!"

Spencer staggered to his feet, rage and fear coursing through him. His razorblade slashed in utter frustration, cutting asunder a pack of agitated Filths. He reached the lagoon's embankment and fell to his knees, peering over the edge for any sign of his friend.

"Phew," Daisy said, staring up at him. "That was close."

She had fallen into one of the blue recycle boats. Still tethered to the bank, it bobbed against the current of the draining Glop.

"I think it's some kind of boat," Daisy said. She reached down and picked up the bristly toilet brush. "What's this for? Is this what they use to destroy the Glop?"

But the Aurans weren't destroying it. The Glop was being recycled, flushed downward to an unknown source.

Spencer squinted across the glowing haze of the lagoon

327

toward the pump house. He needed to stop the recycling process. Maybe he could turn off the pump before any more Glop was drained.

Making a hasty decision, Spencer slid off the muddy bank and dropped into the boat next to Daisy. Rho had said that it was too dangerous to sail while the pump was activated. But they would never make it to the pump house on foot, not with so many enemies between them and their destination.

"We have to get to the far side of the lagoon," Spencer said. "The Aurans are recycling this Glop, and that's going to make more Toxites. I think I can shut it down if we can get inside that pump house."

Spencer swung his razorblade and sliced through the tethering rope. Instantly, the current pulled them away from the bank. Daisy lowered herself to the bottom of the boat as Spencer took the toilet brush from her hand.

Reaching off the back of the recycle bin, he dipped the brush into the thick liquid. The brush spun, kicking up gooey bubbles as it propelled them farther into the lagoon.

There was a shout from the bank, and Spencer took a hasty glance over his shoulder in time to see V sliding down into another boat. She wasn't going to let Spencer escape, even if it meant abandoning the fight for a high-speed boat chase.

"They're after us!" Daisy shouted as V cut her boat free and dipped the brush into the Glop.

Spencer and Daisy were halfway to the pump house when their recycle bin caught a swift eddy. The boat lurched and spun, rocking almost to the point of throwing them out. Spencer dug the toilet brush deeper into the Glop. It was spinning hard, flinging out a wake of sticky liquid, but the boat wasn't going anywhere.

V sped forward, hunched over the blue bin. Her silvery hair blew like a mad scientist's as her boat skipped off waves.

"I thought we were supposed to go *that* way!" Daisy pointed as their boat dragged backward.

"We're caught in a whirlpool!" Spencer frantically shifted the toilet brush from side to side. "It's sucking us down!"

He abandoned the brush, dropping it into the bottom of the boat. They were twirling in circles now, drawing closer to the Broomstaff island, though both were too dizzy and sick to realize just how close.

Daisy's eyes were wide as she stared into the churning muck. "Do you think this is what happened to the *Titanic?*" she asked. "Maybe we should abandon ship and try to swim to shore."

"I don't think we can even survive in Glop," Spencer answered, "let alone swim!"

Then suddenly, mop strings lashed out through the darkness, snaring Spencer around the middle. He would have been jerked out of the boat if his grip hadn't been so solid on the edge of the bin. As it was, his arms felt like they were getting ripped from their sockets.

The mop strings stopped the blue boat from spinning, and Spencer saw that the weapon extended not from V, as he'd expected, but from the Broomstaff island.

Rho held the handle of the mop, bracing herself in the slippery mud. The girl heaved backward, and Spencer felt like he might rip in half. After another heave, the mop strings began to retract naturally, dragging the blue bin out of the dangerous whirlpool and back into calmer waters.

In the next moment, the strings were gone altogether and Spencer tumbled forward onto Daisy. She gave a nervous laugh and reached over the back of the bin, toilet brush in hand. The bristles spun into action, sending them back on course for the pump house.

Rho gave an encouraging wave, and Spencer managed to return the gesture before he saw the incoming boat.

V was closing fast. She had carefully avoided the whirlpool and gained a big advantage. V maneuvered the craft to cut them off, positioning her bin between Spencer and the pump house.

"Dig deep!" Spencer called to Daisy. The girl gritted her teeth and plunged the brush deeper into the Glop, so deep that the heat began to scald her bare hand. The blue bin responded immediately, gathering speed on what seemed like a collision course with V.

Spencer unclipped a broom, rising unsteadily to his feet and taking aim. Dead ahead, the leader of the Aurans scowled at him.

When Spencer was close enough to see her rain-soaked face clearly, he gauged the distance to the pump house, hoping he was close enough. Then he reached back, grabbed Daisy by the arm, and slammed the broom against the bottom of the blue bin boat.

They launched forward, Daisy screaming, then grabbing onto Spencer's back as they soared over V's head. Their empty bin capsized with the shaky launch, sinking out of sight and melting into a streak of blue plastic.

Spencer and Daisy barely reached the shore. They skidded through the mud, broom flying aside as they bumped painfully against the wall of the pump house. Spencer was immediately on his feet. Daisy, slightly stricken, took a second longer. By the time she was up, Spencer had already found the door.

It was a simple brick building, showing signs of decay and erosion that suggested it was quite old. The door was wooden and warped, with bands of iron holding it together. Spencer grabbed the handle and pulled. The door was stiff, but in a moment, the two kids stood on a landing inside the pump house.

The inside was bigger than Spencer expected, with a ladder leading down and another shorter one leading up to a loft. Giant pipes intersected the whole house, twisting and turning in every conceivable angle. The pipes vibrated under the pressure of operation, the joints rattling like they might shake apart at any moment.

At the center of the room was a massive hydraulic pump. The huge cylinder lifted smoothly on an oiled shaft, then slammed down hard, releasing a hiss of sulfuric vapor as it forced the Glop through the pipes and deep into the earth.

"It smells funny in here," Daisy said, crinkling her nose. Spencer couldn't let himself get distracted by gross details.

"There's got to be a switch or something to turn this thing off," he said.

"Maybe up there." Daisy pointed up to the loft.

Spencer nodded. "You check above; I'm going down for a look around."

They tightened their janitorial belts, and Daisy quickly scampered up the short ladder while Spencer began his descent down the long one.

"It just looks like a bunch of gears and pulleys up here!" Daisy shouted before Spencer had even reached the bottom of his ladder. "My dad would love this place."

"Look for a button or a switch!"

Spencer skipped the bottom rung of the ladder and landed on the concrete floor. Here the vapor was thicker, a sickly yellow hue that forced him to squint. He ducked under some pipes and made his way toward the rising and falling pump. He noticed a set of meters and gauges, red needles that spun around, measuring volume and pressure.

"Nothing up here!" Daisy shouted, her voice almost lost in the hiss of the great pump.

"We have to find it!" Spencer called back, running his hands over the meters for any kind of button. "We have to shut this thing down before all the Glop gets recycled!"

"Too late for that!" called a familiar voice.

Spencer whirled around, peering through the hazy vapor to see V standing on the platform above. Daisy was halfway down the ladder. Before she could move, V was on her, pinning the girl against the rungs and holding her fast.

"Come up here, Spencer," V said, "so we can talk about this."

"Spencer! Don't!" Daisy shouted, but V clamped a hand over her mouth.

"I have to shut this down!" Spencer called.

"It's too late. The pump can't be stopped once it's started. The Glop must be recycled," V said. "Circle of life."

Spencer gritted his teeth. "You don't know what you're doing!" he said. "Toxites are born in Glop! You're just making more monsters!"

"Why is that my problem?"

"You're destroying education!"

V shrugged. "I'm just keeping things the way they were when the Founding Witches left."

"That's wrong," Spencer muttered, hardly loud enough for her to hear. "The Witches wouldn't want this." He raised his voice defiantly. "You're out of line, V! And I have to stop you!"

There was only one thing left to do. Lifting one hand in front of his face, Spencer braced himself and spat onto his palm. His hands came together with a resounding clap as he rubbed them briskly together.

His hands were glowing now, fists of golden fire that caused V to release Daisy and step away in fear.

Then Spencer reached out his left hand and pressed it against the rising pump.

CHAPTER 50

"GET OUT OF HERE!"

Spencer felt the oily lubricant smearing across his hand and arm as the pump cylinder rose one final time.

A surge of magic kicked down his arm, lighting the pump like a firework. The metal turned white hot. The huge pump, one minute coursing with unimaginable energy, instantly shut down.

The pump cylinder bucked hard, knocking Spencer back. Then the pump came to a standstill, oozing Glop as the magical power leaked out of the machinery.

Spencer staggered, fighting to remain conscious against the intense drain of energy through his body. He was aware of his success, aware also of V screaming at him from the landing by the door.

He'd done it! Just as Olin had described it, Spencer had opened his full powers like the Dark Aurans.

But there was no time to revel in his success, as Spencer realized that the pump wasn't going to shut down calmly. There was too much pressure in the pipes, too much built-up energy from the Glop.

The pipes began to tremble violently, an elevated hum building through the whole pump house. Spencer caught sight of the gauges and meters, their red needles spinning wildly out of control.

"Get out!" Spencer shouted as the joint between two pipes gave way. It burst with a hiss of sulfuric vapor. The bolts that had held it zinged outward like bullets, puncturing another pipe and burrowing into the wall.

There was a spray of grayish Glop, and Spencer ducked down to avoid the steaming substance. In the course of the explosion, there was a loud crack of splitting timbers. Then the platform was coming down, carrying V with it. Daisy was left above, dangling one-handed from a ladder that now led to nowhere.

The vapor momentarily cleared, and Spencer saw V crumpled under a heap of broken timber.

"Go, Daisy!" Spencer screamed. "Get out!"

He would have gone too, but he couldn't leave V to die like this. Spencer drew a bottle of orange healing spray from his belt and ran to the girl's aid. There was a red gash across her forehead, but he quickly misted it and waited for the healing to happen.

Another pipe exploded, pumping a chug of Glop onto the concrete floor. The walls of the pump house were shuddering and the pressure in the room was mounting.

"Daisy!" Spencer shouted again. "Get out of here! Try to take cover somewhere. This whole place is about to explode!"

Daisy nodded gravely. "I'll be back with help!" She struck her broom against the broken ladder and launched through the doorway. But help would come too late. Spencer had only a few more moments to revive V and make his escape.

Spencer turned away from the fallen girl and checked his janitorial belt for a broom. The clips were empty, and he remembered that he'd used up both brooms just to get to the pump house. With the ladder gone too, he'd have to try climbing up the brick wall. But the floor was a mess of Glop puddles, cutting off any footpath to safety.

Mop strings lashed through the vapor, seizing him around the arm and slamming him against the pump. He slumped to the ground, his shoulder aching from the blow.

V rose through the mist, her mop retracting. "Now you've done it, Spencer Zumbro." V's voice was terrifyingly calm amidst the rattling pipes. "You said you didn't share their powers. You said you weren't a Dark Auran." She grabbed a shiny scrap of metal from the floor and held it out to him. "Look at you now!"

Through the yellowish haze, Spencer saw his reflection in the metal. His hair was silvery white, the telltale sign of an Auran. He reached up instinctively, his hand running through his hair. It must have happened when he had de-Glopified the pump!

"You're just like them now," V muttered. "Trying to

337

take away my glory." V gestured around her. "Destroying this place will accomplish nothing. I will rebuild this pump house, pipe by blasted pipe. And I will use the Dark Aurans to Glopify it for me."

"You're wrong about this, V. I wish you'd understand," Spencer said, feeling the air tighten in the pump house, knowing that in another minute or two it wouldn't matter who was wrong or right because they would both be blown sky-high. "The Dark Aurans aren't evil."

"Enough!" V's face was bathed in sweat and twisted with rage. "We will see who is right and who is wrong," she said. "We will see who is good and who is evil. The Founding Witches will decide."

"The Witches are long gone, V! It's time to make decisions for yourself."

Then there was an earsplitting sound as the wooden roof of the pump house splintered and broke. Amid the shower of shattered timber, Spencer glanced up to see a giant Extension Rubbish swoop through the opening.

There was a rider on its back, smaller than most of the BEM Pluggers he'd seen. As the beast winged around, the figure was clearly visible, long braid blowing out behind her.

"Daisy?"

Spencer didn't even have time to brace himself before one scaly Rubbish foot snatched him in its armored talons. The leathery wings flapped, dispersing the thick vapor and lifting the creature, with Spencer in tow, skyward. They burst into the night through the same hole that the

Extension Rubbish had entered, and Spencer gasped his first breath of fresh air.

"Daisy!" Spencer shouted. "Is that really you?"

The Extension Rubbish craned its long neck, snapping its giant beak at the boy in its grasp. "Bad birdie!" Daisy slapped the Rubbish's neck and twisted the dial on her battery pack. "Don't eat him! We're trying to save him!"

Spencer wanted to laugh! He didn't know how it was possible, but Daisy had somehow mounted an Extension Rubbish and flown to his rescue!

From his aerial view, Spencer could see the battle from a safe distance. The Aurans huddled at the edge of the lagoon, fighting relentlessly against the small agitated Toxites and the Pluggers.

Spencer squinted to find Bookworm and the Rebels making a desperate retreat toward the 7-Up soda can, Sach leading the way. But there was still one figure, isolated and abandoned on the Broomstaff island, her blue bin boat adrift in the now-calm Glop lagoon.

"There!" Spencer shouted, pointing to the little island. "We've got to get Rho!"

Daisy leaned on her Extension Rubbish, sending the creature into a spiral dive. They circled the huge Broomstaff, its coarse bristles weathered and splayed heavenward.

Rho was readying for an attack until she saw the huge creature drop Spencer into the mud and land gracefully a few feet away.

"Good birdie," Daisy said, patting the Rubbish on its bald head. "Polly wanna cracker?"

339

The Extension Rubbish turned and snapped at her, its pinkish eyes vicious in the glow of the Glop. "Yikes!" Daisy twisted the dial all the way to green. "I guess we're still not friends." Electricity flowed down the Glopified cord, and the Rubbish bowed its head contentedly.

"Let's go!" Spencer said, clamoring to his feet and rushing to Rho. He could see the Rubbish's breath beginning to affect Rho, so he clipped out his air freshener and gave a prolonged spray.

The Auran girl paused in thought before turning to Daisy. "You can drop me at the battle with the other Aurans." She pointed across the Glop lagoon. "Sach will make sure the rest of you get safely away."

"No," Spencer said. "You're a traitor now, the other Aurans will hate you!"

"That doesn't matter," Rho said. "I'm going to claim the Spade and attempt to overthrow V. I have some respect among the others. Perhaps a few more will see things the way I do."

"Climb up," Daisy said, helping Rho onto the Extension Rubbish. Spencer grabbed a tuft of black hair on the creature's back, shuddering to think that the beast had never been washed or combed. Then he hoisted himself up behind Rho, barely finding room.

Spencer nestled into the saddle, which seemed to be nothing more than a Glopified floor mat. As soon as he was settled, he felt the magic hold him in place. Spencer was grateful for it, too, because the moment Daisy twisted the dial, the Extension Rubbish lifted off with a lurch that would have sent him tumbling from the monster's back.

"It responds to our movement," Daisy said. "Kind of like the cleaning carts at New Forest Academy. Try to lean with me."

The three kids followed Daisy's directions as she swooped the Extension Rubbish down to where Jersey, Shirley, Sylva, Yorkie, Dela, Netty, Gia, and Lina stood fighting. The Rubbish landed in the mud, and Rho wasted no time in dismounting.

"Rho," Spencer called as she turned away. "What made you change your mind?"

She smiled at him, and for a moment she looked like Jenna, though Spencer could hardly see her that way anymore.

"We've been fighting against the Dark Aurans for such a long time that we couldn't remember how to be peaceable. Then you came along. I got along just fine with you, and that got me thinking. What if it's all just a feud? What if we hate the Dark Aurans simply because we've always hated them? You gave me a second chance," she said. "Maybe Aryl, Olin, and Sach deserve the same."

"Take care of yourself, Rho." The Rubbish spread its wings.

She nodded. "You too."

Then Daisy and Spencer were taking flight once more, swooping down toward Sach and the Rebels hiding in the 7-Up can.

"Plunger!" Daisy shouted. Spencer knew just what she

meant, thinking how great it was that he and Daisy had fought together for so long that they knew how to predict one another.

Spencer unclipped a toilet plunger from his janitorial belt, and Daisy leaned hard, swooping the great bird downward. As they passed the soda can, Spencer thrust with the plunger, clamping solidly to the aluminum side.

With an unbelievable squelching sound, the soda can lifted free of the mud and was airborne. The plunger reduced its weight, making it easy for the Extension Rubbish to bear the whole load away.

Spencer took one final glance over his shoulder at the Broomstaff. The battle still waged at the lagoon's shore. Dozens of injured Toxites were littered among the fallen BEM riders.

No one noticed the flying soda can except for one distant figure emerging from the unstable pump house. She stood at the edge of the lagoon, and, for a moment, Spencer could feel V's angry eyes boring into him.

Then the pump house exploded into a cloud of smoke and scrap. The foundation erupted like a geyser of molten Glop. The sludgy substance flowed over the bank, dripping back into the lagoon where it would wait. Wait for V to rebuild the pump.

CHAPTER 51

"WE HAVE SOMETHING FOR YOU."

Spencer felt as if his arm might fall off. They had been flying for a long time with Spencer bent over the side of the Extension Rubbish, holding the plunger and the soda can. Daisy guided the winged creature past several familiar landmarks, including the garbage arches and lastly the Valley of Tires.

No sooner had they flown past Michelin and Goodyear than they were winging down beside the deep gorge and coming to land on the concrete dumping pad next to the Auran building. It seemed so long ago that the Rebels had been here, watching the Aurans climb out of their dumpsters.

Spencer slid off the side of the Rubbish as his Rebel friends emerged from the soda can, Bookworm and Sach being the last to appear. Daisy jumped down from the saddle, the battery pack still in place with the cord connecting her to the beast.

"What do you think we should do with Birdie?" Daisy asked, pointing at the Extension Rubbish.

"It's a Toxite," Penny said. "We kill it."

Daisy put one hand on the creature's neck. "That doesn't seem fair. She just carried us safely here and now we're going to . . . ?" Daisy drew a finger along the Rubbish's neck like she was decapitating it.

"It's a dangerous beast," Walter reminded her. "Remember, the only reason it isn't attacking us is because it's plugged in."

"I don't know." Daisy shrugged. "Seems kind of friendly to me."

In response, the Extension Rubbish parted its beak and spewed a dark cloud of dust into Daisy's face. When it cleared, the girl was completely covered in black soot. The Rubbish's face was inches from her own, a hungry look in its pterodactyl eyes.

"I could be wrong." Daisy stepped away.

"I'll deal with the Rubbish after you've gone," Sach said. "You guys need to get away while there's still time."

Bernard squinted across the gorge to where the bridge had collapsed on their first day. "I'm guessing my truck is history?"

Sach nodded. "I'm afraid so. Your truck was dragged down with the turning of the landfill."

Bernard's face paled. He tugged on the flaps of his

aviator cap. "Gone? My beauty?" His legs bent stiffly and he sat right down on the ground. Spencer was afraid he might cry.

"We can't go out of here on foot," Alan said. "It's miles of desert in every direction."

"You're taking a different garbage truck," Sach said. "An *Auran* garbage truck."

"The Aurans know how to drive?" Daisy said. "That can't be legal."

"No one's ever caught them," Sach replied. "All the Aurans drive Glopified garbage trucks. When they sit in the cab, the windows create a certain illusion, making it look like an old man behind the wheel."

"Where do you park these trucks?" Walter asked, scanning the area.

"The one you'll be taking is Rho's," Sach said. "It's in Ohio right now."

Penny rolled her eyes. "That's not doing us much good."

"But you can get to it instantly through this dumpster." Sach walked across the concrete dumping pad and pointed into one of the industrial garbage bins. "This dumpster is a portal to the back of the garbage truck. All you have to do is jump in, and you'll come out in Ohio."

Spencer remembered how all the Aurans had climbed out of the dumpsters when Rho had called them. The Aurans must have parked their trucks and jumped through the back to come out in the garbage. Now the Rebels would make the reverse journey to escape.

"Once you're all safely in the truck, I'll attempt to

destroy this dumpster so the Aurans can't follow you through."

"Wait a minute," Spencer said, suddenly realizing what Sach was saying. "You're not coming with us?"

Sach tapped the bronze Pan around his neck. "Sorry, friends. I'm stuck here."

"You don't have to stay," Spencer said. "I can take the Pan off right now." He lifted his left hand to spit again. "I've learned how to de-Glopify. I can set you free!"

Sach shook his head slowly. "There's not enough time."

"Sure, there is," Spencer answered. "It only takes a second."

"The kind of power that you possess has certain limitations," Sach said. "It requires time to regenerate after it has been used."

Spencer lowered his hand. "The pump house," he muttered. "I didn't know . . ."

Sach put a hand on his shoulder. "You did the right thing. If Toxites are really coming from Glop, then the pump house needed to be destroyed."

"How long does it take to regenerate?" Spencer asked.

"A full day or two," answered Sach. He sighed. "Too long for you to stick around. The others will be back by then."

Spencer felt awful about it. He'd had an opportunity to un-Pan each of the Dark Aurans, and instead he'd spent his power on the pump house. "I'll come back for you," he said. "When all this is over, I'll come back and un-Pan you, and Aryl, and Olin. Next week?" He looked to his dad for approval.

Sach shook his head. "You have to be more careful than that," he said. "The girls will be expecting you to return for us. They'll have traps set to get you to the Broomstaff again."

"What should I do, then?" Spencer asked. "When should I come back?"

Sach looked off into the landfill. "For the first time in over two hundred years, there's an Auran who doesn't hate us. After what she did for you, I think Rho will be willing to work with us. We'll use her to convince the other girls that we're not evil," Sach said. "When the time is right, Rho will find you. Then you'll know it's safe to come back and un-Pan us."

Sach stuck out his hand, and Spencer shook it, sealing his promise to come back for the Dark Aurans.

"You best be off." Sach pointed to the dumpster.

Bookworm took two loping steps over to Daisy and made some strange grunting sounds.

She nodded sadly. "I've got to go, buddy."

The Thingamajunk gave its trademark smile, a Lay's potato chip bag sloughing off its shoulder. Before anyone could say a word, the Thingamajunk hoisted itself onto the rim of the dumpster and dove headfirst through the portal.

"I guess Bookworm's coming with us," Walter said.

"I'm not sure how I'm going to explain this to my parents," Daisy said. "They told me not to bring home any more pets."

Bernard stepped up to the edge of Rho's dumpster and grinned like a little kid. "There's nothing I love more than diving headfirst into a pile of trash." He put his hands together and dove into the dumpster, a quick "Geronimo!" escaping his lips before he hit the trash and vanished in the same manner as Bookworm.

Walter and Penny stepped up next. "See you on the other side." Penny put a hand on her uncle's shoulder, and together they leapt into the dumpster and disappeared.

Only Daisy, Spencer, and his dad remained, staring at Sach. It was strange that he appeared as young as Spencer but was actually older than all the Rebels combined.

"I never could figure it out," Daisy said.

Sach raised his eyebrows. "Figure what out?"

"Your name," said Daisy. "The Aurans said they took their names from the thirteen colonies. Are you supposed to be Wisconsin or something?"

Sach couldn't hold back a smile. "I take my name from Massachusetts," he said. "And this is Aryl, named for Maryland." He pointed behind him as Aryl stepped around a pile of trash, right on cue.

"And that is Olin," Sach said, as the final Dark Auran stepped into view. "He was named for North Carolina."

Daisy and Alan drew back with the sudden appearance of the boys, but Spencer recognized them immediately. They strode quietly over to stand beside Sach. All three Dark Aurans in a row.

"Hey there, Spencer," Olin said. "Sorry our chat was cut short." He handed Spencer a folded scrap of paper. "My end of the bargain," he said. "That will tell you how to rescue Marv from the Vortex."

"But I never un-Panned you," Spencer said, remembering his half of the deal.

Olin grinned. "You will. One day."

Spencer nodded.

"We have something for you," Sach said. "Something we've kept hidden from the other Aurans for a very long time."

Aryl reached into his dark cloak and withdrew a book. It was small, and it looked very old. The pages were yellowed and frayed, and the leather cover was cracked. An emblem was painted on the front, faint after years of wear. It was a key ring, with skeletal keys splaying outward like rays from the sun. The covers seemed locked shut, with a small metal clasp sealing the book.

Spencer bent forward and read the title in the dim corner light from the Auran building.

"*Manualis Custodem.*"

"It's the original *Janitor Handbook*," Aryl said. "The unabridged first edition penned by the Founding Witches themselves."

"They had pretty bad handwriting," Daisy said, squinting at the title. "That doesn't look like it says *Janitor Handbook* to me."

"*Manualis Custodem.* The entire work is written in Latin," Olin explained, causing Daisy's eyes to grow even wider.

"This is what the Aurans Panned us for," Sach said. "We stole this from them."

"Why?" Spencer asked.

"They were talking about giving it away," Sach continued. "But we knew how important it was to wait until the right person came looking for it."

"The key to opening the lock is one of the bronze warlock nails. Then you'll need to find a trustworthy person to translate it," Aryl said. "Somewhere in these pages lies the answer you seek: the true location of the Glop source."

Aryl pressed the old book into Spencer's hands.

"Why didn't you tell us earlier?" Alan asked. "Why wait until it was just the three of us?"

"It is safer for fewer to know," Sach answered. "I assume you'll tell the warlock in due time. You'll need his nail to open it. The others should never know. If the *Manualis Custodem* falls into BEM hands, everything is lost."

"What do we do once we find the source?" Alan asked. "Do you know a way to destroy it?"

Olin shook his head. "It can't be destroyed."

"Then why do we need to find it?" Spencer asked.

"The *Manualis Custodem* will tell you what to do," Aryl said. "It will tell you how to bring them back."

"Bring who back?" Daisy asked.

"The Founding Witches," Sach answered. "They're not dead. They're trapped in the source. You have to find them and get them out. This was planned from the beginning. The Witches needed mortals to bring them back. That's why the Aurans developed the thirteen clues. If anyone was resourceful enough to solve them, then they would be given the *Manualis Custodem* so they could find the Witches."

"One hundred and ninety-eight years ago, the Aurans started to waver," Aryl said. "They wanted to be done with their task, and the only way to be released was by bringing back the Witches. They started talking about giving away the *Manualis Custodem*, so anyone could bring back the Witches. But the time wasn't right. So we took the book for safekeeping. We've waited a long time for this day."

"That's why V thinks you went against the Witches," Spencer said. "Why she thinks you're evil."

Olin nodded. "She thought we were trying to stop anyone from finding the Witches. But we weren't. We were just waiting for the right person to do the job. You have to find the source and bring back the Founding Witches." He paused, glancing at Aryl and Sach. "That's the only way this can end."

Spencer tucked the small book into a wide pouch on his janitorial belt. "We'll do it," he said, stepping up to the edge of the dumpster. His mind was swimming with all the things the Dark Aurans had just said.

For a moment, Spencer wanted to be home, sitting in his room without a care in the world. But it would never be that way for him. He was a Dark Auran now, charged to bring back the Founding Witches.

Then his dad put a hand on his shoulder and Daisy stepped up beside him. At least he wasn't alone.

Spencer took a deep breath, turned toward the dumpster, and jumped.

ACKNOWLEDGMENTS

Thanks for reading! I know there was a lot of garbage in this book, but I hope you enjoyed it. I wanted to get it right, so I actually toured a couple of landfills and spent hours doing trashy research. No, literally, research about trash. I even read an operator's manual for a garbage truck. But that's just basic survival knowledge.

Thanks to readers, young and old(er). I love meeting you at schools and book signings. It means a lot when I hear that the series is being enjoyed. Thank you for spreading the books to your friends, neighbors, and families. There's still a ton of excitement to come in books 4 and 5!

The team at Shadow Mountain continues to do an amazing job with this series. Thanks to Chris Schoebinger for his creativity and efforts on my behalf. Thanks to Heidi Taylor for her encouragement and patience with my barrage of emails. Thanks also to Emily Watts for the superb editing. She has the power to appease the red and green squiggly lines under my sentences.

A big thank you to my agent, Rubin Pfeffer, for his wisdom and expertise. And to Deborah Warren, who manages to support me while keeping East/West Agency running smoothly.

I'm a huge fan of Brandon Dorman's artwork. He makes

Janitors look so awesome! I hope I can actually meet him someday so I can thank him face to face!

Thanks to Erin Summerill for taking my new author photo. She made me look better than I actually do. She even spit-combed an errant hair on my head.

I've had so much support from friends and family. I'm so grateful for all of you, for rallying to me time and time again. Your enthusiasm for my projects encourages me and drives me forward!

As always, a special thanks to Connie, for her daily patience with me and my overactive imagination. I wouldn't be where I am without her.

Thanks to my mom for being the recycle police. Sorting plastics awakened my inner garbologist. And thanks to my dad for always hauling me along on his trips to the landfill. It seemed stinky at the time, but apparently it made an impact!

1. Even though Alan Zumbro is back, Spencer wishes he could spend more time with his dad. Who do you like to spend time with? How do those people make you feel?

2. Spencer and Daisy use the phrase, "My socks are warm and fuzzy," as a code phrase. What code phrase would you use? What would it mean?

3. Bernard can study the garbage and get clues about the people who threw it away. What might he learn about your family if he looked through your trash can today?

4. Glopified Windex turns any object to glass. What would you use it on? Why?

5. Bernard has many strange collections that he has gathered from the trash. What do you like to collect? Why?

6. Spencer gets reports from students who are part of the Organization of Janitor Monitors. If you were a monitor, what would you tell Spencer about your school janitor?

7. The map to the landfill is hidden in a paper towel dispenser. If you had an important map, where would you hide it? Where would it lead?

8. The Pluggers ride on huge Extension Toxites. If you were a Plugger, would you want to ride a Rubbish, a Filth, or a Grime? Why?

9. The girl Aurans have been mad at the Dark Aurans

for almost 200 years. How does it feel to hold a grudge? What can you do about it?

10. Instead of trash-talking the Thingamajunk, Daisy shows it kindness, and it becomes her pet. How can talking kindly to others help us?

Take a Sneak Peek at

TYLER WHITESIDES

JANITORS

STRIKE OF THE SWEEPERS

CHAPTER I

"PINK IS NOT STEALTHY."

It was raining. And cold. The parking lot of Welcher Elementary School was a giant puddle, with light from the nearby streetlamps glinting white against the slick blacktop.

"April showers bring May flowers," Alan Zumbro whispered, a poor attempt to lighten the mood.

Spencer scanned the empty parking lot, but there was still no sign of Walter's janitorial van. He turned to Daisy, whose teeth were chattering so loudly it sounded like a machine gun.

"We should get somewhere out of the rain," Spencer said. "We'll be soaked and frozen by the time we get inside."

Daisy's shaking hand reached into a pouch on her janitorial belt. "I have this," she said, withdrawing something and handing it to Spencer.

"You had an umbrella?" Spencer said. "Why didn't you use it?"

"It's pink," answered Daisy, tugging at her sopping black beanie. "Walter said we should wear dark clothes so we could be stealthy."

"Good point," Spencer said. A hot pink umbrella against the dark wall of the school would be like a lighthouse to anyone watching. He handed the umbrella back. "Pink is not stealthy."

The thought of shelter from the rain vanished as headlights flashed across the wet parking lot. Walter's janitorial van careened into view, stopping a few feet from the school's rear doors.

The old warlock stepped out of the vehicle, his bald head instantly shiny from the rain. Alan led Spencer and Daisy from their hiding place against the wall. The four of them ran the short distance to the school doors, and Walter fumbled with some keys. A moment later, they were inside.

"Where's Penny?" Spencer asked. He found it strange she wasn't there, since the warlock rarely went anywhere without his janitor gymnast niece.

"That's Nicole to you," Walter said with a wink. Spencer would never get used to calling his friends by false names. But it was important now. Two weeks ago, Walter Jamison had been rehired as head janitor at Welcher Elementary School. Of course, he was going under his old alias of John Campbell. And Penny was his new assistant janitor, Nicole Jones.

It was by far the best thing that had happened to

Spencer and Daisy since Walter had been fired earlier that year. The kids had spent the last several months working around Mr. Joe, a simple custodian who didn't even know Toxites existed. Now Walter was back at Welcher full-time, hunting the brainwave-sucking creatures and protecting Spencer and Daisy.

"Penny's not coming tonight," Walter said. "This is a matter for the four of us."

Spencer knew there was only one thing that Walter would keep a secret from Penny. It was something that had happened at the Aurans' hidden landfill after Penny and Bernard Weizmann had left. Walter hadn't been there either, but Alan, Spencer, and Daisy had quietly brought him into the secret.

"This is about the *Manualis Custodem*," Walter said, striding off toward the janitorial closet, the Rebels' secret base.

Spencer felt his breath catch in his chest. If the *Manualis Custodem* was the reason for their late-night gathering, then big things were on the horizon. The book had been a gift from the Dark Auran boys. Its pages held a secret that would change everything in the war against the BEM. The *Manualis Custodem* would tell them how to find the Founding Witches and bring them back. Spencer had given the first edition *Janitor Handbook* to Walter almost two months ago. It was written in a foreign language, so the warlock had set out immediately to find a trusted translator. Then came the long, anxious weeks of waiting.

Now, at last, something was happening.

Spencer's wet footsteps left little puddles in the hallway. Walter led them down the stairs and into the cluttered janitorial storage area. Spencer almost slipped on the stairs, but he didn't grab the handrail. There was no telling what kind of germs clung to a public handrail.

Walter grabbed a stack of boxes and slid them aside to reveal a secret door. On the other side, a bare lightbulb flickered on, and the four Rebels moved into the hidden room.

"I received word from our translator last night," Walter said. "Professor DeFleur has finished."

Spencer shared an excited look with his dad. If the translation was complete, then they were one step closer to finding the Founding Witches.

"Such important information cannot be trusted in the mail," Walter said, "so Professor DeFleur arranged to give us the translated manuscript in person."

"He's coming here?" Daisy asked, a residual shiver shaking her voice a bit.

Walter shook his head. "We're going to him."

The old warlock lifted a long-handled squeegee from a rack on the wall. Spencer had seen people use them to clean windows, but he'd never encountered one that was Glopified.

"My latest invention." Walter held the squeegee out for examination. It looked ordinary enough.

"You plan on cleaning some windows?" Daisy asked.

Walter shook his head. "It's for traveling," he said. "Remember the Glopified garbage trucks that the Aurans drive? The backs of their trucks are portals to the dumpsters at the landfill."

Spencer remembered perfectly. They'd escaped from the hidden landfill by jumping into a dumpster. As they had fallen through, they had come out in the back of Rho's garbage truck. The Dark Aurans had destroyed the dumpster behind the Rebels so nobody could follow. Last thing Spencer had heard, Bernard had adopted Rho's garbage truck and was driving it around.

"I was able to figure out a Glop formula that was similar to the garbage truck portal," Walter explained. "I used it on this squeegee."

"We're supposed to jump into a squeegee?" Daisy raised an eyebrow.

"Not exactly," said Walter. "There's a set of two Glopified squeegees. When I run mine across a piece of glass, it creates a magical opening. When the other squeegee is used on a different piece of glass, it creates a portal between the two. We step through our squeegeed glass, and we come out wherever the other squeegee was used."

Alan clapped his hands together, a smile across his bearded face. "Brilliant!" he said. "Why didn't we try something like this sooner?"

"I needed to use the garbage truck as a model to get the right Glop formula," Walter said.

"I could have helped," Spencer said, suddenly feeling left out.

More than two months had passed since he'd discovered his full powers as an Auran. He could Glopify anything with his right hand and de-Glopify with his left. It was as simple as spitting. Literally.

When Spencer became an Auran, Glop was introduced into his bodily systems. Rubbing spit between his hands would activate the Glop and access his powers. It was gross, yes. But Spencer wanted to experiment with it. Walter had forbidden him, talking about a bunch of unknown dangers. Spencer's only experience had been to de-Glopify the Aurans' pump house. And that had left him drained.

"So, who has the second squeegee?" Alan asked.

"Professor Dustin DeFleur," answered Walter.

"A professor dusting the floor?" Daisy said.

Walter looked puzzled. "What? No. Why would he be dusting the floor?"

"That's what you said," Daisy insisted. "Professor dusting the floor."

Walter smiled, finally understanding the confusion. "That's his name. Dustin DeFleur."

"That's got to be a fake name," Spencer said. "Who would name their child Dustin DeFleur?"

"His parents were French," Walter defended. "And don't say anything about his name. He's very sensitive."

"So how is this going to work?" Alan broke in.

Walter stepped over to a rack and retrieved a spray bottle of Glopified window cleaner. In a moment, he had misted the door. It shimmered blue and turned to glass. "The squeegee portal only lasts about fifteen minutes," he said. "One of us should stay here to make sure it doesn't close."

It was quiet for a moment. Then Daisy raised her hand. "Fine, I'll stay."

Walter nodded. "If the portal starts to close, just swipe the squeegee across the glass again."

Spencer checked his janitorial belt. It was loaded with supplies he probably wouldn't need, but it always felt better to be armed when stepping into the unknown. Walter handed the squeegee to Daisy and strapped on his own belt.

"Ready to find out how to bring the Founding Witches back?" Alan said. There were anxious smiles around the room. Then Daisy Gates swiped the Glopified squeegee down the glass door.

ABOUT THE AUTHOR

TYLER WHITESIDES worked as a janitor at a middle school to put himself through college. It was there that he discovered the many secrets and mysteries that can be hidden in a dusty school. Tyler graduated from Utah State University with a degree in music. He enjoys spending time in the mountains, cooking on the barbecue, and vacuuming. Tyler lives in Logan, Utah, with his wife, Connie, a third-grade teacher. He is the author of the Janitors series (*Janitors, Secrets of New Forest Academy, Curse of the Broomstaff,* and the forthcoming *Strike of the Sweepers*).

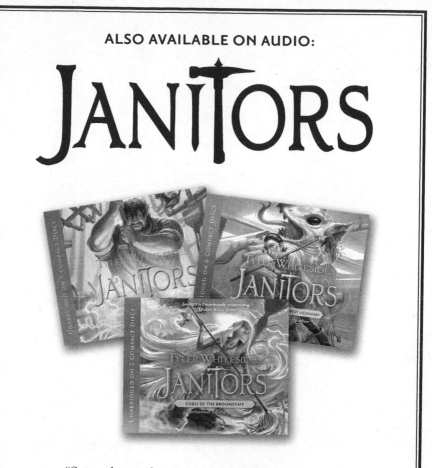